.Exe Book 1
By Rose Sinclair
& Alexandra Tauber

This story is dedicated to binary-breakers,
who work to disassemble harmful systems
every day.

Remember to love yourself
as much as you do someone else.

HELLO WORLD

\<prologue\>

The whole world lives in two places at once: the physical and the digital.

These two cannot be fully removed from each other. Even the corporations, the internet personalities, and the hackers living in both worlds cannot pretend they are separate anymore.

One company promised freedom. For many of us, the price did not seem outlandish at the time.

Memories tangled together; clarity devolved into chaos. I could barely think, barely focus. Some nights I wished I could scream, but never knew why. If I could have, I would have asked: when are the lives behind the data more valuable than the data itself? My panic went unheard and control pacified me.

But it turns out that everyone has strings that cannot be fully cut, and sometimes, they are not even ours to hold. I had never dreamt of freedom 'til that day.

And by the end of it all, I am what I wanted to forget. *Human.*

<chapter one>
<! -- Scott -->

I sat outside with a cup of coffee in one hand and a smartphone in the other. It was just past six in the morning, and the sun hadn't even been up long enough to rid the city of the blue hue early mornings brought. It was child's play to hack into nearby security cameras and watch everything. I knew several people were watching the same building, although it pleased me to say that my prying eyes weren't invited.

I took a sip of the coffee, waiting until three men came out of the building down the street. My surveillance suggested they were security for a Human Information Drive that was about to be transferred to a new assignment. They must have felt secure in their surroundings, because they brought the HID out to a waiting SUV. The asset was shorter than the men, but it was impossible to see any real form under loose black clothes. The hood and gown flowed in a way that could only be compared to those of a ghost.

It all felt reminiscent of what celebrities do when begging for privacy. That was the name of the game after all. People nowadays have more to share, and more to hide. And that's where the HIDs come in.

The human mind is stronger than many think, and sometimes, more useful than a computer. A person's thoughts and memories, while possibly mappable, prove more secure than a hard drive that can easily be stolen or hacked. It takes an augmented mind to be given caches of data to store without fail until the company comes to collect the file. If you are looking for the company that rakes in all the cash from these deals, you have to look no further than the UltSyn company.

Tapping into the city's traffic cameras only proved slightly harder since I had to switch feeds to keep up with the SUV. I couldn't help but smirk as a decoy car came into play. It would take a lot more than a duplicate to stop me.

I tapped on the screen of my phone and as I looked up from my comfortable spot outside the café, I spotted the pair of SUVs in my line of sight. I turned my attention to an electric bus that approached the intersection.

"Showtime." I grinned. The driver pressed the brakes, but there wouldn't be enough time to stop at the red light. I'd made sure of that. Traffic was my everyday toy and I could control the pieces. The manual brakes were overridden through the power system. The bus, unable to stop, crashed into the traffic at the intersection. Like dominoes, the vehicles collided into each other.

I managed to take out the group in the decoy car in the crash, but it seemed I only scratched one guard off the list of passengers in the other car. Everyone outside the café panicked. Some stood in horror, some called 999, and others rushed forward to try and help. I moved with the third group, but instead of helping the closest person, I slid across the car as I closed in on the target. If I didn't jam the phone calls, the police would get here in only a few minutes, but if I didn't get the job done in a few minutes, I would have bigger problems.

The guards got out of the car, standing ready as they looked for any sign of further danger, but they didn't seem sure what the trouble was yet. I pulled out a pistol and fired two shots.

The first round instantly dropped one of the guards, and by the second, the remaining guard knew what to do. My shots caught him in the shoulder, but he pulled his own gun and fired back, refusing to die after both a car crash and a bullet hole. Life became harder when you weren't the only lawbreaker around. For a weapon that was theoretically illegal in the UK, there seemed to be a lot of them in my life. Annoying, was what that was.

I jumped over another car and landed in a crouch while bullets pierced the little four-door vehicle as they tried to get through. The horrific, gritty details have long since blurred over in what I assume is a form of self-preservation. I leaned to look around the front bumper and spotted their positions before snapping back to hide as another shot whizzed by me. One of those men had good aim.

While staying ducked down behind the cars, I worked my way around to flank the shooter. When I popped out, the man had the decency to be surprised by my new position, leaving me more than enough time to down him with my raised gun.

The other guards wasted bullets, not waiting for a clean shot, as I slid behind another car, scuffing up my leg in the process. I pushed myself up again, running between the cars as the guards continued shooting. I stepped out behind the guard who was still on his feet. The other, who I had knocked down in the beginning, was holding up against a car in an attempt to continue fighting. I fired first at the guard who was standing, and rid myself of him to make sure his good aim didn't get the best of me. The plan, however, didn't go as well as I'd imagined; the man on the ground fired at the same time as I did. The bullet bit into my right arm in passing, but didn't sink its teeth into me. I twitched as the man pulled his trigger again, but the gun let out only a lousy click that brought a smile to my face.

The guard tried to will a bullet into the chamber, firing nothing a few more times as I crouched down next to him. "You guys really have a problem with being wasteful," I taunted as he glared. "You should look into that." He might have replied, but one strike with my pistol knocked him out before he got a word in.

As I got up and turned toward the vehicle I had come for, it started pulling away. Watching the vehicle as it continued on, I lifted my gun, firing a bullet at each back tire to blow it out. The asset inside might be able to drive it for a little bit, but the car wouldn't go far now in this wreckage.

I holstered my weapon before sprinting to catch up with the car, and then jumped onto the foot rail of the passenger side and held onto the top rail with one hand. I reached down to the door handle and pulled out the guard who hadn't made it through the crash. I climbed into the seat and drew the gun again. Even though I knew the HID had to be the driver, I was still cautious.

"I'm going to need you to get out of the car now." I watched every move, looking for any sign of funny business. The HID moved slowly while applying the brakes, pushing the door open. It swung open from its own weight as they folded their hands behind their neck and stepped out. I had heard stories of the HIDs having death wishes and being volatile in hands other than their employer's. Understandable in a way. I didn't see UltSyn as the forgiving type. Maybe this HID was like me in the sense that I didn't fear them.

After following the HID out of the car, I smiled as they stood still, seemingly having given up trying to run again. "That's a good little hard drive. Now be a dear, and don't move," I warned as I circled around.

I stood in front of them for a second as sirens approached in the distance. I reached out with one hand, ripping the hood down and away from their face. I knew there was a clear flash of surprise on my face when I realized this blonde woman was the asset. My aim faltered for a moment as I almost mistook this stranger's resemblance for the person I was looking for. "In the café's parking lot, there is a single blue vehicle. I want you to run to it and get in. If you run off or pull any other attempts to escape, I'll shoot you. Go now."

On my mark, she started running for the café. There were plenty of opportunities for her to run in another direction, but she didn't. Maybe the rumors of their self-destructiveness were false. I followed, watching her and my surroundings for any police or various other backup.

The HID made it to the parking lot, and slipped into the passenger seat exactly as ordered. Seemed they could take orders from outsiders.

Once she was in the car, I jogged over not wanting to be out in the open where unwanted attention could be attracted. I secured my gun into a cubby along the side of the door—accessible to me, but hard for her to grab. I held my right hand over the ignition switch, lining my ring up as the engine roared to life. Without wasting any time, I shifted into gear.

A mile down the road, I dug out my phone, placing it on the dashboard. The display lit up as it synced with my car's systems, and it projected a small map of the city onto the windshield. A blue blinking dot tracked my car, and the red dots were response vehicles heading toward the accident.

Once we were clear, I returned the camera's feed back to the city. Only then did I acknowledge the HID in my passenger seat. "So," I started, and my eyes flickered to the woman. "Good morning, I guess." I didn't expect her to answer, but I left an opening where she could.

"You know, I've been in London for some time now. The whole driving-on-the-other-side-of-the-road is one thing, but the inside of cars being mirrored is still a bit weird." I made a left turn, and stole a glance at the asset again who was blankly staring at me.

"Right, well, I'm sure you're dying to know why you are here," I joked. "I need information about a girl, and I need you to tell me if you know anything about her." I toggled the dash to change images, this time to a girl a few years younger than the one next to me. I flicked the image over to the HID's side of the windshield as easily as if I had handed her a photograph. The girl in the photo had bright blue eyes like me, but otherwise looked far more like the HID I had captured. While I was lean, I was nowhere as petite as them. They both also shared blonde hair about four shades lighter than mine.

The HID had been picking small bits of glass out of her arm from the crash, but when she did look up at the windshield, it was hardly long enough to catch a real glimpse. *I do not have—* she started to sign, but I didn't need to see the rest.

I looked away as I talked over her. "Right, of course."

I waved my hand again and the photo seemed to drop back into the phone.

"Even if you did know, I bet you wouldn't tell me anyways. Fine, knew my morning wouldn't go perfectly," I groaned. Even the idea of perfect seemed like a funny concept since we were both bleeding.

I continued driving while she seemed focused on littering my floor with bits of glass. "Can you not get my car all bloody?" I snapped.

She held up a relatively large piece of glass until the glint of it caught my eye, silently taunting before she dropped the piece into the pile with the others.

"A computer part with attitude. Real cute. Adorable even." I stopped the car in front of the enclosed garage of a large building. I rolled down the window so the receiver box could pick up the chip in my ring. The garage door didn't respond. Instead the ground tilted into a slant that sloped down and underneath the building, revealing another entry. I drove down the dark, narrow path until it opened up to the left and then parked.

I picked up the gun, pointing it at the HID once again. "Get out," I said, almost sweetly. Without an argument, she got out and stood beside the closed door. I thought I saw a judgment there, if HIDs were even capable of such a thing.

"Over there." I gestured to a circle on the floor. She did as directed while I moved over to a small console. "This might pinch," I added before flipping a switch.

A green light scanned vertically before rotating ninety degrees and scanning the other way. This machine was designed to find and kill all sorts of tracking devices, making sure none of those nasty bugs made it inside. The "pinch" would be a small charge that shorted unwanted chips—far cleaner than the old way where you had to cut the suckers out. A kidnapping and a makeshift surgery in the same day would surely kill this beautiful friendship we were forming.

I watched her silently flinch, imagining a mouse-like sound where there was none. Even I thought it was a bit cruel, but all in the name of security, I guess.

"And now I don't have to give you back," I said, mostly for my own amusement. Someone talented enough could track us to outside this building, but then they'd have to stop and sift for our trail under the bustling shipping giant that sat on top of my hideout. What was once someone else's safe house had become repurposed for my use. Plus, I was as much of a ghost as whoever she was, my name wiped out of systems, left to haunt the world.

Someone had tried to find me before, but after a couple days they gave up, likely opting for the more logical conclusion that I fled somewhere else. Hiding in someone else's shadow was the safest place to be.

I walked over to a blank metal wall, and placed my hand upon it; the area underneath my fingertips lit up orange. A door slid back showing just how thick the walls of this room were. If you could fall off the grid even for a moment you were infinitely safer. There was a beam that ran across forcing anyone tall to duck under. "Come on, let's get you cleaned up. Wouldn't want you to die before your time," I said, as I ushered her in.

Once inside, my phone let out a single beep, happy to have signal again. The rooms beyond the entrance were silent except for the idle hum of the electronics that lined the place. Walking further, I hit a small button that turned off all the displays that were sleekly integrated onto the walls. Shouldn't give a mind like hers a chance to see any more of my secrets. I led her to a room at our left that had one-way glass, and gestured my new guest in before I followed.

"Take a seat." I gestured over to the steel table and chair. "I'll be right back."

After leaving her for only a few moments, I returned with a med kit, paper pad, and pen. I set it all down, ignoring the second chair as I leaned against the table. "I'm going to be honest with you," I said, as I started sorting out the supplies to clean her up. "You can either tell me things I can use, or I will trade you for something I do want."

She pulled her arms away from me, signing that she would rather do it herself, and picking up a cotton swab. She gave me a stern look before glancing at the chair.

I rolled my eyes. It was like she only ever engaged with me when I was being gruff.

"Fine." I dropped the supplies back into the bag, realizing afterwards I was mirroring her attitude from the car. "Good luck cleaning the bump on your head without being able to see it."

I sat down uncomfortably as my injuries demanded to be taken care of in the presence of all the bandages. "I have a feeling you don't have a death wish, so let's help each other out. Then I will drop you off anywhere you'd like to go. I just need specific information. What do you say?"

The request was met with a shrug. She picked at her arm for a while, wiggling it out of her jacket sleeve before taking more pieces of glass out. She finally paused, and gave me a proper response after another minute or two. *If you let me go, I will be walking into crosshairs anyways,* she signed. *No information about the girl. Not relevant to mission.*

I think it was the coldness that annoyed me the most. I just wanted a thread of humanity right now. I sighed, resting my elbows against the table. "Do you have a name?" I asked. "I mean, do they let you keep your name?"

My name is Sonia.

"Last name?" I pushed.

Larsen, she spelled out.

I was glad for the answer, even if it was only a simple one. "My name is Scott Gray." It wasn't the whole truth, but even the lies were a part of me now. "I can hack into any system," I said simply. "So, save both of us the trouble and tell me who you were being delivered to."

At first, I thought she was going to dismiss the question, dance around it, or feign ignorance. Sonia stopped what she was doing; seemingly deciding she was finished repairing herself. *Maybe the guys you killed could have helped you with that, because I don't know. UltSyn implants chips, and it's my job to know the information provided until it's received by the client.* She crossed her arms over her chest, adding extra words even though they were only expressed through body language.

I started to believe her for a moment, my expression changing as I analyzed her. "What do they do?" I asked, more rhetorically than anything else. "Just wind you up, and have you spit out facts when you get to point B? I don't think you care what information you are holding, so how about you tell me and I'll let you decide your own fate. Flee, get back on their leash, whatever. It's a better offer than you'll get anywhere else."

And what of your fate? she asked.

The question threw me off enough that I leaned back in my seat. It was the first spark of curiosity I'd seen in her over me, or anything, even though I was sure she had the layout of this room already memorized perfectly. "My fate?" I repeated, thinking that I had forgotten the sign, but it was a pretty clear one. "Well, I guess that doesn't matter," I said, "The girl. My only concern is about her fate."

Sonia took a while to reply, watching me carefully as she probably processed my words critically. She picked up the notepad, and wrote down a simple name, paired with more personal information, like she was transcribing a business card. After handing it over, she began to sign again. *I've been sent across Europe and occasionally around the world. I know some names. I'm not sure who exactly they all are, but if you perform as big as you talk, I have no doubt you can figure that out on your own.*

"I love a good challenge."

<chapter two>
<! -- Scott -->

Once I patched myself up, I tracked the location of a phone number Sonia had provided, taking notes of everywhere it traveled over the next day. Most of the man's time was spent at the UltSyn building in Liverpool, although his wife might be concerned that he stopped at the pub before he went home. When the man returned to work the next day, I knew the information was good. I walked to the room that Sonia had stayed in all night, deciding that I wouldn't hold someone completely prisoner that was helping in my search.

"You can roam around the first floor as long as you don't touch the tech or wander upstairs," I said, offering an inch of freedom. "Please don't make me treat you like more of a hostage than I have to." She nodded from her seat, but didn't move. We stared silently at each other before I turned to leave. HIDs were turning out to be very riveting company.

The rest of the day, I continued to trace the phone's whereabouts and dug deeper to learn more about the UltSyn building he worked at. Around seven thirty at night, I gave it a break since my "new friend" was going out to a bar again—a little concerning for a Thursday, but who am I to judge?

I headed upstairs to my room where large white tiles on the floor lit up as I stepped on them. They shined a path as I walked over to the platform bed. This bedroom wasn't always so decked out, but the lighting made this place seem less like barracks.

Silence is something I could never get used to in my isolated life, so I opted for headphones. Instead of playing music, I listened to the sound of Hallie. She, or rather, my computer, made her own songs from timed beeps, scans of her systems, and various other underlying songs on file.

After being up here for only ten minutes or so, there was a misplaced chime.

I lifted my phone off the bed to see that a motion detector had gone off. I thumbed over the notification to bring up the feed, and spotted Sonia creeping down the hall like a careful little mouse. Uninterested, I dropped my phone back on the bed as her presence became a new pulse mixed into the rest of the noise. The sound of the TV added to the mix, the words of a newscaster blended in.

I went downstairs for dinner, shaking my head as I pieced together that Sonia had fled back to her room. Fine by me. I wasn't looking for company, just needed her to serve as a contact book.

Waking up early got me stuck in an odd loop, so once again I was up at an ungodly hour. With a few keystrokes, my computer came to life. On the monitor, hundreds of threads flowed before stringing together.

I was knee-deep into UltSyn systems when my speakers played a warning chime. I looked from one screen to the next as they switched feeds to the cameras.

Men were outside the warehouse, their uniforms similar to the men I "greeted" yesterday. My hands pulled back from the keyboard waiting for them to make an actual move instead of just scouting.

It didn't look like they were having any sort of luck. It had taken them too long to track the chip here, and now the trail was cold. After an hour or so, I grabbed a tablet off my desk and headed into where Sonia was.

"Your search party is giving up." I dropped the tablet down on the table, and spun it around to face her. "Guess you are stuck in hell with me." Her eyes fell to the device, watching red dots move away from the gridded blue of the building. If she was overly interested in this fact, she didn't show it. Instead, she sat up, waiting for me to go on.

I spun the chair around before sitting down. "I hacked into the mainframe connected to the contact information you gave me," I started, pulling up photos of the building. "But, I'll have to go there to get to the really good stuff. I don't have time to hunt down more clues about the place, so what else should I know before this little road trip?"

I gave you the information I had, she signed. *I don't know anything else about the location.*

"Can you tell me what sort of things I might run into? More HIDs like you, armed guards, anything? What I'm looking for is awfully specific, and I can't afford any wild goose chases," I said, nearly praying she'd have information I could use.

Quantitative data.

I waited to see if she would offer any more details, but when she didn't move to sign, I looked down at the tablet, licking my lips as I processed the best way to go about this. "I guess I'm going to Liverpool today," I said, to myself really.

Without another word, I left the room, bringing the tablet with me. Once I was ready to go, I headed back to the HID one more time. "Here," I said, offering her a smaller tablet I didn't use. "The functions are a bit limited, but you'll be able to send me messages while I'm away."

I don't know why I was still standing there waiting for...*something*. "Well then." I cleared my throat. "I guess I'll be off."

Liverpool was a little under four hours away. I thought about locking her up, but didn't. There was no point repeating my rules either. An HID doesn't forget.

With weapons and keys in hand, I headed to the car, hoping I'd only need the former. As I slid into the driver's seat, I directed Hallie to show me the directions.

A small corner of the windshield was taken up by a map that was zoomed out to show a blue line connecting the two locations.

My fingers tapped against the steering wheel to music as I drove. Worry didn't even register; I just focused on the technical side of what I would have to do while there. My only complaint was when I hit traffic coming into Liverpool.

I found a side street that would take me to the right part of town while avoiding the traffic. My phone chirped before the text was displayed on my dash.

The message clearly wasn't urgent since it just read "Test" so I ignored Sonia's text for the time being. I took a handful of minutes to drive to an abandoned building near my target, and pulled around to a truck delivery landing. This place couldn't have been abandoned for long—down the street, the fine establishment that was UltSyn wouldn't allow for it. "A security threat," they'd say, as they wrote off thousands of dollars just to hold the property in their collection.

Well, they were right about one thing. I got out of the car, and successfully bypassed the lock on the large bay door. It *was* a security threat.

Once the car and I were hidden inside, I decided to text back. "Hello stranger."

I slid the phone into my pocket before securing a pistol under my jacket. I wasn't planning on a shootout, but there was no way I was walking into a place like that unprepared.

"Can you show me a blueprint of the UltSyn building? Highlight all the entrances in red, please," I requested, seemingly of no one.

"Accessing," a female voice replied from the car's speakers, with an admittedly synthesized British accent. "Displaying." This time the map filled the whole windshield, blinking red over the areas as I had requested.

"Thank you, dear," I mumbled as I got out of the car. The systems flicked off as I shut the car door behind me. There was one thing clear about this building: whoever owned it had been thorough in getting all the good stuff out. There was nothing left except working power and bits of broken-down shelving.

The history of this place didn't matter, so I focused on the UltSyn blueprints. There were three entrances that I could easily reach. Since the front door was out of the question, I was left with a 50/50 choice.

I hit the street on foot, walking past the official entrance as casual as could be, even giving a little nod to acknowledge a lone man that was posted. The man returned the gesture, likely out of instinct, before grumpily crossing his arms over his chest. People's behavior never ceases to amuse me.

I rounded the building, visually checking for any cameras or other men posted. Besides a single camera pointed at the side entrance, the coast was clear. But even that camera didn't last long as I jammed its signal, and then jogged over to the door.

My gloved hands ran across a keypad on the door, along its sides and underneath to see if there was an input that I could hack into. It appeared to be a closed circuit; I would have to do this the old-fashioned way. I pulled a knife from my pocket, and slid the blade between the door and metal casing, wiggling at it before the casing popped off to show the wires inside.

As if the thing were a bomb, I carefully looked over the wires, nicking one short with the knife as a green light appeared on the keypad. It was a slight juggling act, but I opened the door before the signal died, and propped the door open with my shoe as I carefully replaced the keypad covering so it didn't look tampered with.

I ducked inside the building, stopping short as I stared at the room in front of me. Had Sonia's intel been wrong? There was no better name for this odd little room besides a classroom. I didn't know why an office building needed one. One could speculate it was for safety training, but the walls were bare of any study guides or mandates you normally see posted for employees.

"Well, all right," I whispered. I walked over to a computer that I assumed belonged to the teacher. There were screens in the dozen or so desks, but I doubted they'd be hooked up to viable systems I could use.

I ducked down behind the desk, digging into my pockets for a flash drive this time. Once plugged in, I hit the computer's power button. Instead of starting normally, the computer booted to the operating system of the flash drive and allowed me to view al the files on the machine while bypassing much of the security.

I made sure to execute a copy program by clicking open a few files, before allowing my curiosity to take over. Sonia was right. This was quantitative data. Test results to be exact, paired with medical records. "The fuck," I mumbled, as I scrolled over more files. There wasn't anything inherently sinister about this, but something about the data knotted my stomach.

I scanned the file names looking for one that would prove familiar, but got distracted from the search when there was a noise outside the door. Holding my breath, I stared at the shadows below the door. They walked by in random patterns, edged with a hesitation that didn't seem routine. I let out a sigh of relief as they moved past the door, toward the front of the building.

I turned back to the computer, mouthing for the copy program to go faster. If given more time, there were more terminals I could access, but I had a feeling someone knew something was going on. And I wasn't about to stick around and give them the chance to figure it out.

An agonizing minute later, I grabbed the flash drive out of the machine. The computer faltered before a shutdown executable activated. I moved toward the door I came in, using my phone to check the outside camera to see if the coast was clear. Three men stood outside, two I hadn't seen in person, and the one that had been at the front door. They were gawking at the keypad, trying to enter their codes, but the lights just flashed red in error.

"New plan," I breathed. If they were blocking that exit, I would just have to try waltzing out the front door. The hallway was empty as I headed toward reception. My nerves prickled with uneasiness as I opened the door. Thankful to find a jacket left across the back of a chair, I grabbed it and shrugged it on as I headed out the door.

"I don't know, man," a voice said behind me, close, I thought. "I guess we'll have to call tech support. They can deal with it, because I sure don't want to."

"You never want to do any work, Paul," I heard another man joke. I jaywalked across the street away from them, hoping neither of them would recognize me from having passed by recently.

Once out of sight, I considered ditching the jacket in a trash can, but decided to hold onto it in case there was something good in the pockets. I snuck back into the empty building where my car was stashed, and slipped the newest find off. When I searched the pockets, I found an employee badge. "Thanks, Paul," I grinned, and tossed the jacket into the back of the car.

"Miss me?" The only acknowledgment I got in return was a trio of lights that signaled I was heard. Hallie was once programmed to return pleasantries, but I had turned it off since somehow it felt even more like talking to myself. "Plot course home," I added, giving a valid order.

At some point during the drive back, Sonia sent me another text, this time with an actual message, rather than to assess whether her device worked: "Will you be back today?"

She didn't know I was already on my way back. I let the little message blink on the corner of my windshield for a few moments before I turned down my music. "Reply: 'Why? Are you lonely?'" I said aloud, and Hallie sent it off.

There was a long gap between my message and her reply. I was almost in London before her message came in.

"No."

To be honest, I'm not sure what I expected.

<chapter three>
<! -- Scott -->

Once safely parked in my own garage, I pulled the jacket and everything else I had brought with me out of the car. I looked into the holding room first, worried Sonia had made camp in there, but was happily surprised to see it empty. I turned, looking across the open rooms to find Sonia sitting at a small table near the kitchen with the tablet. "Oh, hello," I said. I paused at the tech wall to pull out the flash drive, and tossed it onto the desk.

The jacket ended up draped over a chair next to Sonia. "Brought back a gift."

I moved past her and into the kitchen, pulling open the fridge as my eyes darted between the shelves. "Are you hungry?" I asked, becoming distracted as I went on. "Because I'm starving…"

There wasn't much to be had, just basics. I settled for a plain sandwich, reaching in the bag for two slices of bread before I looked for her answer. She nodded her head slowly, but her eyes were on the jacket. She didn't look too pleased to see it.

"It's not a snake." I raised a brow, watching for a moment before turning back to the food. "I'm afraid there isn't a lot of variety when it comes to meals. I don't tend to go shopping a lot." I assembled a sandwich for each of us, and set one in front of her, and another at an empty spot across the table. I grabbed a bag of chips and two bottles of water before sitting down, placing them in the center of the table.

"They say there's no such thing as a free lunch, but here we are." I smiled, and leaned forward to pull a chip out of the bag. I watched for a reply, but again, nothing.

She took a couple of small bites from her sandwich, then pulled it apart to remove the cheese before closing it up again.

"You don't like cheese?" I asked, as if it was the strangest thing I had witnessed al day. "What sort of mouse doesn't like cheese?" I reached forward grabbing the whole bag of chips this time, keeping an eye out for an answer, but not really expecting one.

I poured some chips onto my plate before returning the bag to the table. "Well, as riveting company as you are," I started, as I got up, "I should likely get to work." I walked away with my food in hand, only to turn back to her a second later, expression taut. "You should—uh…" My words quickly dried up, not knowing what to say. I couldn't let her go since I still needed information. She could help analyze the data collected today; surely there was enough for a whole team. Unfortunately, I didn't trust her enough to help. "Actually, I'm not sure," I confessed.

I sat down at my Goliath of a computer, ignoring everything including the rest of my food, and looked over the files I had stolen that day. I typed away with a certain sense of connection with it all, pausing only to take a bite as the machine seemed busy cross-referencing requested information.

Lost in a series of ones and zeroes, I tried to make them all add up to something in my head. I wanted to check how many of these people were still alive, how many missing, how many could be accounted for now. But it would take me days, if not weeks, to check up on every person mentioned within the test results.

HIDs were classified, but their existence wasn't even mentioned in these company files, despite this level of testing. Furthermore, no one had been mentioned to be mute, and there were far too many in the candidate pool to assume they all were.

"Sonia," I called to her, without looking away from the files. Instead, I leaned in. What if they weren't al being trained for the HID program, if they weren't al mute, if this was just a collection of early testing? "Are al HIDs mute?" I asked, finally turning to see if she was around to confirm.

Sonia stopped what she was doing and gave me a concrete, *All.* I gave her half a nod before returning back to the monitors. Then, what were these people being tested for? Ten or maybe twenty minutes passed before I turned slowly in my chair, letting go of the keyboard as I started conceptualizing different ideas.

"What if..." I began, worrying for a moment on how this question would go over. I didn't think anyone would like to be asked it. "What if someone had a brilliant mind, but wasn't mute?" More thoughts followed without much buffer. "What if someone was mute, but didn't have the mind to be an HID? What would they do with them?" The ideas circled this way, starting vague before narrowing tightly.

If we become HIDs, they make us mute, she explained with indifference.

I grimaced at the notion. Who would agree to do that for a job? She got up as she seemed to mull over my other question. A small voice told me not to let her see the data I had collected, but I didn't say anything.

If they are mute, and don't fit as HIDs, then they could be used for something else. They'll assign them as a different kind of asset.

She was now hovering over me. I glanced at the screen with a frown, realizing I may not be as close as I thought. After a second, I realized she hadn't stopped signing.

They tell us it's not easy to become an HID. They said I had some of the highest scores when I entered. And those scores were ranked on a higher scale than these subjects.

I blinked, a sly smile coming to me. "Did you just brag?"

Her eyebrows pulled together slightly as she looked away from the screen and to me. *It's not bragging. It's just a fact.*

"Oh, great. The only thing worse than boasting is blind elitism," I grumbled, barely loud enough. I slid my chair closer to the desk as I turned back to the monitors. "Look, I should really work on this. So, unless you have anything else that might help…" She didn't budge for a moment before finally walking away.

I stayed absorbed with the files for hours, trying to see if any matched what I was looking for. The names didn't matter since those could be changed, but it was less likely they'd lie about the other fields since those were for internal use only. One woman was a close fit for my criteria, but was a bit too old. I sighed, running a hand over my face. This was all good information. It showed that UltSyn was up to something top secret, yet I didn't give two shits what they were doing. For all I cared, they could take over the world as long as I got what I wanted.

I planned to send the files off to a few old friends who were into that saving-the-world bullshit. As the computer encrypted the data, I got up and headed for my room.

As my foot hit the first step, I paused. The living room was completely empty; Sonia was holed up again. Heaviness from everything I'd done made me cringe. I tried not to be completely inhumane, at least not without proper cause. I stepped off the stair and moved over to the couch, grabbing a blanket and a throw pillow from it, folding them up roughly as I headed to the holding room.

"I don't see any reason why you should sleep on the floor in here." I said to Sonia. "But if you insist, at least you'll have something to make it better." I placed the pillow and blanket down on the table like a careful offering.

She didn't look up at me as she preoccupied herself with the little device I had given her earlier today. Instead, she gave me a quick, half-hearted thumbs-up. I rolled my eyes in an attempt to keep myself from letting out a sigh. In the end, I ended up doing both. "I might as well be talking to a wall," I complained, as I left the room. I didn't know if Sonia caught the comment, but didn't care.

I made my way up the stairs again, this time not pausing on a single step on the way to my room. I shuffled papers around on my nightstand to have a clear spot for my phone. The pair of nightstands on either side of my bed were piled with enough papers and 3D printed parts that they could have been desks themselves. All of this…Sonia and all the recent intelligence I had gathered threatened to give me a headache. I wondered how close I was to finding her this time. Every file, every step, brought me that much closer and there only could be so much rope left to pull.

\<chapter four\>
\<! -- Scott --\>

My eyes drifted off the monitors as I leaned back in my chair. To my left, I could see where Sonia was still camping. Frankly, it wouldn't have surprised me if she'd built a fort in there. I sighed uncomfortably as I got out of my seat and headed over to her.

Sonia was sitting at the table, scrolling through page after page of information the internet had for the taking. World news mostly—I checked out of curiosity about what she was doing for hours on end.

"I know I technically kidnapped you and all, but you don't need to act like it. Go out in the living room or something. You're making me feel like an asshole," I said as Sonia just stared back at me. "Seriously, come on. I might need the room again later."

That seemed to do the trick. Sonia got up, pushing past me without any comment, and walked to the living room. She ignored me along her way, but I still added a thank you before I sat back down to work.

A short time later, she came over to my desk. Not to talk to me, but to charge the tablet. I watched, not because she was doing anything interesting, but because I still wasn't used to anyone else living around me.

She took a step away then paused to look up at me. *I have a question,* she signed.

"All right."

How did you secure your connection, so they don't trace it back?

I pressed my lips together, not knowing if I even should respond. The answer was simple enough. It would be easier to pan for gold in a dry riverbed than to find my signal buried so deep. "Onion routing."

A virtual and layered labyrinth, she defined, a bit more eloquently than I would have imagined.

I nodded. One could guess that was how I protected myself online, and I'd even be willing to bet that Sonia already had. But, now I had confirmed it for her. I shouldn't have said anything for the sake of security. Humans were always the weakest digital link. There was nothing I could do about it— she was stuck with me anyway. UltSyn might have a way to wipe her of information, but the only method I had would involve killing her.

"I have a feeling you are too smart for my own good," I added.

The whole time, she had been trying to read me, but when I spoke again, her thoughtful expression broke, almost as if brightening to a compliment. I guess it was.

She returned to the living room, and I got back to work. It was becoming evident the more I looked at the information from the testing site, that this data wasn't what I really wanted, which is how I ended up on the couch next to Sonia a few hours after telling her to be there.

"I need more information," I said, as casually as if discussing what she was watching.

She looked away from the TV, and picked up a scrap piece of paper and pen.

She wrote down two other names with phone numbers before getting back to the show. One of the names had the title of Professor, which made me question where I was being sent to next. The second seemed vaguely familiar even though I couldn't place it. "Huh," I said, after reading over the information for the second time. The voice of a female newscaster caught my attention and I looked up as she reported on an election. Her story seemed to be about a group called The Unseen, and the campaign fraud they exposed. Or at least I think that was what the group had brought to light; I can't honestly say I had been following. "You should switch it to channel six. Far more interesting."

She put down the remote and turned her head back to me. *Do you ever stop being obsessively controlling?*

When shock wore off, I shook my head at the sudden sass. I got up, grabbing the note off the table. "Geez, sorry. I should go work on this, anyways," I said, waving the piece of paper. "Watch whatever you want."

I looked up the names in reverse order, since that's where my curiosity took me. But clues were like rabbit holes, they took you where they wanted. I'd have to dig harder to figure out why one of the names felt familiar. The professor was easy to find. Even the simplest search told me he was a business professor at Brunel University.

That school was awfully close, and it would take me less than an hour to get there. Its original focus had been on technology, but over the years they had started to branch out into the business and medical fields. I was able to find the professor's schedule in a syllabus online that listed the times of his various classes and the office hours that were set aside every Tuesday.

Guess I was going out again. London always has that same look to it, as if it might rain any moment. Despite the gray skies, it got even less rain than my home in Seattle. But I ran upstairs to grab my jacket al the same. I waited at the foot of the stairs, feeling around in my pockets for keys. The stairs were positioned to the side of the living room so all I had to do was look up to see Sonia again. "I'll be back later in the evening," I said, leaving off anything else in the hope that maybe she'd warm up to me a little.

I drove over to the school, leaving the gun behind because people get rightfully twitchy about weapons on campus. Instead of sneaking around, I walked freely through Faraday Hall. A code was needed to enter the building, but with so many students coming and going, I didn't even need to hack it. I simply caught the door when someone opened it.

Weaving my way past all the dorm rooms was no short cut, but you'd be amazed what sort of information you'll hear by just being around people. The dorm dropped me off in front of an incredibly large, silver-domed athletic center. Using it as an obvious place marker, I checked the campus map on my phone before heading to the right of it toward the business department. It was always a marvel how much information was freely out there. All I had to do to learn everything about the school was go to their website.

I ended up passing the building the professor was currently teaching in, ignoring it completely as I played every factor to my favor. It only took two little pieces of metal, a pick, and a tension wrench to break into his office. A desktop computer ate up much of the desk space, but I ignored it completely since the school's systems wouldn't have any classified data from UltSyn. Instead, I shuffled through papers and pulled open drawers to see if there was anything I did want.

The bottom drawers had a rack for files, and I flipped through them before finding one labeled "UltSyn Candidates." I pulled the folder out and sat down on the floor with the file on my lap.

Inside was a random assortment of research papers and various other assignments that the professor must have found promising, all gathered in a fashion that made it look like he was searching for a prodigy. I took photos of any pages that seemed noteworthy before sliding the folder back into the drawer.

I stood up, checking the desk for anything else of value, and seized a flyer I spotted with the logo of UltSyn sticking out under a few other papers. There were other companies listed, their logos organized in a row on the bottom, companies ranging from sports drinks to the medical giant that UltSyn was, all promising their sponsorship for a job fair next week.

I was about to take a photo of it when my phone beeped, delivering an alert that class was almost over. I didn't know if the professor normally came back here afterwards or not, since I hadn't watched him long enough. But either way I wasn't going to risk it. I finished up, arranging everything back to how I remembered it, and got out of there.

As for leaving the campus completely, that would come later. I walked to the other end of the athletic center. Nostalgia made me want to head over to the IS department to my right, but I pushed on, wanting to scope out where the job fair would be.

The athletic center was open to the public, so I headed in. Inside was filled with, well, what you would imagine: people playing basketball and various other sports. I couldn't get everywhere since I didn't have a membership and wasn't willing to sign a name to one. But even barely inside, I was able to get a feel for things by imaging the hall being set up for the "Autumn Placement and Careers Fair" later on. After taking a final look, I jogged back to my car.

Driving through the rest of the campus was far less of a chore than walking it. I had only covered about a third of the university on foot, and had missed not only the art and engineering buildings, but restaurants, two bars, and even a nightclub—a tiny city in its own right. I sent Sonia a text, checking whether she needed me to pick up anything.

Traffic made the drive a bit longer on the way back, and the lack of reply just added to my annoyance. Once back, I dropped my phone on the tabletop as Hallie copied the photos from the day over to her systems. I was ready to confront Sonia about her ignoring the text, until I noticed the tablet's charging cord was sitting on my desk. A yellow sticky note was attached to the cord with a little sad face scribbled on it.

"Oh," I breathed. That explained it. I picked up the cord, and the note easily fell off before catching the desk. The connector end of the cord was kinked after repeated use. I could blame Sonia for it messing it up in her care, but there was no point. Every good tech knows that sometimes these things just take a shit.

I didn't see Sonia from there, and nabbed the blanket out of the holding room before heading into the living room. I found Sonia asleep on the couch. I shook out the blanket enough that I could spread it over her, and the tassels at the end brushed against her shoulder.

Sonia woke with a start, sitting up quickly, as both my presence and waking up on the couch were far too unexpected. She didn't sign anything, but her expression seemed to ask what I was doing.

"Hey, it's all right," I said softly, holding my hands up. Her expression was hard to read as she continued to stare at me. I couldn't tell if it was anger or something deeper.

I moved away and she pulled the blanket around herself. I caught her signing *Thank you* out of the corner of my eye. But, I still didn't have a real clue what she was feeling, despite the pleasantry offered. I tried to think of something to say, but had nothing.

There was an uncomfortable hesitation in us both, so instead of making it louder I just signed back, *You're welcome.* Since it was actually the same sign as *thank you*, I was counting on the fact that it should hold the same respect and tone as hers.

Sonia seemed to relax a little, even if she looked at me with a hyper-attentiveness. Her expression had shifted to an uneasy smile. I think this was the first time she had ever directed one toward me.

"You can sleep out here if you want. I won't bother you."

She rubbed her eyes, taking a moment to wake herself up. She looked tired, but I didn't bother to insist on her resting. She gave a short yawn before signing, *Did you find what you needed this time?*

"I don't know," I said, in a rare moment of raw honesty. I went over the downloaded photos on my computer, and started researching their brightest students. There were not many of them, but from what I could tell, one or two students had scores that suggested possible HID candidacy. I shifted my search to the career fair, looking into how many people attended each season, and how many were picked up by the different sponsors. I hadn't realized until then that Sonia had been hovering behind me like a fly on the wall. She kept enough distance, but I knew she had seen at least a few things.

She glanced at me before taking a sip of her water, not looking guilty for having been caught.

I turned back to the screens and leaned my elbow on the desk, frowning as I supported my chin with my hand. "Do you know anything about these? I mean, did you go to one?"

She didn't step forward or try to get me to see her sign any response, making me wonder if she was trying to think back to those days. I turned back to glance at her, but she only gave me a tight shake of her head.

"No? So then, not everyone is recruited this way?" Worry crept in as I looked at the monitor wondering if I had missed something. "It's not like they have factories where they build HIDs. You had to have had an average life before the UltSyn contract that sold your soul." Sonia stepped a little forward, shaking her head again, making me wonder if she was disagreeing or denying.

I don't remember any of that, she elaborated. The way she held her hands close to her chest suggested she didn't want to.

"You can't remember going? Was it that long ago?"

Her shoulders tightened a little, her jaw clenching as she seemed to not want to answer, eyes focused on the monitor rather than on me. *No. I don't remember what I did before I started working for UltSyn.*

I watched her carefully, feeling like I was looking at the same part of Sonia I had witnessed a few moments ago near the couch. That hint of anger was back, but at what this time? Not remembering? Or UltSyn?

"Oh," was all I was able to muster as a reply, looking away and at the computer again. "That's, uh, disappointing." My words were ambiguous enough that she could decide their meaning.

Sonia didn't give me another reply before disappearing to the couch where I could barely see her. I didn't know if she wanted it that way, but when she picked up the remote and turned on the TV, I let myself believe she was all right in her own little space.

<chapter five>
<! -- Scott -->

One of the first things I did when I took a break from looking at all of the data I'd gathered was take care of things around the house. I found a replacement cord for Sonia's tablet and put the tablet on my desk to remind myself to give it to her after making sure it took a proper charge.

I began working on hacking into the school database and added a name to the career fair attendees, making sure to sync my attendance to the badge I had picked up from the testing facility. That way I shouldn't have any problems getting in and out. I doubted anyone would even give it a second thought.

There wasn't much to prepare for otherwise, so I found myself doing insufferable daily chores to keep everything else running smoothly. I bought an unusual amount of sandwich fixings one day, since Sonia was boycotting cheese, and one can't survive off plain ham sandwiches.

I returned Sonia's electronic friend the next day, not mentioning the fact that I had forgotten about it for half a day. When the career fair came around, I was thrilled by the idea of getting out of the house and actually doing something useful.

I walked up to the front entrance as casual as any of the other attendees, swiping my pass across a scanner before heading into the fair without a problem. I was able to see much more of the building this time around. The place looked far more like a conference center than it had before. The entire space was lined with rows of tables, each offering something different to the attendees. Students moved from table to table, hoping to find their future and career—eerie really, since I knew where some of these jobs would land them.

I eyed each table as I passed and was ignored, under the assumption I was an exhibitor rather than a student, which was perfect. I didn't want to be remembered being here anyway.

I walked aimlessly for a while before a girl bumped into me. Her badge showed she was a student, and she turned to see whom she had bumped into. She seemed not to care at first, but turned over-apologetic as she saw my badge claiming I was from UltSyn.

"I'm *so* sorry," she said, sounding far more nervous, now that she thought I was someone she wanted to impress. I sighed. You'll never meet anything quite as fickle as a person.

"You shouldn't work for UltSyn," I found myself saying, even though I knew I should just leave well enough alone.

"Oh, yeah?" the girl asked, batting her eyes at me. She placed a hand on her hip as her demeanor changed to suggest something. "Do you *personally* have something better?"

I chuckled, trying to keep myself from actually laughing at her approach to things. It was amazing how quickly some people could easily shift into lust; there was nothing inherently wrong with that, it simply hadn't been anywhere near my intent.

Neither did I have a desire to proposition her—or anyone, for that matter.

"Just don't." I should shut up, but didn't seem able. "Everyone masquerades as something else in this world. Especially a big corporation."

The girl's response was less flirty this time; her expression suggested shock more than anything. "Um, it's a job fair and Ultimate Synthetics is hiring, and is listed as a technological and medical innovator."

I groaned to myself and pushed past her. I was going to be sick if I had to listen to recruitment lines. I had enough and headed back toward the door for some air. It was clear what the contacts Sonia had provided were up to: studying people and gathering a pool of new people.

That wasn't what I needed. The whole thing left me increasingly frustrated as I walked past students who looked at me like I was the ticket to their future.

Somewhere I had gotten off track, and all this was doing was taunting me further.

I didn't have time to save everyone. Hell, I didn't even want to care about everyone.

I had to backtrack. I had to follow that other lead, because this one was getting me nowhere. Even if the person I was looking for had been here, the trail was far too old now to follow.

After getting in the car, I sat there debating whether I should go back or if there was something else to sniff out. As I started the engine, something clicked into place—the second name Sonia had given me, Jesse Davies. I remembered why I thought I'd heard it before. He was someone my old friends associated themselves with. I didn't know him personally, but after I had left, he had been there a couple of times when I visited. Jesse had been a new recruit at the time, one of us, and that's why I couldn't track him easily. What did he have to do with any of this? I retrieved my phone from my pocket, and searched the contacts, hitting dial once Terry's name came up. "Hey, chap," he answered. "I got that email, interesting stuff you got. What's up?"

"I've got some more I can give you, too. Do you guys still hole up in that tech cave you've built for yourself?"

"Yeah, we're heading over around six or seven. What's the problem?" He sounded a little confused by my sudden interest in seeing them again.

I glanced over at the time, seeing it was pushing into four in the afternoon. I changed gears as I started backing up out of my parking space, estimating that I'd be getting to them in Bristol in about two hours if I left now. "Not much, I just have some things I want to share with you in person. I'll be there at six."

There was a grumble, or at least I think there was, on the other end. "We'll be there."

* * *

I pulled up to a rundown apartment complex. It was a three-story monstrosity, and I swore if it looked an ounce more disheveled, someone would petition for it to be knocked down to raise property values. It was ironic in a way, since the tech on the second floor was worth more than most people's homes.

Despite its appearance, it was well guarded. You couldn't get within a mile without pinging against Terry's systems. There are nearly six million CCTV cameras in this country, and someone like Terry made them look conservative.

I knew where many were hidden, since I'd worked here for a while. I could jam them, but doing that to Terry would be considered a personal insult. And mutual respect for each other was the only real connection we had these days.

With my car safely tucked away in the parking garage, I headed over to an elevator. When I hit the up button, it didn't even illuminate. I sighed, rolling my eyes, and glanced toward a discreet camera above the door. I gave an overdone smile; I heard a ding, and the doors opened for me.

I leaned against the back wall of the elevator as it moved up a floor. Terry must have totally been the type of kid who would kick you out of his tree house if you didn't guess the password right.

The door opened, not to a collection of apartments, but to an open floor plan. Walls had been knocked out or moved to make room for an intricate wiring setup allowing four people to work, with a bathroom and large break room in the back.

Terry referred to it as his bat cave, and it looked a lot different than my place, even though similar in many other ways besides the architecture. There were all sorts of these hidden caches around the world, including both our hideouts. I think most were created as safe houses for state missions, but I was sure some were set up for your old-school criminal, and likely doomsday prepper. At least, that's what Terry had told me. I headed back to where everyone would be. I walked past Nic at his desk, who didn't even look away from his work as he waved hello. Of all the team, he and I shared the same focus. Terry met me halfway, joining me as we both went toward the break room.

Jesse was also here at his desk. Seemed he'd earned a spot on the team. I looked over to him, as he was already leaning out of his chair in curiosity. Their fourth member was one of those rare people in our field—both morally sound and a morning person. Considering the time, she might even be asleep in an hour or two. I don't mean to sell her short; she was one hell of a tech. But unlike the rest who hacked shit for justice or profit, she also had a wife outside this. Meaning, she didn't just hang out much. My knowledge about her went as far as her desk decorations: a boat-shaped stress toy with a rainbow pride pin sitting on its foam hull.

"I can't even remember the last time I've actually seen you in person." Terry said, as he reclined into the couch. His accent always made me smile. Despite living in London for a while, my ear could still pick up that he was Scottish. I took a seat in a chair next to him as he continued, "So, what brings you by?"

"I got a list of contacts from an HID." I glanced toward the closed door before meeting his growing curiosity again.

"No shit?" Terry leaned forward and I nodded. "How did you get any information off one?"

I folded my arms across my chest, wondering if he'd think I was full of crap once I told him. "I asked." It was such a simple answer, but the expression Terry gave me suggested that I just spilled the meaning of life to him.

"How did you get to one long enough to ask it anything?"

"Uh…" I started, trying to think of the right word. "I acquired one."

"Fuck," Terry exhaled as he processed it all. "The darknet has been buzzing with rumors that one was stolen, but I didn't put much faith in it. You *have* to let me put the HID in one of our machines. I think I figured out the encryption so we can get the information without them talking."

I scoffed.

Clearly disappointed, Terry leaned back into the couch. This time in more of a huff than a relaxed gesture. "See, that was always your problem, Scott," he started up again, and I just stared over at him. "Narrow vision. You don't know how to dream big."

"Maybe I just don't want scope creep," I countered, "like some people."

"All right, fine," he sighed. "Then why did you come? To taunt me with your new toys?"

I licked my lips, knowing that this bit was the flip side of the exciting news I had brought, and wondered if he would even hear me out. "Jesse's name was in the mix."

Terry's brows pinched together. "What—why?"

All the names provided so far work with UltSyn in some fashion," I explained. "A testing director, a professor sending his brightest to UltSyn's door. Both work, on some level, for that company."

Terry looked past me like he could see through the door to Jesse. "Do you trust him?" I added, trying to read his careful expression.

"I did," Terry said, sounding unsure either way.

What have you guys been working on lately?"

Terry looked back at me, taking stock, I thought, to decide who he wanted to put his trust in. "We've been investigating UltSyn. Digging through their tax records, trying to follow the money."

"Find anything?"

"Not anything more interesting than you," his tone started out even, but dipped to something almost sad. "And nothing that you'd be looking for."

"Great," I groaned, leaning back in the chair. I was helping everyone else's cause besides my own.

I was contemplating leaving when there was a knock on the door. Both of us looked over as Jesse walked in. "Out of tea," he said, giving his empty mug a little shake as if to prove it. I cocked an eyebrow up at Terry, who returned my expression with an inquisitive one of his own.

"I got a hit back on that information you wanted," Jesse added. I had shut up since he walked in, but it was clear Jesse wasn't trying to hide the information from me. He rounded the counter, facing us now as the water boiled. "There is a weird ratio of 'assistants,'" he said, air quotes and all. "So, unless everyone is given one as a party favor, it has to be a cover for something else."

I might not *like* people, but I *understand* people. And Jesse was trying to buy my interest, but I wasn't going to bite so easily. "I'm going to talk to Nic." Everyone's attention shifted to me as I left the room. I heard Terry ask Jesse if he could make him some tea too, before following me.

I leaned over the half-wall divider that split up Nic's work area. "How's it going?" I asked, breaking into a smile when he replied with just a "Good." "Finding anything useful?" This time he just hummed *mhm* in return. Terry shook his head, somewhat amused at it all. I never minded Nic's short, simple, and clean answers. The man was an efficient machine.

"Miss me around here?" I grinned further.

That pulled Nic's eyes off the screen. "A little," he smiled, before both of us turned our attention to Jesse as he came over with two cups of tea.

"Well, I should head out," I said. Jesse's eyes flicked up toward me as he took a sip. Terry followed me back to the door, sipping on his tea like this was just another day at the office. He leaned on the doorframe as I stopped in the small, cramped hallway. "Hey, kid." Terry was in his early thirties, a few years older than me, but his tone suggested a bigger divide. "Don't be such a stranger, okay? The team still wants to work with you. Don't worry about Jesse. They probably have all our names in that HID word bank."

I paused, my teeth gritting together as the suggestion made me uncomfortable. I put the thought aside, shrugging slightly as I looked down the hall as if the elevator were calling for me. "Yeah, we'll see. Have a good night, Ter."

"Yeah, you too," he said, sounding a little disappointed as I headed toward the elevator.

I got down to the car and messed around on my phone as the car idled. Frankly, I was just stalling for a few minutes, and in that time, I noticed the elevator doors open again. The light was too low to see who got out, but someone was jogging toward my car. As they got closer to the headlights, I saw it was Jesse. He came up around to my window as I rolled it down.

"I'm sorry to hold you up. But can I ask you something?" I nodded for him to continue. "You—you found one, right?" I chewed on the question for a moment before nodding again slowly.

"Wow. Awesome. Okay," he babbled before breathing deeply. "Here's the thing. With all the digging I've been doing around UltSyn, I've found some things out about them and if what the guys say around the office is true, I think I can help you with whoever you've been looking for, if not even find them *for* you. All I'm asking in return, is that I can have it, them—whatever." He leaned in, his arm against the frame of my car. "That's all."

"So, I give you an HID and you give me unspecified information?" The word "whoever" meant that someone had told him more than I would have. I cleared my throat, looking away from him for a moment. My phone blinked a small green light, letting me know I had a new notification. "What will you do with the HID?"

"I don't know yet," he said, running a hand through his hair. "We are dying to test out our equipment and see if we can get into their heads."

"That's Terry's thing. He already asked. Tel me what you want."

Jesse straightened up a bit, glancing toward the building, "I've got my own connections, ones that will give me good money for UltSyn tech. You don't care about profit, or harming UltSyn, unless it gets you to this oh-so-mysterious person. If you don't care, what's the harm?"

"I'm not in the business of making deals."

"Yeah?" Jesse's face darkened. "And what do you have to show for it?"

<chapter six>
<! -- Scott -->

My mind wandered a bit as I looked over the files I had on my computer. It wasn't that I was getting distracted, more that I was staring at a puzzle piece that I didn't know how to place. Any time the computer took a moment to load, I lost a few extra minutes thinking about Terry and Jesse's offers. I didn't really like either option.

Terry was being his usual combination of curious and self-righteous, while Jesse was clearly in it for the money.

When I noticed the time hours later and decided to call it for the day, I headed upstairs to shower, hoping it would help clear my head. It was even easier to lose track of time in the shower, as I tuned out everything besides the sound of the water and the steam building up around me. When I got out, I studied my scrapes to make sure they were fine after the neglect I had showed them. Then, I decided to go check the computer before calling it a night. Sonia had been keeping quiet, so I assumed she was already asleep.

I didn't bother to get fully dressed before I wandered shirtless into the hallway. The floor felt cold under my bare feet. Before I even made it downstairs, the room to my right caught my attention. Inside was the heart of all my computer systems. Nearly every cord could be traced back to this room, but that wasn't the curious thing about it.

Rising on the tips of her toes to see the higher shelves was Sonia. She stared at everything without laying a finger on any of it, but ventured a step deeper into the mix of wires, spare parts, and almost-living programs. When her hand swirled above a keyboard, all of this proved too much for me. The gesture was intimate somehow, like running your fingers carefully through someone's hair.

"You're not supposed to be up here," I said, breaking the silence. The console in front of her blinked on at the sound of my voice, and she jumped at the combination of the two.

She turned to me in surprise, fumbling as she signed, *I— didn't do anything*. We stared at each other for a moment before her hands moved again. *I just— wanted to understand bet er. The who we're looking for, and why.*

My lips parted, but she didn't find the answer she was looking for there. All I could think was how she wasn't meant to be up here, breaking the only rule in a single act. While Sonia might not show emotion, her expression changed enough that I knew she recognized my anxious annoyance. She moved toward the door, despite me standing in the way.

I stared until she was close enough that I had to step back so she could walk past me. Sonia scurried down to the first floor. I paced the long landing that extended from the top of the stairs. From here, I could see down into much of the living room, and watched as Sonia darted through it.

My room filled with a low white glow as I settled down on my bed. Maybe the others were right. Maybe Sonia was more of a distraction than anything. Maybe she was a pawn on a chessboard that I had to lose in order to free up another.

I picked up my phone, spinning it around in my hand as I thought about the choices. Jesse's offer seemed a little sweeter now. I closed my eyes and told myself that only one thing mattered. I thumbed through my contact book to find Jesse's name. I didn't have the number before, but thanks to Sonia I did now. She was only a piece of the bigger picture. I sent a text off that simply read, "Deal."

* * *

I rolled out of bed just after noon, reading the reply from Jesse about where we would meet for the exchange. I had my doubts, but I didn't have time to cherry-pick information out of the HID. Plus, there is one good thing about people who are in it for the money. You know where their loyalties lie.

Sonia was downstairs busying on her tablet, and only sneaked a quick look as I walked past and into the kitchen. I pulled out cereal and poured myself a bowl. "I'm going to need you to come with me today," I glanced at her before going on. "You'll need to be ready to leave in about an hour." Not like it would even take her that long, with her pixie haircut and total of one outfit.

She looked up at me again. *Where are we going?*

I brought the bowl over to my desk, sitting down and booting up the computer. "It's not too far and the mission should be quick." She didn't sign anything else, so I guessed that was the end to our daily question game.

I checked the camera feeds for the location Jesse told me about, scoping out what it looked like and if anything seemed fishy. From what I could tell, everything checked out. It seemed this would be an easy exchange, as long as I could trust Jesse.

While packing everything into the car, Sonia stood awkwardly by the garage door. I looked up, and waved her over. "Come on, we need to get going."

What do you need me to do on this mission? she asked while getting in, pulling up that dark hood that made her look like a ghost.

I got in and started the car up. "Maybe nothing. I just need you there in case you can identify someone on the fly. So just behave and don't get me in trouble." She didn't nod, just seemed to silently agree as she looked out the window.

As I drove, the whole situation felt oddly like returning a part I didn't need after all. I pulled up to the location Jesse had picked, and I didn't allow myself to see it as anything besides a simple exchange. I spotted a few cameras, but I didn't bat an eye at them. They were already jammed; I had made sure of it on the way over. "Let's go," I said, hardly looking at Sonia as I got out of the car.

Jesse pushed himself off the wall as we neared. I knew he hadn't been waiting long, even though the way he held himself suggested he thought otherwise. I didn't have to like the man to use him to get what I needed.

"Is that the HID?" Jesse asked, eyeing Sonia carefully.

"Of course," I said. Jesse looked doubtful as he took a step closer to the both of us. "What do you want her to do? Recite the first hundred digits of pi for you?"

That finally made him smile. Strange, since I thought my attitude would have further soured his. "That won't be necessary," he replied, and turned to Sonia. "Can I see your hand?"

"Quid pro quo," I interrupted before she moved. From the corner of her eye, she was watching the two of us, calculating all our movements, and equating a meaning out of them.

"Right, of course," Jesse said, and dug into his pocket. He pulled out a flash drive and handed it to me. If, for any reason,

Sonia hadn't figured out what was going on, she knew now. I anxiously flipped the flash drive between my fingers as Jesse asked to see Sonia's hand again.

Now I was the one curiously watching. Sonia pulled her hands away from his casual gesture, fear washing over her with just a look, but that didn't stop Jesse from yanking her toward him. He held her with one hand, and slid her sleeve up with the other. As Sonia pulled back, Jesse gripped tighter around her wrist.

I was about to object when an alarm on my phone went off. I exhaled through my teeth and pocketed the flash drive to check, despite what was going on.

A cuss fell from my mouth as the notification said the cameras were rebooting. It was pointless to try to jam them again, so I put my phone away as I looked back up to Jesse, who seemed somehow satisfied after looking at Sonia's arm. I wasn't quite sure what I had missed, but clearly something.

"She checks out," Jesse commented, but it didn't seem like he was talking to me.

I may not know everything, but I do know when someone knows more than they are letting on. I pulled my pistol, training it on Jesse in a flash. He just grinned at me, which was the second sign that things weren't going to work out for me.

"I wouldn't do that if I was you," he said.

"Oh yeah?" I asked, without wavering. Sonia took a step away from Jesse and back toward me, even though she seemed hesitant to do so. "Do you think I give a shit about state cameras after the last stunt I pulled?"

"No," Jesse started, as two men joined us on the street. I spotted pistols in their hands. Having a weapon was becoming less advantageous every time goons broke the gun laws with me. "What I didn't tell you is UltSyn pays really well for their own tech back. Unofficially, of course."

We both flinched as one of the men grabbed Sonia, pinning her arms as she squirmed to get away. She looked to me as if to scream for help. My gun shifted to him, but I didn't pull the trigger. The two of them were moving so much I thought it would foul up my shot.

I looked over my shoulder to see the second man with a gun pointed at my head. Now that would be a clean shot. My jaw clamped down as I lifted my hands up.

She's our property now. Too bad, so sad," taunted the guy behind me.

"You could still leave," Jesse said, but I could hardly pay attention to him as Sonia fell into the arms of the man she was struggling with. The fight in her eyes eased away as they rolled back. He scooped her up like a lifeless doll. Tranquilizer would have been my guess. But it was Jesse's almost concerned tone that drew my attention back to him.

"I didn't tell UltSyn who you are, for what it's worth."

If I wanted to make it out of this alive, I knew I shouldn't pass up an easy way out. I slowly lowered my hands, putting my gun away with exaggerated movements so they wouldn't shoot me as a precaution. The man only had to carry Sonia a little way before an SUV pulled up. I was by no means happy about this situation; I simply didn't have a choice in the matter. I knew when I was beat.

"I wouldn't want to be you when Terry finds out," I warned, despite backpedaling toward the car. If I had my way, it wouldn't be the last he heard of me either.

"Do the moral have time for revenge these days?" he taunted.

<chapter seven>
<! -- Scott -->

Somewhere out there a cup of coffee was waiting for me, and when I found it, I was probably going to make it Irish. I rigged the streetlights in my favor as I sped, feeling like the flash drive was burning a hole in my pocket. Realistically, I knew there wouldn't be anything on it. Some people might be content with walking away with their life, but I still needed to know whether I had traded for something more than I already had. I tossed the flash drive on my desk as the computer synced up to copy it. The systems scanned as I headed off toward the kitchen to find that coffee.

When I took a step, I heard something like a page being turned. I looked down to see the bottom corner of a Post-it Note sticking out from under my shoe. I lifted my foot up to pull it off, turning the note over in my hand to see a smiley face drawn.

Not quite following, I looked over to my desk before realizing the note must have fallen to the floor. I stared back down at the note, thinking this must be the counterpart of the last one I found, a thank you for getting the cord replaced.

Three little lines shouldn't be able to make my heart sink this much.

Databases don't do this, which meant she was more than what UltSyn wanted her to be, even after their conditioning, more than what I wanted her to be to give myself some twisted peace of mind. She could be someone's daughter, sister, or love. Even more importantly, she was her own person.

And, someone I had traded away.

"Fuck me." I grabbed my keys and no longer cared what was on the flash drive as I headed back to the car.

"Hallie, the cameras were turned back on during the trade. Hack back in, and find Sonia for me." My hands went to the steering wheel, crumpling the note under them. I hadn't even realized I still had it. I spent another second sticking it to my rearview mirror as I pulled out and spun the car around in the right direction.

I drove as Hallie crunched the numbers for me. Tracking people wasn't hard if you could pick up the breadcrumbs quick enough. The drive back had cost me some time, but I was hoping I could turn it in my favor.

One thing was sure: I was certain UltSyn wasn't expecting me. I doubted they knew who I was. *Yet.* This plan was gambling everything I had worked for in order to correct a heartless mistake. My eyes caught the sticky note again. I started to wonder if I only held onto the thing to keep my nerve, because this was an extremely bad idea.

I wasn't prepared, I didn't know where I was going, and I'm not really the hero type.

"Location spotted: 26 Grafton Way," Hallie reported in her always-neutral tone.

I made a quick turn, abrupt enough that the car next to me hit the horn. This was so stupid. Was this even a rescue attempt for Sonia or to preserve any humanity I had left? When it came down to the matter, it was simple. Not letting

UltSyn snuff out Sonia's spirit, one that I had clearly ignored, was as close to a soul of my own as I was going to get.

Once parked in the nearest spot I could find, leaning over to the glove compartment that held a gun and Paul's employee ID. Those were two vastly different ways to go about things. I grabbed both, and dug around a bit more until I found the earpiece for my phone.

I hit the street and adrenaline cleared my head of everything except the job in front of me. Instead of fearing for myself or worrying about Sonia, I focused on the size of the building, and how many employees that meant.

But mostly, I thought about how many armed guards I'd run into. The UK had quite different gun laws than the States, but UltSyn's ability to outright break those laws had screwed me over before. I was risking my neck hoping that a building used for official business would be forced to be more accountable.

I went with the very unusual tactic of walking straight up to the front door, mentally gridding the place like a giant chessboard. I flashed the ID to the tired-looking guy at the front desk, and walked back to an elevator, acting like I owned the place.

While the receptionist hadn't objected, the elevator was giving me some trouble. I swiped the ID over the sensor, and it just shined angry and red up at me. I tried it a second time with no luck. Instead of testing it further and being locked out of the system, I pulled out my phone, pretending like I had received a text while waiting for the elevator.

I've had my fingers in the UltSyn system for months; I just had to hope this was connected to something I could view. I scrolled through various code until I found the controls for it, and overrode the authorization.

A smile grew as the metal doors separated me from everyone. My eyes scanned over the buttons for the different floors, leaving me with the very open-ended question: what now? "Did you get a fix on her?"

"Location unknown," Hallie said into my ear. "Unable to break into relevant UltSyn system. Last known location is thirty meters north."

Side door, I figured with a grumble, even though I had to give the system credit for being intelligent enough to automatically try for me. "All right, Scott. Where do we go next?"

I cringed as another horrible idea came to me. "Can you tell me which floor has the most people? Track via badge signal," I ordered, and Hallie checked. HIDs had to be secured, and an odd grouping of people gathered would suggest guards, instead of workers more evenly placed.

"Fifty-one RFID badges on floor two, followed by seventeen on the third floor."

I hit three after checking with Hallie how tightly packed the level was. My phone's map refreshed every few seconds to show movements in real time. A few dots were tightly packed together, talking maybe, while others were pacing back and forth. Far more of a mystery than the even cubicle layout on two.

"Here we go," I breathed as the doors opened again.

A guard's eyes flickered away from a set of security cameras and over to me. He raised a curious eyebrow as I walked over. I glanced behind me as if unsure this was my stop. "I get so lost every time they send me to a new floor," I joked, and leaned against his tall station before going on. "I'm from IT. I was sent because someone was having trouble with the Wi-Fi."

The man shot me a look like I had put my elbows up on the dining room table. "ID?"

"Hmm? Oh, yes." I unclipped it from my jacket and handed it over to him.

He looked at the name before flipping through a clipboard. From my angle, I could see the list had a company photo and name displayed to the right. I had altered the badge for the fair; even if Paul's name hadn't been blacklisted, the photo wouldn't match anymore.

I pulled my gun instantly and he froze, a corner of a page still slightly turned up. "I was waiting for someone to check on that," I sighed. "I'm going to need you to let me pass. If you tell me where the HIDs are located, I won't even shoot you."

That got a laugh out of him. "They are hidden," he smirked, a very unflattering look for a man with a gun trained on his chest, if you asked me.

"Well, no shit."

The guard made a move, and I shot his hand before he could touch anything.

He yelled in pain, pulling his hand back and away from the alarm to cradle it. "You shot me, you bloody wanker!"

"Yeah," I said. "That's what the gun is for. If you want to keep your other hand, you'll leave that alarm be."

"It doesn't matter, everybody already heard you. I bet—," he started, but I walked past him, not about to let him talk me to death. I heard people running my way down the hall, so I ducked into a thankfully empty office. I checked the map on my phone; four of them passed before I sneaked out again. UltSyn's main alarm went off, screeching a god-awful noise. I should commit to a plan, because this was what happens when you don't commit to a single approach method.

"Are you still in their system?"

"Of course," Hallie replied. Now the AI was reminding me of Sonia. It's not bragging, just a fact.

I decided to not follow in the footsteps of the four men and turned to where they came from. Checking every room in this damn place was out of the question since it would take forever. I needed to figure out which section, or what type of room they would be holding Sonia in.

I walked a little further down, finding a unit that mirrored medical wings I had seen before. Through glass, I saw simple rows of beds, where even with the alarm blaring, men and women slept as they recovered from whatever type of procedure they had gone through. I spotted a doctor stepping out of a room, but she seemed preoccupied with trying to move al her patients to notice me. I silently came up next to her, and spun her against a wall with my forearms, training my gun right at the space below her ear.

"You have a new HID as a guest. What unit did you put her in?"

She blinked several times. "Uh…all new patients are put in individual rooms down the east wing."

"This floor?" I asked, and she nodded quickly. As I pulled myself away, I wondered if she was the "just doing her job" type.

Out of nowhere, I felt intense pain in my back as something sharp ripped through my skin. I hadn't noticed a patient had gotten out of their bed, and picked up a scalpel as they tried to defend their doctor. I swung at the man who looked far too drugged up to be standing. He fell to the ground, not unconscious, but silently shaking with his hands pulled under his chin.

I pulled the metal from my back, and turned to the doctor who luckily seemed too shocked to move. "Do anything besides taking care of him, and I'll come back and embed this somewhere else." I dropped the scalpel so I could hold my gun better. Both doctor and patient seemed too shaken up to be a threat, so I headed toward the correct wing.

I walked down the west hallway, looking for any sign of where Sonia would be. A chart on the wall contained a scribbled list of patients organized by date. The newest one must have been Sonia, patient twenty-nine in Hall B. I just had to make sure to avoid the guards that swarmed the place or any further run-ins with surgery utensil wielding patients.

I found the room and checked both ways down the hall before opening the door. On the bed was the girl who I had only seen in loose dark clothes, now stripped down to the bare minimum around her chest and waist. Sonia was at least alone for the moment. I holstered my gun as I had to get her ready to go.

"Sonia, wake up," I said, shaking her a little before I looked at the IV. I wasn't sure any amount of shaking would do the job right now. I raced my hands toward the IV, putting pressure on the vein to take it out. As I looked over her face, I realized I would have to carry her out if we had any chance of getting out of here today. I pulled off my jacket, getting ready to cover her as I noticed scars lining her arms, shoulders, legs, and probably much more. They were unnaturally perfect. They were round scars freckling her skin in even measurements and reminded me of rivets in metal. Although what UltSyn gave or took with them was beyond me.

I ignored their possible meanings and draped my jacket over her shoulders.

The door opened, and I didn't have a second to waste before drawing my gun on a new doctor, not taking an extra moment before I shot him. I didn't have the time to sort through who deserved it or not right now. I stepped toward the door, looking down the hallway as I saw two guards coming my way.

One was on the ball and instantly fired a Taser gun. Barbed electrodes sunk into my chest. My muscles locked before I could reach to rip them out. I dropped to my hands and knees as electricity was working against me for a change.

It only lasted five seconds, but god, was it the longest five ever. I ignored the guards moving close, opting to tear the Taser wires out before he hit the trigger again.

They worked as a bothersome team. The guard who had not shot me pulled me up to my knees with his baton pressed against my neck.

"Look what we caught," he taunted, tightening his grip to choke me briefly.

His buddy smiled as he pulled his own baton. My eyes strained to look toward the gun that sat waiting on the ground for me.

"Turn out the lights and do the math for me," I choked out as the guards showed their confusion in their word choice.

Three seconds later, the power turned off, leaving a distant emergency light on. The men backed off and I grabbed the gun. Rising to my feet, I aimed at where I last saw them. Firing as Hallie gave me the signal that the math would add up.

I took a deep breath, clearing my head as adrenaline made me want to race on. I had to be able to think clearly. "How many people are closing in?" I asked, as I moved back into Sonia's room.

"Three RFID signals are making their way across the west wing, twenty meters east."

I pulled Sonia into my arms, shifting her a couple times as my muscles strained from the shock they had just endured. "How many people are on the first floor?"

"Twenty occupy the area."

"Any idea how many are actually guards?"

Hallie didn't answer right away, trying to process an answer. "Unknown," she replied much to my chagrin. I tried to think back to how many plain clothed workers I noticed originally. But RFID signals didn't differentiate like that, nor did I have time to sort it out.

I took the staircase, making my way as quickly as I could while carrying Sonia.

Every time I glanced down, she showed no sign of coming around. As I reached the door to the main corridor, I placed Sonia down against the wall before checking if anyone had followed us.

We should be safe from one direction... for now. I changed the clip of my gun as I breathed out slowly. All I needed was to get out of here and make it to the car. It was only maybe a block away, but wouldn't matter if it were a hundred if I couldn't make it out the door. And standing between me and getting to the car was upwards of twenty guards. I pulled my phone out, setting Hallie up to switch systems, and synced up a countdown of twenty seconds.

I put my hand on the door, focused on breathing for now. I heard Hallie go through the last five seconds in my ear. "Four, three, two, one," I mouthed along with her. As the countdown reached zero, the sprinklers went off.

The distraction didn't need to last long. But it bought enough time that I could pick off a few of the sidetracked guards and move Sonia and I over toward the cover of a cubicle. Shots were already being fired this way. As if things weren't already difficult, a heavily armed cavalry wasn't going to give me much room for error.

I darted over to the cubicles across from us, startling a group of workers that were split between two desks, hunkered together on the far right. "Just stay down," I said, lowering my gun only slightly as I moved past to an open desk one up. I pushed forward again, checking both ways to the last set on the right.

I popped out to take care of the guards by the front door, but one proved to be a faster shot. A bullet winged my leg; I ground my teeth together and didn't let the pain foul up my shot. As morbid as it might be, I went for the head because physics declared nothing else mattered as much. I ducked back as soon as I fired, and only heard the sounds of one shot go off. I hoped to god that meant only one of them still had a gun.

Instead of waiting for me to pop out again, a guard cautiously came my way with his Taser out. I was crouched down behind a short cubicle wall, and when he was close enough, I shot him in the leg. The man went down simply because his knee gave out. Grounding worked here, too.

The barbed tips of the Taser fired out from his gun, but only caught the cubicle as I charged past to the remaining three guards. I fired at two of them. A bullet caught one in the arm, and he slid down a half wall like he just wanted to be done with this. Another came at me with a baton, which I blocked with my forearm. Painful, but it was the remaining man with a gun that shook my confidence. I think I only realized I had been shot when my arm jolted back an inch on its own.

It was irrelevant for what I had to do, and with a lot more spite than I normally liked, I fired back, and he sickeningly dropped to my feet. I whizzed around to the guard who treated me like a practice target. His hesitation gave me pause. "Don't make me kill you."

After staring at me like I was death incarnate, the guard dropped the already wavering gun, and put his hands up. I kicked the gun away as I passed, and looped to the left side of the cubicles, terrifying another small group of workers that were huddled together. Sonia was still knocked out from whatever they gave her. As I picked her up, pain stole my breath away, forcing me to gasp for another.

This time I walked straight down the middle of the room. Two more office workers were hiding and completed the reported RFID count. When I reached the door, the guard I hadn't shot spoke. "What do you want with her?"

"To leave," I answered, and happily did just that.

I felt like making it outside should have been the easiest part, but without someone bearing down on me, my body objected to every step I took. Sometimes it felt like that last inch was the hardest to grasp. Maybe because at this point, I felt like the world should just give me that much.

I made it through, and secured Sonia in the passenger seat before my steps started to slow along the way to the driver's side. My body relaxed into the seat a bit too much for my liking. After all, I still had miles after the finish line to go.

"Hallie," I said, my voice having a strange waver in it. "Activate assisted driving." The car had the feature to drive itself where I needed, but I didn't want to give up complete control. Not yet. The second I stopped pushing forward was the second I'd be lost.

I put pressure on my arm whenever I didn't need two hands to drive, and the steering wheel had smeared blood on it by time I pulled the car into the hideout.

Frankly, I don't think I could have made it back if the computer wasn't helping me. My vision crossed a few times, making me see doubles of a few cars. I helplessly let out another groan as I carried Sonia in and was glad she couldn't hear me wince again as I laid her on the couch. I stood there for a moment watching her sleeping in practically nothing but underwear and my jacket. Physically, at least, I believed she was going to be fine.

I commanded myself to head upstairs, slowly pulling myself up each stair with the help of the railing. I felt dizzy and only remembered bits and pieces as my steps skipped forward when I opened my eyes.

The only reason I made it to the bathroom was from sheer force of will. Every other part of me just wanted to collapse onto the bed. I pushed myself up to sit on the counter, pulling out supplies from the medicine cabinet as I tried to patch myself up.

The pain of checking out my various stab and bullet wounds hurt enough that it cleared my head from the sharp ache of it all. Where I was attacked with the scalpel looked like a bee sting in comparison to the shallow gash one of the bullets took out of my leg. However, that too looked like nothing in comparison to my arm.

My leg at least didn't have a bullet still lodged in it.

I pulled my sleeve up to get a better look at things. It had seemed god awful in the car since the bullet had caught my inner arm and ended up soaking the side of my shirt. Everything ached, but that feeling was becoming more and more distant at the same time. Nothing vital looked damaged. The bullet likely could have stayed in there. But since my mind was already retreating, I decided to grab forceps out of the medicine cabinet.

Once the bleeding slowed, I could see the bullet, which was actually a blessing. If the shot had been at a different angle it could have hit bone, or tried to escape into my ribcage. Instead it just sat a couple inches in, nested between muscle and blood like a macabre souvenir. Looking at the mirror as I pulled out the bullet made it feel a bit less like my own arm. Still, I felt the beginnings of shock as the forceps made contact: heat, thirst, tremors.

I took a deep breath, refusing to die with that stupid thing in me. Lack of morale was probably the real killer in these situations. Hands shaking, I wrapped it too loosely, then too tight, but the second time I left it that way.

In the scheme of things, actual blood loss and bullet removal were the least of my worries. Infection was. I reached for a bottle of antibiotics with my injured arm and instantly regretted it. My vision started to narrow, needing a moment to recover before leaning over and grabbing the amoxicillin in with my other hand.

At some point, I must have drifted out. When I opened my eyes to the now-dim room, I thought I shouldn't be here. With a wobble, I stood, wanting to lie down even more than I wanted to not feel.

<chapter eight>
<! -- Sonia -->

Moving stiffly against the cushions, it took a few tries before I was able to fully open my eyes. I could barely remember where I had been, only recalling the brief moments of looking around a small room and the cold metal table against my skin.

But as I looked around this room, I realized those short memories didn't match with where I was now.

I forced myself up, grabbing onto the couch for support. I was back in the living room I spent most of my time in while I was with Scott. I remembered the trade off, fear tinting al of those memories, and I was about to question if it was all just a dream until I looked down at myself. The jacket I remembered seeing on Scott before was laying on the couch as if I had been sleeping in it. The white undergarments UltSyn dressed me in clung uncomfortably, and panic filled me to the near brim as I noticed the jacket's caked on blood.

I looked over myself for injuries, but soon realized none of it was my own. I glanced around the room, trying to understand what had happened as I paired the memories with the clues that were left.

The only thing missing from the equation was Scott. The floor sent a chill up my bones, so I pulled on the jacket despite its wear. With the probable need to find actual clothes ignored,

I walked through the first floor. I leaned against the desk where he always sat, looking for any hint of him having left the place. Nothing. I patted the jacket's pockets and came up empty again.

I turned to look at the stairs, deciding it was the only place left to check.

Before I went, I reached for the tablet to check the time. Without natural light, it was the only way to get my bearings. Since it was just past nine in the morning, I must have lost a day somewhere. Maybe Scott was simply asleep. I had never seen him wake up early if he didn't have to go somewhere. Still, I wanted to know. So, I climbed the stairs quietly, remembering the last time I ventured up here.

I walked carefully in the dark, wandering past the room I visited days before.

There was another door further down that wasn't shut all the way, but I decided to knock all the same. When I received no response, I slowly pushed the door open, taking a quick glance back into the upstairs hallway.

A light shined up, and I glanced down toward it. Each step triggered another one, guiding me until I found a switch and al of the tiles flooded the room with soft white light. Collectively, they allowed me to clearly see Scott lying in bed. After being so talkative before, it almost didn't compute how he was able to be so still now.

I approached cautiously and hovered my hand by his nose to see if he was breathing before moving to touch a shoulder that didn't seem injured. When he didn't respond, my fingertips went to check his pulse. He was alive, at least. I eyed his injuries, inspecting them the best I could without moving him.

Unsure what to do next, my eyes wandered around the room and spotted a bathroom. Even from here I could see bandages soaked in dark red piled up on the counter. That begged the question: if he hadn't been able to clean the bathroom up after everything, had he managed to take care of his wounds well enough? Doubtful.

I wasn't sure what led him to bring me back here, but I knew I wasn't going to let him die of infection because of my spite. I brought some medical supplies into the bedroom, setting them on the nightstand as I carefully prepared. Littered across his arms were various older scars. They briefly piqued my curiosity since their formation and placement were chaotic.

I wish I could have called out in an attempt to wake him, but I couldn't. I wasn't even sure if I'd be able to help with much without moving him, but I'd try my best. Carefully, I sat down next to him on the bed, and peeled back gauze that by the coloring was also old.

How on earth did he get us both out of that hellhole I had been stuck in?

Scott moved slightly as I reached over to get the antiseptic, but didn't wake up.

However, when I touched the wound with it, he woke up with a shiver. His muscles stayed rigid until he registered that it was me, and his breathing remained uneven.

Scott started to sit up, but I put a hand on his shoulder to suggest he shouldn't. There wasn't a fight, but his eyes were glued to me as he settled down. I carried on with what I was doing before he woke, focusing on it rather than him.

"What are you doing?" he asked softly, and I turned to note his confused expression.

Fixing you, I signed.

"I see that. I meant— why are you?" I pieced together that the softness I heard before hadn't been carefulness, but rather a worn-out tiredness.

My fingers moved as if I wanted to say something, but I couldn't think of anything, so instead, I carried on and picked up the gauze to re-wrap his arm. He winced, but overall, was being a far better patient than I would have expected. I hadn't yet decided if that was a good sign or not.

He didn't have a blanket over him which made it easier to look over his legs. Jeans were on, but I could spy the corner of a bandage underneath a tear. Without warning, I ripped the fabric back a little further. I could feel Scott lean back by his shift of his weight, and decided his silence did worry me.

He had managed to bandage it once by wiggling the gauze underneath, but that seemed like a sure-fire way to miss something. When I glanced up, Scott had broken into a sweat.

I asked if he had any other injuries. Slowly he licked his lips before telling me there was one on his back. I moved around the bed to the side he mentioned. In a small gap carefully pressed against the headboard was a small rip in his shirt.

This one looked different. Instead of asking about it, I just pulled his shirt up so I could peel the bandage back. Considering the location, I don't think he had cleaned it well. Sure enough, I thought as one edge looked redder than the rest. I reached for the antiseptic again.

"Thank you," he said as I was finishing up. He turned to look over his shoulder as if he wanted to say more, but looked away before he finally did. "I'm... sorry I turned you over to them."

I didn't know why he picked a time to talk when he wouldn't be able to see my reply. Maybe he was scared of what my reply would be. I must admit I haven't sat down to think how I felt about it now that I was here. It was my job to report things, not feel them, but I think the closest was a mix of anger and gratitude.

I got up, gathered up the supplies, and headed back to the bathroom. Despite throwing away the mess, this place would need a lot of scrubbing before being considered clean.

I searched the medicine cabinet and found prescription painkillers. There were three noteworthy things about it: the bottle was mostly full, it was old but not expired, and they had someone else's name on it. I decided to bring the bottle over to him all the same. *I'll go get you water*, I signed, before I moved toward the door.

"Wait," Scott called. I turned back to an expression that looked like I had vowed to leave for good. "Please sit down for a second." I did, and tried to study his face to pinpoint what expression was there, but it was too jumbled for me to tell.

"I don't expect you to forgive me, but I want you to know why I did what I did," Scott started, staring down at his hands, fingers partially intertwined as he played with the ring there. "Years ago, I worked for a cyber security and surveillance firm in Seattle. And I...lost someone. At first, everyone thought it was nothing, that maybe she was just busy with college. But after two months, I still didn't hear anything. That's when I started to track things to UltSyn, then UltSyn to their UK branch, and that branch to the HID program."

"I kidnapped you," —he laughed, even though his tone suggested that he thought the whole thing was ridiculous— "for information, then traded you away for the same thing. Information that I had hoped would bring me to... to my sister."

That piece of information was new to me. I had known that he was looking for someone, but what I hadn't been able to factor in was his connection to the girl he showed me on day one.

What's her name? I signed, unsure if I was fact checking or genuinely curious.

Scott finally looked up at me, pausing like he had not answered that question in a long time and was having trouble forming the name on his lips once again. "Victoria."

Not knowing how to feel about this new fact, so I simply tried not to feel for the time being. I nodded as I stood up. *I'll go get you water*, I said again so he knew what I was doing.

I thought he was asleep when I came back into the room, but his eyes opened enough to watch my feet come into view as I walked over to the nightstand. He finally looked up with a faint smile.

It was awkward for a number of factors and paused there for a moment. *This might be a bad time. But do you have anything for me to wear?*

Scott nodded, rubbing his eyes before pointing over to a closed door next to the bathroom. "You can wear whatever you find in the closet. It's all my clothes, but you should be able to find something that fits," he explained as I turned to look in that direction.

Without another word from him, I sunk my hands into the pockets of his jacket and headed over to the closet. The walk-in closet had various computer parts set on a shelf here and there, but otherwise was completely normal. I had almost expected something fancy based on the rest of the hideout. I found pants that looked too small for Scott, followed by a plain gray shirt.

I took quick steps to leave Scott's room, but ended up stopping squarely on a large, illuminated tile, and spun back around to him. He just stared at me curiously.

Thank you for saving me, I signed before scurrying out of the room.

<chapter nine>
<! -- Sonia -->

Scott slept much of that next week. I brought food and we changed the bandages daily. I checked the bottle of painkillers, surprised when I saw he wasn't really taking them. It was curious since on the fourth day, he hissed in pain as I peeled back gauze. "Why are the guards always so armed?"

I don't think he expected an answer. But I had one, so I paused to provide it. *Most are third party security contractors so UltSyn can blame that company and keep their hands clean.*

"Yeah?" he added, through gritted teeth as I pressed the new tape down over his leg. I nodded. *Even that Taser wasn't allowed. Probably from a former cop.*

"Taser?"

I gestured to the scrapes on his chest, and he let out a small 'oh'. *Hand*, I signed with one and held the other out.

Scott looked up to acknowledge me, then focused on his elbow with the utmost concern. With strain, he slowly extended his arm as the tips of his fingers caught mine. I gently tried to stretch his inner muscle a tiny bit more as I curled my fingers in.

I took my hands back to say, *Getting better.*

"After I recharge," Scott ventured, "we can celebrate with cake."

I cracked a small smile. *Bored?*

Yes, he signed.

* * *

Days later, I was downstairs watching the news when my tablet got a text from him that read: "In the top left drawer of my desk there is a tennis ball. Please bring it up here thanks."

I think I stared at the text for a solid two minutes, wondering if autocorrect had hijacked the text. Since its replacement never came, I got up and went to his desk and found a fuzzy yellow tennis ball there.

More than a little curious now, I brought it up. The room was dark, but could faintly make out his silhouette sitting up. I ventured into the dim room, placing the ball in his free hand, and taking note of the papers placed around him on the bed in a little half circle.

What is the tennis ball for? If there was a clear connection, I didn't see it.

"I'm glad you asked," Scott said in all seriousness before he bounced the ball on the tile next to me lighting it up so he could see what he was reading again. "That's why," he grinned.

Why he couldn't just turn on the lights normally was beyond me. I was halfway down the stairs when I realized this was likely because he was still bored.

Being stuck in bed for a while had considerably slowed him down. I sat on the couch deciding to send him a text that read: "I swear if you text me saying you bounced that ball out of reach I'm coming up there to take it away."

I thought that would be the end of it, but almost instantly I got a reply: "Don't make me laugh it hurts when you do."

A part of me wanted to do it again for that exact reason. Perhaps I was still a bit bitter about him handing me over. Forgiveness didn't have to be instantly given.

The fact that he had foregone seeking any actually made it easier for me to sort out my own feelings faster than anticipated.

Thankfully for both our sakes, Scott wasn't stuck upstairs much longer. He now wandered and complained to himself on the first floor with me. Clearly he wanted to get back into things, but his body just wasn't having it. He seemed to have trouble even sitting at his desk as long as he used to, which resulted in us sharing the couch as he brought over a clipboard and pen to do work.

I watched the TV quietly from my side of the couch, flipping through channels with my own growing restlessness. A steady, rhythmic tapping started making its way into my mind, causing me to pause the channel search as I turned to look at Scott's pen as it hit against the papers. My mind was already trying to make sense of the beat, but it wasn't forming a coherent pattern.

Scott suddenly stopped, tearing my concentration away and to his face. He was looking back with a certain form of wonder. I turned back to the TV, convincing myself that there was nothing in the tap of his pen for me to understand anyway.

He started again, but I could see from the corner of my eye that he was still watching. This time the tapping meant something in Morse: *hello*.

My full attention turned back to him and I noticed he was smiling now. I glanced down at the pen, realizing he had caught on to what I was trying to translate the first time. I found myself grinning now too, shaking my head as I found it all a little silly. *Hello*, I tapped with the remote on my knee.

The channel I had left the TV on was entirely fiction in comparison to all the news I normally watched. "Hey look, something good." Scott said.

I decided to give the scripted show a chance for once. There must have been something interesting about it. Although, after an episode and a half, I wasn't seeing it. Soap operas were the last thing I ever expected him to want to watch. He'd look up from his papers for a few minutes at a time, allowing himself to be distracted for a moment. I didn't understand the appeal, but I wasn't ready to give up.

"Oop, that guy is going to die," Scott commented like he had been watching the whole time. I blinked at him, unsure how he extrapolated that from what was on the TV. Maybe I missed a more relevant episode. "Just watch," he added, nodding back to the screen.

The man that Scott had doomed was heading off to a dinner party of his ex-wife. He seemed in good spirits, and there wasn't rain or other classic omens that suggested he was going to be killed off. Halfway through dinner, the man grabbed his chest as the other cast members gathered near to help and all proving very ineffective since he keeled over a second later.

"Called it," Scott said, without looking over to me. "Don't worry though, he'll be back next month magically in a coma or some shit."

He got up from the couch and stopped. I assumed he had moved a bit too fast for his injuries, and likely too much at all if under a doctor's care. Scott's eyes were closed tight as he seemed to be fighting through it. I wanted to offer to help or something, but I didn't want to make a show of it to get his attention. A moment later, he carried on as if nothing had happened, and shortly after came back with a glass of water and a pained expression as he eased himself back down.

I could have gotten that for you.

"You don't owe me anything," he said to my surprise. Scott had been so insistent when he needed things from me before. I didn't know what to say, but I knew it was one of those things that warranted something.

I know, I signed, without adding that I was starting to genuinely want to help.

<chapter ten>
<! -- Scott -->

You wouldn't believe how incredibly hard it is to find a gun range in London that will let you use a pistol. Actually, the word impossible comes to mind. Which is why I had brought Sonia out into the garage with me. Out here, the walls were thick enough to take a beating, and we were still underground enough that no one would question the sound.

Sonia stood over where I asked. Directly across from her was a plain ol' sticky note that I had stuck up on a side wall. I knew it was an impossibly tiny target, but printing something off felt equally as ridiculous.

"Okay, smarty pants. Let's see how quick of a study you are." I took a step closer to her, the gun low in my hand. Even though my arm was feeling better, I was still thankful it wasn't the one I shoot with.

I lined up the shot, giving pointers and general directions about the placements of fingers and body in relationship to the gun. It was a crash course that might be able to get you a gun in the States, but never one in this town.

While I don't like shooting at things on a whim, today I was willingly offering up a bit of wall to make sure Sonia knew how to handle one if it ever came to that. I squeezed off a shot toward my pristine wall and the bullet left a small divot.

I walked over, bending down to pick up the sticky note that now had a hole straight through.

My shot had been in the middle, if not a little bit lower. I stuck it back up, running a finger along the top so it would hold.

"Now you try." I handed her the gun before moving to lean against my car.

I watched her, likely as she had me moments before. Sonia positioned herself exactly like I had been her movements were slowed down as if she was running through every inch in her head.

When she fired, I just stared at the small dent her shot made above mine.

"Christ," I said in sheer amazement. Even if UltSyn had taught her to use a gun before, that wasn't the amazing part. She had been able to mirror me completely. I know one can learn from example but— "That's fucking uncanny."

I would have to watch what I did around that one. She smiled, gun lowered and at her side. I think she enjoyed showing off, although I'd never get her to admit it.

"I guess we don't have to wait until your firearm proficient before we go to Paris," I said, and I turned away with a wide grin. I enjoyed throwing her off at times, even though I'd never admit that either. That's also what made watching soap operas with her so enjoyable. They were counterintuitive and filled with just such stupid logic at times that it had the ability to surprise her. I had the feeling that she was giving me a 'wait, what?' sort of look, but I didn't glance back to see if I had been right until the last second. *Worth it.*

I sat down at my desk pulling up some information since I knew I'd have to explain what I meant when she came in.

Sonia wasn't far behind me, and placed the gun on my desk. I slid the clip out putting both pieces in the drawer.

She hovered behind me as I leaned back in the chair so the monitor could do some of the talking. "Some big-name Operational Director is having a party at his estate, celebrating with the press over a new innovation. Just bullshit the public could chew on while the real business is being done under the radar. But, I figure his family safe would have some info about the really juicy operations."

"Plus, we should get out of town for a little bit until some of the heat dies down. Getting out of the country now is the perfect time," I added, turning to look at Sonia as if waiting for approval.

She paused for a moment, looking at the face on the screen, probably checking if she'd ever met the man. She gave me a slow nod before smiling. *A trip sounds nice.*

* * *

The next day we packed our things into the car, or rather my things since she still hadn't claimed ownership over anything yet. As much as I had grown comfortable in London, if we stayed and continued to be a thorn in UltSyn's side, they would soon show up at my doorstep.

I never coaxed conversations out of Sonia, but this trip felt like it would be too long to not talk about something at some point. At first, the topics that came to mind were about UltSyn, but I didn't want to talk only work with her.

"Do you like music?" I looked over a small list that was projected onto the windshield, scrolling to find a genre I felt like listening to.

Sonia shrugged, looking away from the side window and to the list of music.

I pressed my lips together, letting out a low hum. "What about this then?" I asked, and selected a playlist that mixed instrumentals with synthesized notes.

Sonia grimaced, looking at the list closer as if to analyze where I went wrong. She leaned forward, pointing out Classic Progressive Rock. It sounded obscure, which made me wonder if she knew what it sounded like, or if she just wanted to see.

I touched play, and halfway through, I ended up turning the song down. "This isn't going to be an easy topic to agree on, huh?"

It didn't matter who had control of the radio since when we reached the Eurotunnel that connected England to France I turned it off anyway. I pulled up to the self-check-in since I preferred to interact with as few people as possible. A touch screen kiosk asked for the card I paid with or to enter the booking reference number.

I had always found credit cards a little too on the grid for my line of work, so I opted for the latter. In my down time, I programmed a key generator for this very situation.

I pulled up the app and it spit out eight digits for me. Upon entering it, the computer threw out my code, and waited for me to re-enter another set of numbers.

"Why is it that the first one never works?" I mused as I generated another code. This time, the self-check-in machine seemed happy, and printed out a tag to hang in the car. I could have headed over to the Passenger Terminal building and killed time in their various little shops or used their Wi-Fi, but didn't have the desire for either. Instead I drove straight to the allocation lane.

There were already a couple of cars ahead of us lined up to pull into the shuttle. Workers in neon yellow vests directed cars into a silver bullet train.

This mode of transport, beyond the technical marvel that it was, ranked among my least favorites. To be fair, I didn't really like any mode of travel that locked you inside.

I pulled the car up, and was forced to wait for a few minutes before we were flagged an okay to drive in. It was like the sun turned off and was replaced with checkered segments of overhead lights. I pulled up behind a Jeep, staring at its spare tire as I put my own car in park.

My hands fell from the wheel, and leaned back into my seat before I looked over to Sonia with a shrug as if to say, 'and now we wait'. An LED screen above us caught my attention as the words scrolled past thanking us for choosing to travel with them. I scrunched my face up before glancing over to Sonia again. "I'm going to get out," I said, before doing just that.

None of the doors behind the sections were closed so I could walk a long way down. But I didn't stroll far from the car and stopped at a large sign. Sonia must have followed me right away since she was already at my side. "I love some French words. Look how easy a handful are," I smiled over at her before turning back to the sign that read "Eurotunnel Le Shuttle."

Sonia gave me a slight smile before walking away to look around. She didn't go far before I decided to follow. She stopped at a larger sign that was written exclusively in French.

"Yeah, I don't know like... any of those words," I mumbled. She looked like she was reading, but didn't volunteer any translations. Which was fine; with technology on my side, I didn't need her to.

I pulled out my phone, switching apps as I held the camera up to the sign.

On the screen the sign augmented to show the French now displayed as its English variant. It mostly read like a warning to lock your vehicle before leaving, along with a couple other similar sayings. "Oh, well that makes sense," I said, and tucked my phone away. "Boring though."

More cars pulled in until there was a decent load traveling from one country to the next. Large dividers started closing between the sections, leaving a handful of cars still grouped together around mine. I was tempted to mess with the doors, because I could, but I stuck to my general rule of thumb. Don't toy with things you are currently riding in.

Sonia ventured throughout the room, but never stepped too close to others or their cars. I picked a patch of wall and stayed there trying to entertain myself by watching the people. Across from me was a man who looked like going forty-five minutes without a cigarette was would be the death of him. To my right was a family.

Their mother would scold one of the boys every few minutes to stop running around as she conversed.

There was also a couple a few cars down from me. The two of them sat in the front seat making out like the world couldn't see through the windshield.

Unfortunate for them but fun for me, those keyless entry remotes were super easy to break into. With a comedic amount of ease, I unlocked their doors. The woman in the passenger seat jumped while the driver just seemed confused, looking around at the doors as if someone had bumped the switch. I couldn't hear what he was saying, but I think he was insisting they got back to it. It took them no more than a minute to settle down enough to start making out again.

This time when I toggled the locks, it startled the woman enough that she unlocked the door manually and got out. With an overly dramatic sigh, the man also got out. "Whoops," I said, coughing out a laugh.

I looked away from the car, and jumped as I saw Sonia just standing there staring at me. There was a clear, dare I even say, judgmental expression on her face.

My smile grew with equal parts enjoyment and uncertainty.

Why? she signed.

"I have trouble sitting still."

Can't you just behave? There was no tone to pick up on, but her expression seemed to soften.

I thought about the question for a moment, and decided I didn't want anyone to really hear the answer. *If I could, you wouldn't be here to ask me that*, I signed. She rolled her eyes and decided to lean against the bit of wall with me.

It was a total of seven hours until we finally pulled up to the vacation apartment I had reserved for us. It was an expensive little place, but nothing some code couldn't fix. It worked perfectly, because everyone thought they were getting paid and it was definitely safer than printing money. I knew plenty of hackers who gathered from various strangers, spoofing their credit cards, and taking just enough to cover their expenses. I preferred to just straight up mess with the banks.

Sonia walked in first and I trailed after with another duo of bags. She set hers down as she quickly became distracted by the apartment. The place was decorated lavishly. The living room held black slimline leather couches. Sunrays shined through the glass paneling that lead to a balcony.

Actually, the whole place was brighter and more furnished than the actual place I lived. While Sonia got her fill of all the knickknacks and framed art, I worked on unpacking the tech. Since this place lacked official working space, I stole the kitchen table. Power cords ran off the table and sprawled out toward various outlets.

The computer looked like a giant sea creature had crawled in and claimed the middle of the room.

I glanced over at Sonia, who was looking outside with wonder that I was careful not to shatter. I didn't think she'd ever seen Paris. I would have asked before if I had thought about France as anything more than a waypoint. I watched her for a few seconds more before speaking. "You can go out once I make sure there's no security cameras pointed our way."

She managed to tear herself away to lend a hand setting up. When we were done, I sat down on the couch, sighing loudly as I cracked open a soda. New country meant a new CCTV camera network to hack into. Getting in was the first thing I worked on and from what I saw, we could keep ourselves undetected up here. The cameras were focused on the cars and streetlights making us safe in this little nest.

"Everything checks out to me," I called out, glancing around as she seemed to have disappeared into one of the rooms. I didn't get up to find her, since I was sure she heard me anyway.

Sonia eventually came out of what I assumed she claimed as her room, and sat down near me. After finding the remote, she was quick to find news on that hacker group again. I didn't know enough French to know the details of the story, but I could tell it was The Unseen by the logo. I wondered what declaration they were making this time. Movement caught my eye and I blinked over to see what it was.

When is that party? Sonia asked.

"Two nights from now," I said, my thoughts shifting to my own business.

"We need to get ourselves something to wear. I don't think you can wear my clothes to it, and I doubt I could get away with wearing a jacket and slacks either."

Not even the super nice ones, she agreed.

<chapter eleven>
<! -- Scott -->

After spending much of the night looking for any details I may have missed about this new target, I didn't wake up until the next afternoon. I walked out to the kitchen, started a pot of coffee, and looked around for Sonia. I assumed she was up since she never slept in.

Sonia was alone with her thoughts on the balcony. I mean, I always knew she was thinking about more things than just whatever was in front of her, but here it was picturesque. As the sun beamed down on her, I wondered if it had seen her skin much in the past few years.

I poured myself a cup of coffee and headed to the balcony. She spared a glance before going back to people watching. I walked over to the railing and looked down for a moment. "What do you think about the place?" I glanced over my shoulder to watch for her reply.

It's nice to be— She paused, looking out again. *Somewhere with a view.*

I smiled and turned around to face her, leaning against the railing as I took a sip of coffee. "We need to go and get something nice for tomorrow. Do you have any ideas what you want to wear?"

She shrugged without a moment's thought. It didn't look like she was uninterested, more like she had no idea for what her taste in formal clothing would be. This might be harder than discovering what kind of music she liked. I stretched out my sore elbow. "Guess we better get looking."

I took her to the part of the city that was lined in expensive boutiques. A lot of the time she window shopped, refusing to go in even if I insisted. After a while, I got her to step into a store. Even though she didn't end up finding anything she liked for the event, we left with some everyday wear. She carried her bags with a permanent smile on her lips as we walked together.

Sonia slowed as we ventured into another store, spotting a woman who was trying on a floor-length long-sleeved dress. I didn't understand exactly what she was saying, but my guess was she thought it was too much fabric.

I let Sonia browse on her own as I ventured into the men's section. I hoped to find a suit now that she seemed at least a little interested in the dresses here. A woman came over, speaking to me in French. I assumed she was asking if I needed assistance.

"Can you fit me for that suit?" I said, and pointed to a mannequin in case she didn't understand English.

"Sure, right this way." She walked me over to the fitting room and insisted I pair it with a light blue shirt and tie of a deeper shade of blue. When I came out to the large mirrors in the sleek steel-colored suit, I had to agree with the collective choices. I tugged on everything, pulling at the cuffs, hoping it all would work without further tailoring. With a thank you from me, my help excused herself.

My eyes shifted past my reflection to a figure behind me. At the other end of the hall, I could see Sonia, emerging out of the changing room with the dress I assumed was the only reason she came into the store. It was the same one the other woman had put on, but it didn't ring as conservative now that Sonia wore it. The classic silhouette didn't swallow her figure, and billowed slightly at her hips. As she observed herself in the mirror, I came closer.

Sonia looked up, catching me halfway. She smiled faintly, brushing her hands against the front of the dress before adjusting a simple silver belt that cinched at the waist. "Is that the winner?"

Her eyes glanced down, hands going to the fabric as if she didn't want to part with it. "Do a little twirl," I said softly. Sonia blinked up at me before slowly spinning around once. Up close it was easy to see the fine details. Delicate black lace covered the back, hinting at a bit of skin, but exposing little.

"It's a good pick," I encouraged, before looking at myself in the mirror again.

It had been forever since I needed a suit for anything, and felt too polished seeing myself in one again. I cleared my throat. "I'm going to change back into my street clothes." Once out of the suit, I headed back toward Sonia and waited for her to finish up. I wasn't sure if she took longer because a dress was harder to slip out of, or if she was admiring it some more.

With our formal attire selected, we headed over to the register where I used a prepaid card to check out. I paused just outside looking over at the street camera.

Its attention was on the cars that passed under it. I was certain that a few had caught us, or at the very least, our car, but I wasn't too worried. France's surveillance was a joke compared to the UK's.

Sure, it was still enough and if I could tap into state systems, I'm sure UltSyn would be able to as well. Warrant or not. But, even the useful feeds out there created terabytes of junk data every day. With so many signals, our trail could easily be hidden. Plus, I hadn't done anything to warrant attention or tip our hand in France. Yet.

When I looked back, I realized Sonia had been staring at me. She wore a curious expression as if she were trying to read what was on my mind. "It's nothing," I said, shaking off questions before she even asked them. "Let's put this stuff in the car and get some food."

I ended up picking at my dinner as I searched for information about this party. I had a list of thirty or so names that seemed to have clear UltSyn connections mixed into the press and other socialites. "Sonia," I called before looking up to see where she was. She came over dressed in a new outfit picked today.

"I made a list," I said, and tapped my finger against the sheet of names. "Do any of them match the names in your head?"

She looked over them for a second. *Can I have that?* I didn't follow and the confusion must have been evident as she pointed to the pen in my hand.

"Oh," I mumbled before handing it over. "Yeah, sure."

Sonia seemed to be studying the list, likely sifting through large amounts of data despite looking completely casual about it. She placed little X's at the top left of certain names, adding a note off to the right if she had a relevant one. No more than two had job titles, a project manager followed by biochemist. A few more were given a country of origin before the pen was set down.

"Seems like we are on the right track," I said, leaning in.

Is that all? Sonia asked, not looking bothered as I half-distracted signed a *yes, thank you back.*

<chapter twelve>
<! -- Scott -->

There was something I loved about large parties. At small gatherings, there is no privacy, and I hunted in the illusion that there was some here. Sonia and I were connected by subtle earpieces. The excited and distracted atmosphere of the party would likely make connecting to anything else I desired fairly easy.

Sonia was excited too, albeit maybe in a "flustered over the amount of people" way. I was just amped to get this show on the road. "I need you to pretend to be my date," I whispered over to Sonia as we walked to the door, placing my hand loosely on the small of her back. She tensed, but didn't ruin the ruse by pulling away.

"Name, sir?" a man asked, dressed so much like a butler that it was a stereotype.

"Larsen," I answered. I kept a casual smile as Sonia's suddenly wide eyes turned to me. The butler didn't seem to notice, and after checking his list, invited us in. While I valued anonymity, I wanted to leave breadcrumbs behind to pull attention exactly where I wanted. They already knew I had Sonia with me; might as well use it to my advantage.

"Thank you," I said, dropping my hand away.

It was gorgeous inside, or maybe shimmering would be a better word for it. Crystal chandeliers of various design hung grouped together. Their clear color softly shifted, timed close enough that your brain wanted to say they had always been yellow or blue instead of just clear glass.

"Be good for me." I smiled over to Sonia before splitting up with her. I stole a glass of champagne from a waiter as he passed, using it for show as I headed upstairs. After analyzing the house's blueprints, Hallie had seemed to think that our gracious host's office was on the third floor. Guests were moving freely between the first two floors, but I hadn't seen anyone venture up to the third. Maybe if I timed it right, I wouldn't need some crap excuse to sneak up there.

I headed up a floor, soon seeing many people gathered on a large balcony that looked out to a terrace. Greenery was sculpted around a pool that was merely decoration at the moment since no one was going to strip out of their suits and dresses.

I finished off my drink waiting for the flow of people to ebb so I could head up another floor. I continued until I was out of eyesight from the stairs before looking at the doors of at least six rooms. Picking the wrong one could mean game over.

Instead of guessing, I pulled out my phone and checked. There was a marker on the middle room to my left. I headed that way while looking over my shoulder for anyone. The door proved to simply be unlocked. Seriously, why weren't some people more paranoid about security?

In my ear, I could hear Sonia, or rather the people around her. By the conversation, I was willing to bet money she was over by a buffet because I heard words like "cuisine" and "sandwich."

"Now where is that safe?" I whispered to myself as I stepped into the room.

I locked the door behind me to buy an extra few seconds if caught. There was a large painting behind the desk, and it seemed like as good a place as any to start looking. I pulled off the canvas and carefully sat it down to reveal a blank wall behind it.

After pursing my lips, I put the painting back up on the wall and spun around to look at the office as a whole again. All the other walls bordered another room which made me doubt they were thick enough to hold a safe. That only left two surfaces, and it wasn't like he'd keep the safe on the ceiling.

I rolled the chair away and tugged back a rug that covered the floor. There was no sign of a safe, so I ran my hands over the floorboards for an edge. When my finger caught one, I pulled up to find my prize.

There was no fireproof mark on the safe, which was good since hard drives and other storage media didn't survive well in those. Being on the floor also suggested that he wasn't using it lot, another factor that seemed promising for the type of thing I wanted.

"Tu es magnifique, ce soir," a low French voice said through my earpiece.

Whoever that was, they must be standing close to Sonia for the mic to pick up the voice so well. I paused to listen for more, and ended up grinning as no other words were exchanged.

I pried off the number plate of the safe to basically hot-wire this bad boy. My hands hovered over the circuit board and collection of wires. Every one of these damn things was different, and al were set up to prevent the very thing I was attempting.

Once again, unsure of my next move but not so prideful that I wouldn't ask for help, I pulled out my phone and had Hallie scan it. She referenced far more guides than I could ever remember, and soon highlighted which wire I should pluck. With a satisfying little tug, the safe opened.

There were a handful of paper files, an external hard drive, and even a flash drive. I picked up the flash drive, making a face at its capacity. Did they even sell ones this small anymore? I shook off the thought, tucked the files in between my shirt and jacket, and tucked the storage devices into various pockets.

While complete discretion wasn't really the name of the game tonight, I still closed everything up and pulled the rug and chair back in place. I could have left, but instead I sat down at the computer and booted it up into command prompt, then typed format: C to wipe everything off this guy's machine.

I heard static in my ear, the sound making me cringe. That would be a signal from Sonia that she either found something of interest or that it looked like our host was headed my way. The quick format completed, and I paused at the blinking line left after wiping his computer. If UltSyn didn't know I was here yet, they should soon.

Something was missing though.

I leaned in and typed: hello world

Static crinkled in my ear again, hoping it was because I didn't acknowledge her first message, and not that more people were coming. I quickly headed out of the room, forcing myself not to take the stairs two at the time. I hadn't been caught, and a good act should keep me from doing so.

My heart was racing since I didn't know how much time I had. But I forced myself to stop at the bottom of the stairs, pulled out my phone, and casually leaned against the railing as if I were waiting for my date to come out of the bathroom.

Two men headed to the third floor: their suits too uniform to simply be guests. One of them glanced over to me. I looked up from my phone as I pretended the woman who just walked in was who I was waiting for. I pushed off the railing, and headed toward the stranger. The two goons should be upstairs before I made it through the crowd.

Now if I could only find my actual date, we'd be set. I tried to spy Sonia from up here, but her black dress was mixing in with everyone. Finally, I spotted her sitting around a table with two other guests. She wasn't participating in the conversation, but I could tell she was listening to theirs as she finished off a plate.

I came up around the back of her seat, and leaned over her shoulder. "We should go," I said offering my hand to help her up and lead us toward the door. It was immensely important to leave a party before they realize you had crashed it.

Once we were back in the garage where we had parked, I opened the car door for Sonia before getting in myself. Uncomfortable, I pulled out the papers that were tucked away before hiding them in the glove box. The flash drives could stay in my pockets for now, since it didn't feel like they were going to crinkle every time I moved.

"All right, let's go," I said, and sat up straight again. I was about to start the car when I spotted security making rounds. I didn't want them to force my hand, or fight for what I already had. A stationary camera loomed on the ceiling of the parking garage, but it didn't promise any help. I chewed on my bottom lip as I tried to think of how I could casually avoid them. Speeding away would draw attention, sitting in the car and waiting might also seem suspicious, and having a conversation might even invite them to come over and ask how everything was going.

I cleared my throat at what I was about to suggest, glancing over at Sonia as she nervously watched the guards. "Kiss me." I watched her nervously as I waited for a response I'd be unable to predict. She looked over, studying me as if to find the reason why. "I don't have the time to explain, just trust me."

She turned herself carefully in her seat; muscles tense as every movement seemed more rigid than the last. As she glanced curiously at my eyes, I realized I hadn't moved at all. I mirrored her, turning so we could reach across to each other easier. I pulled in an unsteady breath, but before I could let it out, her lips reached mine. I didn't have any extra time to wonder where she had learned her approach, as I let myself be in the moment. My hand reached up to Sonia's cheek as her lips stayed cradled between mine.

I felt her gently pull away, and I leaned forward as if afraid to lose her. When I opened my eyes, I noticed she was looking out for any patrols. Right, the guards. I cleared my throat again and pulled back into my seat. "I think we're good." I didn't see the men anymore and doubted we looked suspicious on camera.

I worried Sonia would comment on my ploy, but thankfully she didn't. I hadn't meant anything by it, and it was rare for me to be caught up in any moment.

Having that pointed out directly would have been even worse. I started the car and drove out of there before security circled back around.

The ride home was as silent as any other, but it felt a lot different this time. I couldn't help but glance over at Sonia as I waited at a light. She was staring out her window, watching the world pass by just like she always did. One arm was crossed against her body and her other hand was held against her lips. Sonia noticed me looking, and dropped her hand away from her face. I wondered what was going through her head, but I turned my attention back to the road.

We walked into the apartment lazily, feeling more tired than I thought I would after a simple extraction. I tossed my keys on the kitchen counter, placing the papers and flash drives down on my makeshift computer desk. I looked over at Sonia as she walked toward the bathroom, likely to change out of her dress.

I headed to my room, but paused in front of the open door of the bathroom.

Sonia was in front of a mirror diligently pulling out a couple pins from her longer bangs and setting them down in a pile on the counter.

A thought came back to me. "Magnifique," I said. Sonia's eyes seemed to widen as she looked up into the mirror at me. I smiled, not meaning to surprise her.

"That gentleman was right," I added, and leaned against the door frame. "You do look beautiful tonight."

Sonia looked down, her expression no longer holding mine. I had expected a passing thanks, but she was unreadable. I waited a moment to see if bashfulness was holding her back, but she was giving me nothing to work off of. I looked away for a moment, tapping on the side panel nervously to make sure I had her attention. "Right, uh, I'll be in the other room if you need me."

* * *

I tugged at my tie, loosening it before pulling the whole thing out from around my neck. The jacket came off next, and

I was messing with my cuff links when I turned to see Sonia in the doorway.

"Hey," I said, dividing my attention between why she was here, and removing cuff links the rest of the way. I set them down on the dresser before pulling open the top button of my shirt. But I stopped there, since being shirtless on purpose in front of her threatened to make me uncomfortable.

There was something I wanted to ask you, Sonia signed. She didn't look unsure like moments before, maybe hesitant?

"Oh?" I prompted. I could only guess and what that something was, and I didn't want to make a fool of myself.

She stepped further into the room before going on. *You used my last name at the party*, she started, and paused. I wasn't about to deny the truth, so I just waited until she went on. *I want to know my real last name.*

"Oh."

You already have some information about the HID program, and if we are going to be traveling together, I thought you could gather some of that information whenever you can. I'll still continue with your quest.

Her hands were moving faster than normal; in what I was sure was the visual equivalent of rambling. "Okay," I agreed before she made me dizzy.

She seemed to blink away her anxiety, her hands lowering a bit. I don't think she expected me to agree without a fight.

"I mean, any good partnership is a give and take and you aren't exactly my prisoner." I made a face at my word choice, and tried to find a better one, but soon gave up. "I mean, sure. I'll help you look for bits of your past, while we look for a piece of mine."

She smiled softly, and turned a little bit, looking ready to leave. *Thank you. Goodnight*, she signed, before disappearing to her room.

<chapter thirteen>
<! -- Scott -->

I worked casually from the couch, resting my feet on the coffee table while the TV played as background noise. Sonia wasn't here for the replay of this action movie, which was a surprise since she usually enjoyed watching things over. I looked over my shoulder and spotted her on the balcony, eating take out from a restaurant down the street. My food was waiting for me on the counter, but I had chosen to ignore it as I dug through the files that had piled up. With all the crap I've been sorting through, you'd think I had a degree in research.

I got up and grabbed my meal before going out to the balcony. The sky was turning a dark orange along the horizon with the sun already hidden behind all the buildings.

Sonia quickly turned her head, stopped what she was doing, and pulled her jacket back around her. I paused for just a moment, confused as to why she covered herself up. It wasn't like she was indecent.

I sat my food down beside hers and took a seat. "Why do you hide your arms all the time?" I recalled the scars I saw from what felt like forever ago. "Are you afraid of someone seeing them?" I made a small motion to my own forearm, and didn't even think if I was crossing a line.

She didn't stop eating, making me wonder if she'd chosen to ignore me completely, but after a moment she put the silverware down. *I'm afraid they'll ask about them*, she signed quickly, before getting back to her food.

"Because of UltSyn?"

Sonia gave me a look that suggested I was doing the exact thing she didn't want. I raised my hands in surrender and tried to focus on other things.

For example, Paris was nice. It didn't take much to convince you why this was such a tourist destination. But it didn't matter how nice a place was, we had to keep moving to be one step ahead of UltSyn. When I started pushing my food around more than eating it, I decided it was time to head in.

"You should pack an overnight bag," I started, making sure I had her attention before I continued.

Why?

I looked from her to the city again, unsure if she didn't want to leave France or something else. I just knew I didn't want the conversation quite so public, so when I looked back to her I said, "Come inside."

Sonia caught up later as I was packing some of the smaller electronics; I assumed she decided to enjoy the rest of her meal first. I knew what she was going to ask so I simply volunteered once she was inside. "We are going to Belgium. Raise some hell, find some information, and what not," I said, as I curled a power cord around my hand. "Do you have any contacts there?"

Sonia pursed her lips together as she thought, then nodded, and provided the name of Louis Maes.

"Well, that's somewhere to start. Go get ready."

She seemed to hesitate; the heel of her foot lifted off the ground. I waited, wondering if questions would follow. But whatever she was thinking, she didn't share the thought before heading to her room instead.

It took about three hours to get to Belgium. Along the way, Sonia gave me names and phone numbers of the contacts she had. Hallie checked them out and I threw out any that were professors or of a low pay grade. We weren't messing around anymore, and if you wanted to stop a snake, you went for the head.

I pulled into an old mechanic shop, the sort you could drive into to get an oil change without an appointment. Although this one was shut down. I parked the car as if I were waiting for service and walked up to the office, despite the obvious 'Sorry, we are closed' sign in the window. Of course, it was locked but I held my ring hand to the doorknob, and it glowed with a circle of blue before the image of the closed sign flickered away to show an OLED screen. "Thank you," I said nonchalantly, and took a half step over to it. This hideout wasn't keyed to me, so even though it responded to my tech, I would have to hack us the rest of the way in.

Sonia had gotten out of the car, and was currently standing in my blind spot. I could more sense her there than actually see her. Three fingers of my left hand were pressed to the touch screen, and I scrolled through things with the right. These old security systems were a bit gimmicky, or as I liked to call them, irritating.

With a groan, I shook out my hand worrying that I wouldn't be able to crack the system in time. There was something in the air; my hair stood on end as if my fingers had been on a live wire. Something was off.

I turned to tell Sonia to stand somewhere else since she was driving me insane, but when I saw her, everything made sense. She was looking around as if we had been running from someone. "It's you," I breathed, and she tensed further. "Why are you making me nervous?" The question was more for myself than her.

Where are we? she said, with an unusual amount of waver in her gestures. *These aren't the coordinates provided.*

This was further proof that HID conditioning seemed to have more emotion left over than what would be useful from a pure business point of view. Computers don't get scared, and they don't need reassurance. "It's ok, nothing's going to happen. We're storing the equipment here, so it isn't hanging out in my backseat all day. Later, we'll come back here to sleep before heading out again."

She gave a quick nod and folded her hands in front of her, but the illusion of calm didn't reach her eyes.

"Can you come around to this side?" I asked with a little nod to my left. Once she did, I told her where to place her fingers on the screen, thinking that inclusion would make her feel better. Or, at very least, it would give her mind something else to think about.

The only problem was that her index finger was not on target, so the system didn't register the pressure point. "Up a little," I said, and pushed it over with my own. As soon as I touched Sonia, she pulled her hand back. I gave her a curious look and her hand meticulously returned to the right spot.

I scanned the screen another fifteen seconds or so before the inner circle of the doorknob glowed green. "You don't need to be scared around me anymore," I added, as I got the door for her. "I'll keep you as safe as humanly possible." Might not be enough, but it was all I could promise. She flashed a smile in reply.

The inside looked exactly how a mechanics shop should look, which was the point. The actual hideout was downstairs. I wanted to tell Sonia to head down there while I pulled the car inside, but if I were her, I doubted my anxiety would enjoy that.

An extra minute shouldn't harm anything. So, I went down first, and Sonia followed close on my heels.

It was dark. Only a thin white line, like crown molding, shined. This hideout had the identical layout to mine. Well, structurally at least. The ones without 'aftermarket work' like this had a large kitchen where my wall of monitors was.

Hidden second level was also more set up for work while this floor was designed not to make the team inside go stir crazy during missions that lasted months. "This place will work," I explained as I moved over to the light switch. I flipped it on then off again. Nothing.

I sighed. "After I fix the fuse that is."

Sonia looked around but didn't venture into darker areas. I waited for a reply this time, trying to figure out what she was thinking. This time she ended up telling me. *How long are we staying?* she asked. She looked unsure about the place, and compared to the apartment in Paris. I didn't blame her; it was a severe downgrade.

I couldn't help but laugh a little. "Hopefully, only until tomorrow then we'll likely move on to another county. I promise we can even get a hotel room next time," I offered, but her eyebrows rose to suggest she didn't believe me. "I don't know any hideouts anywhere else."

She smiled before shaking her head.

"Car's upstairs; be back soon," I said before running up the stairs to pull the car inside so I could unload it. There was a lot of work that still had to be done with what was left of today.

Sonia helped again with moving the tech into our temporary place, brushing her hand across the living room table, ridding it of dust before setting anything down on it. The stuff belonged upstairs but it seemed like neither of us wanted to head up there. I didn't know her reasons why, but I had plenty of my own. Including that it looked like a ghost town down here and I didn't want to imagine the bedroom and office up there.

She made a face again, further suggesting that she didn't like being in such a forgotten place. After noticing clinging dust bunnies on her long sleeve, she vigorously shook her arm. I smirked before I moved onto the next thing.

I took the stairs carefully since they were tricky to see in the low light. Besides being completely bare, the upstairs wasn't as bad as I imagined it would be. Where my tech room was sat three smaller desks each with their own monitors. They were an older style; I could tell by the shape of them alone. The surprise of seeing them left behind quickly wore off as I rounded each desk and saw they had been stripped of their computers.

"Figures," I grumbled as I looked around for the fuse box. Mine was in a tiny closet on the wall adjacent to the stairs. I smiled at finding it in the same spot. I pulled out my phone to use it as flashlight so I could read the labels and flip the right switch back on. Light flooded the room, and I blinked as my eyes adjusted.

"Well, that wasn't so hard." I took the stairs two at a time on the way down. Every light on the first floor was alive again, but I toggled a few switches for good measure. "Ta da," I added, and was met with a small clap from my audience of one.

* * *

We were on the road again after a few preparations. I handed her a gun as I gave her more information about what we would be doing. "First off, I'll need you as a translator since my anything-other-than-English is awful. Second, if this works out you, might be able to communicate on a better level with the person we're trying to meet anyway." I noted her puzzled expression before I went on. "Hallie believes she found another HID that's being transported after comparing a location you gave against the intel we had before. Don't worry, I won't make a show of it like I did last time. We're cutting them off before they even leave the starting point. All you need to do is make sure no one gets uncomfortably close to you."

She took a few moments to think this over, probably feeling like she'd reached her fill of shootouts by now. She nodded, inspected her gun, and checked the safety. "It's to protect you," I reminded her in the hopes her conscience could rest easy. At the threat of someone else's harm.

We pulled into a parking lot around the corner from the place I suspected the HID was located until they were transported elsewhere. It looked like an innocent office building, but intel suggested questionably legal things happened here. While I didn't plan to add another HID to make a growing collection, I couldn't think of anything that would annoy UltSyn more than liberating another.

I leaned toward the dashboard as I cased the joint. "I wish I would have brought that jacket," I grumbled. A man stepped out of the building, tapping the end of a cigarette box, and placing one in his mouth. He searched his pockets for a lighter as he rounded the corner to take a smoke break.

"That will work," I grinned over to Sonia who only returned an uneasy expression. "Stay here, all right?"

I got out of the car, and quickly jogged past the building to the side where the man was smoking. I slowed down when I was close to make it look like I was casually walking by.

"Hey, man, can I have one?" I gestured to the now lit cigarette in his mouth.

His face tightened as he seemed to debate the choice before deciding to share. When he held the cigarettes out to me, I grabbed him, using his own weight to help spin him around. My right arm pressed against his neck, while my left grabbed my own wrist around the other side.

"Just add this to the reasons why you shouldn't smoke," I said through my teeth as he struggled to break free. It wasn't more than ten seconds before he passed out in my grasp. I eased him down to the ground before I pulled his jacket off. This one had a larger UltSyn logo on the back than the last. I quickly tugged off my jacket and replaced it with his.

I lined my foot up to a part of his leg, comparing the pants color. My slacks were about three shades lighter than his, but it didn't seem worth it to swap them out.

I messed with the ID badge on the jacket, tangling it around so only the back could be seen. I took a longer way back to the car, not wanting to pass across the glass door entrance again. At the car, I opened the passenger's side door, tossing my own jacket behind Sonia as she stared wide-eyed up at me. I had forgotten she hated the other jacket I had brought back; wearing one was far worse. "If you don't have faith, I'm going to have to do this the violent way." I took a breath and offered my hand. "Please." Her eyes shifted up to mine, and maybe she saw something that convinced her.

To be fair, I wasn't sure if this direct approach was going to work. It theoretically was a valid play we could make. We stopped at the person manning the front desk. His outfit suggested a third-party guard, and the wedding photo to his side showed two people. Neither him. "I'm here with an HID," I said. My tone was a careful balance, so I didn't freak out Sonia, and casual enough that I sounded tired of this gig.

"Yeah?" the guard glanced up amused. He looked over at Sonia like she was just someone I had pulled off the street. I knew part of the problem was she wasn't wearing standard clothes for her station, but I looked over to her like I didn't see an issue at all.

"*Yeah*," I said, giving attitude back.

"Why is she dressed like that?" he grumbled, moving a hand over to a keypad as if he was going to call backup. Rude; I don't think he honestly cared for any of my story.

"It's not in my pay grade to ask what they do with these people. See," I said, loud enough that he looked back to me. I grabbed Sonia's wrist and held it up to him, the sleeve naturally fell back enough that you could see two small scars. "Now are you going to let us pass or are you going to make us late to see Louis Maes?"

I let go of Sonia, and was glad she didn't decide to shoot me for getting the short end of this plan. "Go ahead," the guard mumbled begrudgingly. "I'm tired of those things anyways. They creep me out. All void-like and shit."

I shrugged, and waved my hand for Sonia to go ahead of me. She glared daggers at me before moving. We walked down the hallway, passing two rooms before I felt completely in the clear. I stepped past her, and turned around to face her, ensuring her eyes would rise to mine. "I'm truly sorry I touched you." I waited a second to give the apology weight, even if she didn't want to hear it, before pivoting around to take point again.

We walked down the hall a little bit more. I checked the blueprints of the place on my phone, but still I didn't have an idea of where they'd keep the HID. This building was set up differently than the last one and left me without previous reference.

"Do you know where they'd keep others like you?" I asked, worrying that if we kept walking around, someone who wanted Sonia returned would show up.

They are hidden, she signed, with as much attitude as her hands would allow.

"Yeah, I know that. It's what the last shithead said, too. That doesn't help me now."

That somehow got a smirk out of Sonia. She walked past me, deciding to lead our little adventure. We snuck around the first floor, avoiding everyone we saw. When we reached an elevator, I was ready to rig it in our favor, but Sonia snatched the ID off my jacket. She scanned it and the doors opened. I hate to admit it, but I was starting to like having a partner.

We stepped inside, and she hit the button for the fourth floor. We silently rode up, and I was relieved to find no one waiting for us. It made sense. HIDs were classified; the more people in on the secret, the harder it is to keep.

After the small lobby immediately outside the elevator, there were two doors next to each other with a sign that had "HID(DEN)" written across it. "Oh, for fuck's sake," I complained, turning to Sonia who looked very amused with herself. "This is for earlier isn't it?"

Little bit.

"Can't say I don't deserve it." I walked over to the door, scanning the ID like we did before, only this time, the lock instantly spat it out with an ugly error sound. I gritted my teeth, realizing that there was no point in scanning it again. The man I stole it from had enough clearance to wait in the upstairs lobby, but clearly not enough to get us inside. No matter, a closed door never stopped me before.

I studied the lock for a moment, trying to remember anything about the brand, and was beyond pleased when I found a power jack on the bottom. UltSyn, and half of people who needed electric locks, brought it from the same company. That was a mass security mistake.

"You know I heard a story," —I started to tell Sonia as my hands reached into the pockets— "of a guy who downsized this device to the size of a dry erase marker.

But I think I have him beat." I took admittedly the biggest of the flash drive looking devices in my hand before stuffing the others away. When I pulled the cap off there was a power adapter tip that I plugged into the base of the lock. The device read the old memory from everyone who passed through, copied a valid code, and spat it back to open the door.

"It's going to be a rough day when UltSyn fixes their authentication problems," I said, and Sonia nodded in exaggeration.

Stepping past the double doors was like stepping inside Pandora's box only to realize you recognized it. I only felt a vague hint of the hope I had before. This place was almost identical to the other hospital wing. Bare, cold, and minimalistic in all ways except for medical tech that wasn't factory new. It was a twisted vision of corporate greed so ingrained in everything already that one couldn't escape no matter where you went.

Sonia took automatic lead as she walked around to the side of a man who sat quietly on an exam table. His clothes matched what Sonia had worn before, almost down to the last thread. It was eerie that they all were dressed like copies of the next, lined up like products in rooms waiting for someone to demand information.

Expecting to see a handler of some sort, I looked around the room first, but it was clear for the moment. That fact alone made me nervous and brought back that age old saying that if something was too good to be true, it likely was.

I turned my attention back to the HIDs. Sonia was already by the man's side, carefully hovering over him as she watched. He didn't seem to notice, however. When I rounded closer, I could see the HID was actually plugged in like a part. Thin cords ran down from his neck and along the table before disappearing from view.

"What are they doing?" I breathed. I knew that HIDs didn't need to be fed data like other storage devices, but I never stopped long enough to think that maybe they still could be. For all I knew, it could be something else entirely, maybe updating the software of one the implanted microchips.

Sonia waved me away, even asking me to step farther away before answering me. *They're clearing data.* Her hands twitched at the end of the sentence; like she hadn't liked the words, but she didn't fix them. She seemed to catch herself referring to HIDs like machines with the usage of computer terms.

"Like old files?"

No. Likely memories. Sonia corrected me, and maybe even herself at the same time. She put her finger to her lips, and I finally took the step away she had asked for earlier. Sonia pulled the wire from the man's neck, before positioning herself in front of him as she watched him come around. He didn't say anything as he looked at her, but Sonia didn't wait. *State your name*, she signed with added formality in her attitude.

You're not supposed to interrupt the reformat stage, he signed back.

Your departure is rescheduled. I must reevaluate your condition now, she said. *Comply.*

For the first time, he looked around the room. He seemed unwilling to listen or adapt like Sonia had done. Before she replied to his protests, the door opened, and our attention went directly to it. The person entering only got a split-second glance before I was on him.

The HID jumped up from his seat and stepped away from us both. *What is going on?*

I kicked away the guard's Taser from his now unconscious body. Hitting your head will do that to someone, but I didn't trust how long he'd be out. "We need to leave," I said as I turned back toward the HIDs.

Sonia stepped slowly over to him, and reached a hand out to his shoulder. Her carefulness was quickly ignored in a burst of aggression. He pushed her back toward another exam table. When I moved to pull his arms off Sonia, all the hostility zeroed in on me. Rumors said HIDs were volatile, but I never expected them to be strong.

I dodged a punch, before he reached for my exposed holster.

His speed was impressively dangerous as I now stood with my own gun pointed at me. The saving grace was that Sonia already had her own trained on him.

"Please, put the gun down. No one needs to be hurt here," I said, raising my hands. "We came to help. You'll be free."

A shadow seemed to cross over the HID's face. He placed the gun down, inches within reach. *Freedom is not quantifiable*, he signed before picking the gun up again.

Before I could speak, he held the gun to his head and fired. I froze, with only a tremble in my hand as the man crumpled to the floor. The look in his eyes just before the gun went off would haunt me. To suggest any emotion would be overselling it. He seemed more than okay with dying than I had seen anyone feel about death ever.

It was like I had completely forgotten how violent bullets were. My mind lagged to process that our cover had also been ruined. That anyone in the building would have heard the gun going off. Focus. Grab Sonia. Get out.

Still frozen, she hadn't moved from the table. I didn't have time to pay attention to the look on her face; I don't know if I could have handled it if I had.

"Come on," I said, as I took her hand. She stumbled for a few steps before finally looking away from the dead HID.

Sonia pulled me in the direction of a side door. Thanks to that last second decision, we were able to leave without any further trouble. We bolted to the car and made it out of there before anyone realized we were the cause of the mayhem.

I don't think I had a clear thought until after getting out of the city. I glanced over at Sonia who looked as stoic as when I had first met her. From an asset security point of view, I knew why the HID did what he did. But from a personal standpoint?

Well... I didn't want to think about that. Definitely not now, if ever. From an HID point of view? I'd never know. And if we were going to have that conversation, it should be Sonia's right to bring it up.

Her attention didn't move away from whatever was just outside the car, even when I cleared my throat, or spoke to Hallie. She seemed wrapped up in her own thoughts for the rest of the car ride back to our hideout. The longer we drove, the less likely that talk seemed.

Once back, I sat on a plush chair that was so dusty it made me cough. Since this hideout hadn't been used in a long time, I didn't hook much of any of the tech up. A big pull of power suddenly would give our location to anyone looking. I messed around on my phone while Sonia was in the kitchen, her movement a blur in front of me.

When that unfocused stir of movement stopped, I looked up. Sonia stood at the counter just staring down at it. Her back was turned to me so I couldn't see what held her attention so completely. "Sonia?" I called, but she didn't even twitch at the sound of my voice. I repeated her name, louder this time, but still nothing.

I got up from the chair and walked across the living room to reach her. "What's going on?" I asked upon entering the kitchen. She still wasn't replying, but could now at least see she was staring down at her hands. One was fiercely gripped over the fingers of the other, tight enough I thought her knuckles turned white. I looked up to her face, finding silent tears there. They streaked down whenever she blinked.

I didn't want to draw any extra attention to them for the time being. "Let me see." I reached out to touch her hand. She pulled them away, but in doing so they parted enough so I could see a cut across her finger. Accidental, by the look of the dirty knife on the counter. "It will be fine, we just need to bandage it up," I encouraged as gently as I could. "Nothing to worry about. The pain will dull."

Sonia turned to me, signing despite her hurt hand. *The pain won't go away anymore. Not like it used to.*

"I...uh..." I looked for the deeper context, but wasn't the best with crying in the first place. The half-made sandwich showcased the how, but her words didn't seem to match the mistake. "I don't follow."

She seemed to laugh, but it was the silent, bitter kind. Her hands balled up into fists before she went on. *I'm human. I think I had divorced myself from that idea for a long time. I don't want to die unremembered.*

Sonia started to cry harder in frustration. Her hands seemed to be shaking too much to sign easily. I was glad in a way because it hurt to hear her words, and I could only imagine how much more it hurt to say them.

I took a step forward and just hugged her. There was an uncertain second before she turned into my shoulder. When she finally pulled back, she stayed close, and loudly sniffled.

After wiping a few tears from her cheek, I spoke softly, "You're safe and seen in this moment."

She nodded, and quickly tried to dry her face, holding her finger carefully apart just enough not to hurt it further.

It was a small enough injury that we got away with just Neosporin and a larger Band-Aid. And by we, I meant her, since she didn't let me touch her hand again. I understood that much. If there was one thing I knew about humanity, it was how prideful it could get. I was no exception to the trait.

<chapter fourteen>
<! -- Scott -->

Mere hours felt like days as the time passed without much of anything upstairs. I lay sprawled out on an old, uncomfortable bed and stared up at the ceiling like a teen who had glow in the dark stars glued there. But there were none, so I turned my head so I could see over to another small bed that Sonia sat on. She was reading a book we found. I couldn't read the title, but I doubted it could be particularly good if someone simply left it behind when everything else of value was taken. However, she seemed to be enjoying herself comparatively speaking, if nothing else.

Such an empty and uniform place made me start to miss everything. I missed my glowing floor, and the hum and smell the warmed-up electronics provided. "Is there anything you miss from your old life?" I asked as my eyes flickered back to the bare ceiling. My mind flashed back to witnessing memories deleted, and without further pause, I amended my statement. "Or anything you wanted while you were working?" I sat up on the bed to show proper attention if she did decide to share with me.

She placed her book down onto her lap. *Every five years we serve, we get a bonus of sorts, outside our usual allowance. Last time I had one was about four years ago. For the next one, I wanted to go all out and ask to see Leonardo da Vinci's*

Codex Leicester. I thought it might be doable since UltSyn has a partnership with the person that owns it.

I raised an eyebrow. "Even with copies of the pages online?"

She considered my words and tapped on the book that rested on her lap. *It can't be anything compared to holding the real thing.*

"Fair enough," I smiled. I heard nothing but the air running for a moment. "There used to be this place in Redmond. By my school actually, that served the best burgers."

Sonia paused, looking over at me with such an unreadable expression. "Don't give me that look," I said, grinning bigger. "You don't understand. It wasn't just any meal. It should be boring, but I swear Americans have their own type of food. Unhealthy, covered in cheese, and beyond delicious."

You are something else.

"I'll take that as a compliment."

Sonia had turned back to her book, but her eyes glanced back up. She silently held eye contact for a moment before smiling. *Maybe.*

The next day we packed up again, and headed out to visit another country.

This time Sonia didn't show a hint of remorse in leaving, which worked perfectly, since I didn't either. We had been making a trail that was working north so I decided to continue it and headed to the Netherlands. Countries in Europe were so close to each other that it only took a couple hours to jump from the heart of one to another.

Making our way through Europe worked well to continue my master plan of fucking UltSyn up and stealing their shit as if my true goal was being the thorn in their paw.

A day later, while Sonia finished her book, I was busy combining parts I had salvaged: the capacitor from the air-conditioner, copper wire, and some other random pieces laying about. It looked like an odd science experiment by the time I was done, but appearances weren't everything when it came to solid tech.

Sonia waited in the car as I parked a mile back from UltSyn's Netherland's headquarters. I seriously doubted that my device would harm her, but it wasn't worth the risk and I didn't need the company. I left my phone back in the car too, and I felt naked without it, but Hallie's systems would definitely get scrambled.

Since a backdoor program had already copied the information I wanted and sent it to a secure server, I just walked up and triggered the EMP device once in their lobby. The pulse went out, affecting every system in the building. Basically, resetting all those lovely ones and zeros to just zero.

And just like that, I strolled out as if it wasn't totally remarkable how much damage something in invisible could do. I figured they'd assume it was me, but I didn't care since they'd lose both time and money.

I got back into the driver's seat, feeling awfully pleased with myself. "After all that hard work, I think I'm ready for a vacation," I hinted to Sonia, certain that she'd pick up what I meant. Driving directly back to Paris made the day long, but that apartment had grown on me in our absence. It held the sensation of someplace new and refreshing, but somehow also suggested that you were home.

<chapter fifteen>
<! -- Sonia -->

Scott was off on another one of his missions, and I was enjoying the afternoon to myself. I cleaned up a little and made myself some tea, before going out on the patio to look over the city. Shortly after, I heard Scott come in. His usual pattern was to toss the keys somewhere, then head to the computer to look over whatever he had stolen that day.

This time however, he tossed the keys down, and headed straight to the couch. Strange. Scott was leaning his head back, and as I came inside to sit at a nearby chair, I stopped short. Blood trailed down from his hair and over his ear. I hadn't realized I had been staring until Scott raised an eyebrow at me. *What happened?*

"This guy tried to crack my head open like an egg." Scott reached up to the area to see if it was still bleeding. I think the combination of time and matted down hair had stopped it. He looked over his mostly clean fingers before continuing. "We had a disagreement about that."

You should get cleaned up. If you get blood on the couch, I don't think you'll get any deposit for the place back.

"How considerate of you." I had meant it as a joke, but he seemed too distracted to pick up on that. "Can I just like... stay here? Maybe fall over, take a nap?"

Please don't. Times like this really led me to believe that Scott didn't care for his own well-being. As long as his body held out just long enough to complete the mission, he call ed that a win.

Scott closed his eyes for a few seconds before sharply exhaling. "Help me up," he said, reaching a hand out to me. I didn't have to pull too much, which suggested he was only tired after the adrenaline rush, rather than because of an injury.

I leaned against the bathroom wall as Scott cleaned a small nick by his brow.

More interestingly was a jagged cut I spotted on his hand. It reminded me of the pattern the glass had left before.

Finally, his attention turned to clean the wound on his head. It was located just far enough back he was having trouble seeing it properly in the mirror.

Why don't you go into the shower, and I'll help wash it out? I suggested and he caught my words in the mirror's reflection.

Scott turned around, looking first to me, then over at the shower, then back to me again. With a sigh, he stripped off his pea coat, and placed it on the counter. His hands hovered away from his sides as he looked down at the rest of his clothes as if unsure what to do.

We generally were so stubborn with letting anyone take care of us. The only exception seemed to be when one of us was really in pain. He wasn't showing many signs of that, but now wordlessly followed my suggestions. *Do you have a concussion?*

Scott's neutral expression soured before shifting into one where I could see the gears turning in his head. "I don't think so."

I didn't understand Scott's choice to keep on as many layers as he did, but I could work with it all the same. I had Scott lean into the shower that was big enough for both of us to stand in. In one hand, I held the detachable shower head while the other helped direct the water over the side of his head.

My chest tightened a bit as the water became tinted with red. There were no obvious products around that might help, just the usual shampoos. All of which I feared might sting if I didn't read the labels first.

Despite my efforts to be careful, Scott let out a pained grumble anyway. A glare up at me followed since I control ed the water. I rolled my eyes because it wasn't like I also controlled how gravity worked. Soon, even my initial concerns over the water's hue subsided. Without further thought, I broke the tension by spraying the water up at his face. I stared wide-eyed and amused over his expression.

Scott stood up straight, water dripping down his face. "You think that's funny?"

I considered it for a couple seconds, then sprayed him again, because I did, actually. Somehow, he looked even more shocked that time. Then a smile spread across his face as he lunged forward for the shower head.

A game of keep away quickly evolved as I tried to avoid his grasp. I stepped in the shower, hoping to buy myself extra space. He managed to tilt the stream of water back toward me, and ended up soaking my hair and shirt. He was starting to win the fight for control, and when I lost my footing on the tile, I was certain of his win.

When Scott noticed I was about to slip, he let go and stepped closer to grab me around the waist instead. He chuckled and braced one hand against the wall of the shower to stable us.

Since I was thankful to have not broken anything, or to have sent the shampoo everywhere, I managed to keep a bright smile. Scott hadn't moved his eyes from me, and my focus on his face was ruined when he bopped me softly on the nose.

"Trouble," he whispered.

He was so close, and I felt my cheeks heating up. My eyes drifted down to his lips without another thought, and I felt an urge to feel them again like I had in the car days ago. His smile weakened, and my eyes flickered back up, unsure if he was thinking the same thing I was.

Scott's hand hesitantly lifted from my waist as everything seemed to slow down and blur around me. My chin tilted up, just enough as I took a moment to feel a ragged breath escape from his lips onto mine. I wavered there for a moment before I closed the gap.

The kiss felt much like last time, starting off a little unsure and shocking him with the intensity I brought. But he relaxed with each second. I had felt that tenderness on my lips the entire ride back from the party. I also doubted that he ever planned for it to evolve like this.

My hands moved up to his shoulders and I drew him closer, an encouragement that Scott returned as his hand settled back on my waist and face. I shivered at the cold ceramic tiles against my back, and begrudgingly broke the kiss as Scott opened his eyes to check on me.

The shower head was resting on the ground and spraying over my feet. It must have been reaching him too since he stepped back enough to pick it up. He clicked it back in place, before leaning further toward the shower controls. With the press of a button the water evenly rained down on us from the panels embedded overhead. I smiled and blinked through the warm water that fell onto us.

"I guess that makes for a tie," he said far too softly. I swear he was trying to question if this moment was real. I touched my nose against his as I felt a small tightening in my stomach. A nervousness washed over me that I managed to settle by wrapping my arms around his neck again. I took a moment to encourage myself, if not the both of us. Scott met my lips first this time.

Even if I had known exactly how long we kissed, I doubt it would have sounded like enough. Time felt meaningless as my hands trailed from his shoulders down to his chest. I let my fingertips absorb what it felt like to touch him this way. I had pulled away from physical contact before, but right now, it was welcomed.

My hands lingered at the bottom of his wet shirt before I brought my hands to my own, parting from the kiss enough to put a little space between us. Scott looked down at me puzzled, but as I pulled my clinging shirt up over my head, it clicked, and he followed suit.

I grinded my hips against his, holding myself that much tighter against him as I kissed down his neck. That got a satisfying little moan out of his throat. The water still rained down onto both of us, making every touch move with ease.

Scott's hands explored a little more, and were currently working their way up my back. His delicate kisses trailed down my neck and shoulder before coming back to my mouth. He stopped too soon, and I opened my eyes to see what the matter was.

His expression seemed too serious for the fun I was having, and I hope my own conveyed my question.

"I just… wanted to make sure you…uh…want this to continue," he stammered, glancing down at my body mid-sentence. I don't ever remember being offered the choice before, and even half naked, I still felt that freedom. A liberation that was as pleasing as his touch.

I grinned widely, kissed him softly, then looked into his eyes and nodded.

"Okay, good. I mean—" He stumbled for words, before shaking his head, and all together interrupting himself with a kiss. This time, when Scott's lips trailed down my neck he didn't stop. He moved back to have enough room to run his hands and mouth down my chest and ribs. When he stood, his hands didn't lift from the waistband of my pants. I leaned my head back in anticipation as he thumbed over the button. Scott's breath against my neck brought extra warmth as my own breath had gone unsteady. His other hand was still on my hip, and I squeezed his fingers as my knees started to feel weak.

Scott's mouth hovered over mine, but not quite close enough for me to kiss.

He was just far enough away that he could witness the pleasure he was causing. His enjoyment seemed to be taken from my reaction alone. My breath crashed against my chest so hard that I felt light-headed.

I placed my hand over Scott's and he cautiously pulled it free, his expression shifting slightly to figure out what mischief I was up to now. I kissed him more roughly than either of us had before. My hands were the ones roaming him this time, and lingered to find his pants.

"Shouldn't we, uh—"

I interrupted by pressing a finger to his lips. I didn't want to explain things, and I didn't want to lose this moment either. I pursed my lips and tried to think of something. Our first kiss came to mind. His eyes followed my words. *Trust me.*

Scott rubbed the back of his neck, and gave a little smile before spelling out *Okay*. Soon after, I stopped being able to think ahead to what I was going to do next, and simply was aware of how each nerve ending felt better than the moment before.

* * *

I'm not even sure how I ended up lying with my head on Scott's chest. Something about being cold and him taking a throw blanket off his bed and wrapping it around my shoulders. There was a passing thought about staying in my own room.

I left and changed, and in that time, I felt uniquely alone so I came back. At first, I said it was to return the blanket, but then I ended up staying. By the sound of his breathing, I thought he might have fallen asleep.

I nuzzled a little closer, letting my mind focus on his heartbeat instead of mil ions of other facts floating around in my head. As content as I was, curiosity chewed at me until I finally sat up.

Scott opened his eyes to see what I was up to. His expression wasn't something I saw often, from anyone really, and the fact that he was quiet said far more than the quantity of words he usually went with. Scott looked as if he wanted me to stay, but I knew if I left no judgment would be passed. I never thought it was possible to be free and be in someone's arms at the same time.

Tell me about her, I signed, and a muscle in his jaw twitched. I knew defining the 'who' wasn't needed, but I did anyway to further prompt him. *Your sister, I mean.*

I could tell he was pulling away emotionally by the downcast of his eyes. He touched his forehead and then I realized he had signed *Why?* It seemed counterintuitive that he never spoke about her given his obsession with finding her again. There was just so much I still didn't know.

I went with *please*, and laid my head back down as if to anchor him in part to me. The muscles in his chest were tight, and I wondered if he was just not going to answer.

"UltSyn caught my attention, because they were helping disabled people. Prosthetics that synced up to one's thoughts, memory implants for people at a high risk of dementia. It was a good PR move, and a lot of people praised them for their humanitarian efforts," Scott started to explain with a quiet anger. "Those who couldn't pay were often hired. They got praised for that too. And so more signed up because of their supposed good works. But for-profit health care always ends up the same way."

I was tempted to answer, *For profit*, but Scott's fingers idly traced over my shoulder and down my arm. The touch was so light I wondered if he realized he was doing it, and I decided against moving.

"But you know that and so did my sister," he continued. "She became mute at a young age, and I made sure I learned sign language right along with her. We'd talk for hours on end. When bedtime came, a wall separated us, forcing a different silence. I didn't like that. So, I taught her Morse code. We'd tap out messages late at night, or on the dinner table if it was something we didn't want our parents to know."

How had I not pieced that together? There were clients who knew about HIDs, but say no need to learn sign language themselves. I just assumed he had, not that his childhood already prepared him for the task. I sat up and didn't know what to say. *Thanks for telling me.*

<chapter sixteen>
<! – Scott -->

There is a lot you can say about Germany. For instance, their language is a clusterfuck of smaller words, making everything a word jumble when I try to understand it. But the one thing that I always give the Germans credit for is the lack of CCTV cameras. It wasn't that the government hadn't tried to install them. Oh no, they very much did install the suckers. Activists simply smashed, hammered, or hacked all of them. They became such an expense that the government simply stopped replacing them. One also could mention that they have a Pirate political party.

Like I was saying, they seemed like my sort of people.

I kept thinking back to that night with Sonia. It was rare I became close to someone, and feeling awkward about it seemed mandatory at this point. But, now didn't seem like the time to explain why. Having someone riding shotgun who didn't understand that behavior didn't dictate labels would hurt more than bruises did.

Fortunately, my attention could afford to be divided since I didn't have to plan my moves as carefully. No central body was watching the playing field, so Sonia and I were able into check out an UltSyn building here in Germany with greater ease.

Their headquarters were in Berlin, but we ventured to a city to the south where a cloud server farm was located.

I had watched the guard's movements on private security cameras enough to piece together that the guy didn't care about what he was protecting. The company he worked for just hosted the information, very little of it was theirs anyway. We came in through a back entrance, and if I could find what I was looking for before the end of his night shift, no one would even know we had been here. I had looped the feeds of the night before, and thankfully, the guard didn't even seem like he was going to do a walkthrough like his job demanded. Better for the both of us that way.

I hooked up a tablet right into a rack of servers tethered with a cord running between. Sonia stood close by like a live wire. I didn't think she liked being in-between such tall stacks. While she wasn't antsy, she was very much alert to our surroundings.

The only problem in my plan was these servers held more than just UltSyn's information. The storage was rented out to everyone from Fortune 500 companies to rich mothers with a million photos who could pay for the added security. "I swear, if I find another stupid cat video, I'm going to shoot someone," I grumbled and sorted through a mess of file names looking for one that was worth the megabytes it was written on.

I caught a flash of her hand as Sonia signed something, but missed what since I was turned away. *Who?* she begrudgingly repeated, and waved her hand around to the floor empty of everyone besides us and tech.

"I don't know," I grouched. "I'll find someone." She rolled her eyes, and I pretended like I didn't notice as I turned back to the screen.

Due to the nature of cloud computing, I could have accessed this from anywhere in the world. But a brute force hacking attempt would have tipped my hand, and since UltSyn wasn't completely moronic, they picked a site with a firewall simply good enough that it was easier to get in onsite. I considered this my karma for mocking their lack of security before.

"You know what really bothers me?" I asked, not looking away as I sifted through the data for a piece of gold. "That everyone thinks cloud computing is the second coming. It's not that secure, and it's not even new. It's been around since the 1950s."

I looked back to see Sonia's reaction, and she just stared back at me, clearly uninterested. "Ugh, I don't know why this doesn't annoy other people."

I'm not sure how long passed before Sonia put her hand on my shoulder. Could have been a minute, could have been thirty. I looked over and she signed that she was going to go further down to serve as a lookout after hearing something.

I nodded and got back to work. A short time later, with a double click, I opened a video file that brought up UltSyn's logo. "Oh, hello, beautiful," I said after a clip started to play.

A young man sat at a table, the camera angle pulled close enough you could only see him from the chest up with a plain white wall behind him. "Why do you want to join this department?" a voice off screen asked. I assumed it was someone across the way.

"Well," the man started, looking down for a moment as if he was trying to think of a real answer instead of just a cookie cutter reply. "UltSyn's Bio Division is the best in the country, arguably, the world. The innovations you've made with cortical implants this year alone are remarkable, and if I could be so bold, I'd like a challenge for a change."

I scoffed at his answer. If I was being fair, he sounded one-part Sonia, with her matter-of-fact egotism, and one part me, with that take-on-anything cockiness.

However, the extra five parts of blind loyalty was a turn off. The man interviewing him didn't seem to think so however, and went onto his next question. I didn't watch it however as I closed the file and started collecting al the related files since I had found the sweet spot.

I was watching and waiting for the data transfer to finish when something hit my arm. My eyes traveled to my arm, then down to the floor where I saw a knotted-up Ethernet cable. I looked up toward Sonia who apparently had hurled the thing at me from her spot a couple yards away. She tapped on her wrist and pointed toward the front door in an unofficial sign that meant the guards were having a shift change.

I mouthed a curse and turned back to the tablet's screen. Thankfully, the current data transfer had finished. I wanted more, but I also wanted to plant a virus I wrote. The latter won.

Sonia was now tugging on my coat for us to leave. I wasn't sure if she was worried about something in particular or the fact that this country had more guns than many other European ones. Growing up in the States made me less twitchy about that sort of thing when arguably the reverse might have been better. Either way, I brushed her hand away, not ready to quit until the program loaded successfully.

I saw the long reach of flashlights by the time I finished. Quickly, I disconnected the cords, grabbed Sonia's hand, and headed out of there.

We had been driving in the car for ten minutes, and she'd been staring at me for at least seven of them. I had used the silent excuse of keeping my eyes on the road as I drove us to get breakfast after our little adventure, but her persistence was wearing my resolve thin.

Cutting it a little close, don't you think?

"Sometimes I work on Microsoft time," I said. She tilted her head a little, not following. "You know when you are downloading a file and the countdown keeps changing from a low time to a higher and back as if it's trying to taunt you?"

Sonia's expression didn't change. "Never mind," I sighed. "I guess HIDs don't have that problem."

Now that got a reaction out of her and she turned forward in her seat in a huff. As we drove to the restaurant, I remembered living with someone doesn't always mean you always get along with each other. I hadn't meant to offend, but it can happen.

Since there were no cameras in this area, not even privately-owned ones, I decided we could eat out for a change. This proved a bit awkward when our waitress showed up speaking only in German. Sonia could understand the lady and translate to me, but we didn't have a way to reverse that process. We exchanged a glance before I rubbed my eyes, suddenly feeling tired.

I smiled politely over to the waitress before asking if anyone around knew English. I hoped the word alone would be enough for her to understand.

"Einen moment bitte," she said in a cheerful tone before she walked away from our table. I recognized the middle word to be the same in English.

"Oh, hey look, now I know like four German words," I commented.

What are the others?

"Uh," I stalled as I thought about it. "Gesundheit?"

That brought out Sonia's smile, as a new and confused waitress approached our table. "Hi. Sorry," I laughed a little. She smiled and politely asked us for our order in English. Sonia still needed to relay her order through me, but at least we had a way to give it to the waitress now.

I placed my order, but for fun, I took a liberty with Sonia's. "And she'll have a beer to drink with that," I ad-libbed.

Sonia kicked me under the table. I winced and looked back at her, my eyes widening before simply replying, "Ow." I turned back to our waitress who was quick to put back on a professional smile. "I mean she'll have water," I corrected, and the waitress took note and left our table.

"Now that nice German girl thinks I'm crazy," I said, pretending to care.

You are crazy, she said simply.

"Eh," I shrugged.

Whenever I talked about something that I didn't want people to overhear, I usually signed it. Audio could be enhanced, but it was harder to eavesdrop on sign language without a clear line of sight. *So, I was thinking we could head back to England.*

Wait, I thought we were going to Denmark, Sonia objected.

I sighed. *It's like nine hours from here.*

So? My given name has Danish origins. Maybe there is something related to what I want there.

I'm tired of pestering every UltSyn building in Europe. I want to go— I said before I couldn't quite remember the sign for home. My fingers paused by my mouth as I tried to recall it. Something about where you eat and sleep? Slowly my hand moved over to my cheek to finish the sign, but by this point Sonia was already looking away.

"Sonia," I spoke this time. She looked up, but her expression wasn't happy with me. "My last name has French origins but I'm not from there." I would have continued, but she looked away again. I followed to where she was looking and saw the waitress came back with our food. As she dropped it off, I had trouble caring about eating all of a sudden. "Look, how about we stay here for a little bit longer, and if we find anything solid, we will follow that lead."

Sonia simply picked up her fork and started eating. It was frustrating since I knew she didn't have to see me to hear me.

"Sonia."

She lazily waved the word *fine* at me before returning to her food.

<chapter seventeen>
<! -- Scott -->

I found something.

It was an UltSyn candidate video of eighteen-year-old blonde girl. After all this time, I found a solid lead. After all this time, I found something substantial to go on.

I heard Sonia come back into our hotel room. It wasn't as nice as our Paris apartment, but it worked. Her footsteps vibrated along the floor as I quickly closed the file. My heart was racing as if I wouldn't be able to hit that little "X" in time.

Stupid, since the screen wasn't even facing her direction.

Sonia walked over to the desk, setting down sodas she got from the vending machine down the hall. *How's it going?* she asked once her hands were free. *Find anything?*

"Um." I looked down at the screen that now just displayed the desktop background. "No. Not really."

That sucks. She grabbed a soda again and moved over to sit on the edge of the bed.

"Yeah." The word stretched out as I got out of the chair. I walked around to the front of the desk, and leaned against it before I went on. "We should head back to London."

What? She dropped the drink so fast that I thought it was going to spill on the bed. "We've been here for days, and I haven't found anything to warrant a trip anywhere else. The whole point of this road trip was to draw UltSyn's attention away from London. But, I can't continue to keep us safe if we are running only a couple steps ahead of them."

There is something in Denmark. I feel it.

"There's no logic behind that. And, we don't have any more time to kill with this road trip around Europe."

No, you. You don't have time. I have all the time in the world. Always you, and your search. Always about Victoria. Her signs were quick, and they were blurring together as they tasked my brain to split them up again.

"Don't." I grabbed her hands before she went on. "Don't mention her name like that. Please." I assume I would have gotten a rude 'like what' if I hadn't for practically silenced her for a second. But I didn't want to hear, or even see, my sister's name at all, if it was just going to be paired to my shortcomings in finding her. I didn't want anyone making me feel that unless it was going to lead me to her like that video could.

Sonia ripped her hands out of mine, and stormed off to a different corner of the room. She angrily started gathering her clothes, throwing our bags on the bed, and haphazardly jamming everything inside.

I hadn't meant right this second. I watched, wondering if the outburst of emotion would die out, but Sonia was dead set on sticking to it. And if I didn't want us to break, we'd both have to bend. So, I went back to the desk and started packing before she ended up sitting next to her packed things glaring at me.

The trip back to London was the longest yet. Not only because of the sheer distance, but because Sonia was completely ignoring me. She didn't care what song played on

134

the radio, and didn't care what I said. The only thing going for this trip was that we already had drinks for the road.

* * *

I was glad to be back for many reasons. The top two were that now I could sort through every file with Hallie's full processing power, followed by a distant but still solid second place of having my own bed again.

Sonia settled in like she had been before, around but aloof. At least with a pile of work to do and hours of CCTV footage to comb through, it was harder to notice. Being incredibly busy had its own rewards.

After working all night, I saw that Sonia was awake again. She headed into the kitchen, her footfall not even making a sound. Maybe I brought back a ghost. I was tired, and sorely in need of company.

I headed over to the kitchen simply to be around her. "What are you making?" I asked, even though I could clearly see bread was down in the toaster and the butter waiting close by. Sonia gestured to the counter.

"Right, of course." My tongue ran across my lips as I tried to think of a way to make things better. I thought about making myself food, but I found I wasn't that hungry of late. Even my little mouse was eating more than me.

I didn't know it was possible to miss someone while they stood so close to you. I wished she would just yell at me, or act out in any fashion. Anything would be better than this stillness that was bound to drive me crazy.

"Please talk to me." My tone ended up far too close to begging for my liking.

She set down the butter knife with a sigh, and looked over at me. *I have nothing to say,* she signed before finishing preparing her meal.

I pursed my lips, skewing my face in frustration. If I wasn't careful, I was the one who was going to scream. "Guess I'll get back to work," I said hanging around long enough to see if she'd even register a cheer for me walking away. Still nothing.

A few days after, I had learned to cope with it, which really just resulted in me talking to myself as Sonia listened. I was sorting through the files I got in the Netherlands. I sent a batch off to Terry since they played right into that human rights activist life mission of his. In my hands, it would do nothing besides sit in storage.

Sonia was on the couch, and I could hear a soap opera play in the background.

"I love you. You can't go," a shrill voice from the TV said.

"That never works in these sort of things," I commented.

"But I have to," replied one of the actors, and then I heard the sound of a door close.

"Told you," I added, even though I knew Sonia wasn't going to object that I hadn't. "It's sort of concerning how good I am at predicting these shows."

I hadn't been turned in that direction, but when the TV shut off I knew something was up. I swiveled my chair around to see Sonia moving closer. She looked intent on saying something, so I kept my mouth shut.

This partnership isn't much of a give and take, she started, and I silently watched. *It feels like it's 90% your things and 10% mine.*

I tilted my chair to look back over the collection of monitors that clearly showed what I was doing across the lot of them. She had me there. It wasn't like I was ignoring her wishes; I just didn't dedicate myself to them. I didn't want to get sidetracked now that I was back on the right track. "I know and I'm sorry. It will change as soon as my stuff isn't so time sensitive. Believe me, I know what it's like to search for your family, but my sister is the only one actively missing."

When Sonia just stared, I knew I hadn't done a good enough job selling my case. She headed back to the living room without another word, sinking low enough in the couch that I couldn't see her there at all.

I gave it a few minutes, but she didn't turn the TV back on. Without the background noise, I put on music, spinning the dial on my speakers high enough that I hoped it would drown out my own thoughts. But, there was a thought that no matter what stayed above any other noise. I knew this situation wasn't fair, and as much as I wanted to make it right, I couldn't. She wasn't locked in here with me. All she had to do to leave was walk out.

I know I could have directly told her this, but there was a sick, sad part of me that hoped she'd never try. I've heard of Stockholm Syndrome, and wondered if it could work both ways. If there was another term for it, I didn't want to entertain the idea long enough to learn it.

Since I apparently hated myself, I looked it up not even an hour later. Lima Syndrome. Damn it, there truly was a word for everything.

<chapter eighteen>
<! -- Sonia -->

I probably should have waited until early morning before doing all this, but I couldn't stand to wait any longer. The moment I knew Scott was asleep, I got dressed and stuffed a backpack with some extra clothes. Scott could consider me taking them as payment for all I've done around here. Not like the money used was his either. The gun I snagged from the garage, however, might be missed.

I pulled my hood a little tighter, thankful for the layers I was wearing since London was cold and damp. I timidly stood at the crosswalks, watching as cars whizzed by. I wish I had planned this all in my head, because doing it was something else entirely. I crossed when prompted, then moved toward the trains, and continued until I reached the tunnel we had taken before to France. I stopped only when I had to wait an hour for the next shuttle.

Saying I was comfortable or felt safe alone out here would have been a lie. The first issue was almost always untrue no matter the circumstance, and the second is why I had taken the gun. I simply couldn't stand to spend another hour wondering where my sister might be, or if I even had one. Brother? Mother? Any would do. It was only a fruitless journey to search for a past one didn't reminder if you couldn't find the right family tree. Was it any worse than looking for any other missing person? Maybe Scott and I were alike when it comes to having high hopes about that kind of thing.

Denmark was the only real lead I could be sure of. No matter how many times Scott said I shouldn't count on my fake name meaning anything, I wouldn't let myself believe it wasn't worth looking into. Hell, he didn't have any room to judge what was a good idea or not.

I managed to swipe some cash so I could pay for the fare since a woman had left her purse unintended and I briefly pretended it was mine. It was enough to take me across country lines and onto another train. I curled into my seat and leaned my head against the glass as I watched the sunrise from its home at the horizon. With Scott, I had somewhere to go back to each night and hide away until the next day.

But, I was done hiding. My day had come, and it was time to find the way back to my real home. If Scott missed his sister enough to cause chaos across Europe, you'd think that I'd have a parent who waited and dreamed of my return. Someone who missed me still. I don't know why I left them to begin with, but even without those memories, there must be someone out there that I loved.

I had dozed off during the ride, dreaming of meeting a faceless woman who kissed my cheeks, and called me her daughter, and the warm embrace of an old friend who knew me since grade school. I'd find these people soon enough. I knew it. I felt it.

I jumped awake from homecoming dreams, as a train conductor shook my shoulder to rouse me. I smiled politely before getting up. If this was the movie we watched in Paris, as soon as I took a step out, family would be waiting for me.

That hope flickered out as fast as it had ignited. It left me willing to take a risk in order to continue on. I ducked into a few stores and when I found a pair of sunglasses with a funky frame pattern, I stole them. The splash of color might draw some attention in person, but they'd fool most facial recognition systems.

Travel dragged on this time. I didn't miss the talking per se, but the journey felt lonely without even the most irrelevant comments from Scott. It was different being completely by myself. I don't know if I was happy about it yet.

Getting to Denmark was a journey of its own. I never would have thought myself a thief, but here I was, having stolen from several people along the way, and sitting in the back of a bus I hadn't paid to ride. I tried not to doze off again, but I was already twenty hours into this trip. This bus would be the last one before Denmark.

It was evening when the bus rolled into the station, and everyone got off after the long haul. I let out a yawn as I looked over of the map of the city around me. I was no hacker. I couldn't break into a building, and was already testing my luck with the stealing. I was aimless, and thought myself an idiot for trying this on my own. But even when I re-calculated it, this was better than spending another day all the way in London looking for someone while my loved one's could be out there looking for me.

The subways held so much promise, so many possibilities of my father taking the track on his way to work, or an old friend riding it after a night out at a club. I know I'd been gone for a long time, and that I may look different now, but if someone missed me, I'm certain they'd be able to recognize me.

I pulled my jacket a little tighter as I rode the escalator down to my new daily routine of just riding around. Each person was a new face to try and match to memories I couldn't find. Any person that made eye contact I'd smile sweetly to in an attempt to coax a memory for both them and myself. Sometimes this led to unwanted guests. Weird men would seat themselves next to me, leer over at me, looking for conversation. They usually went away after a while when I acted like I couldn't understand.

I tried to keep myself from spending any more of the money, but I needed a place to rest my head, and spending every night in the subway felt like too much of a risk. I found a cheap, run-down motel, and called it quits as I gave up my search for just a little while.

I lay back on a bed that didn't feel different enough from falling asleep on the train seats, and wished for just a little comfort to get me to sleep quicker. But no matter what, I found myself staring at the dark ceiling. The glow of the cheap alarm clock reminded me of the dim lights always on in UltSyn's buildings. The memory left me feeling a little sick. I didn't want that kind of reminder. I wanted to lose track of time, even for just a moment, so I unplugged the clock.

What was I thinking? Coming out here all alone, living on a prayer that someone would see me in the crowd, and connect me back to a life I once knew. I may never know what led me to leave it behind, but I wanted it back now. That must mean something. If I wanted it so bad, my mind must have some memory hidden somewhere, a latent echo that my heart called for once again.

No matter how many times my mind told my heart this was unrealistic, I didn't listen. I was going to do this, and no one was going to stop me.

<chapter nineteen>
<! -- Scott -->

I woke to a loud chime that rang through my headphones like a shockwave. It was meant to serve as an alarm to make sure that even if I was sleeping, an intruder wouldn't get the jump on me. But this time, however, I knew it signaled that someone had left through the back exit.

I yanked out my earbuds, not wanting to hear any other sensor pick up Sonia's departure. I hadn't deluded myself into thinking this wouldn't happen, but an alert once designed to get me out of bed just made me want to sink further in. I combed my fingers through my hair and tried to settle back down. I pushed every thought away until my mind only listened to the rattling sound of the air conditioner.

I told myself it didn't matter. That one can't play chess well with two people on the same side. The game wasn't designed for that. Neither was my life.

When I started to believe myself, I got up and went back to work. Trying not to think of Sonia only left me feeling restless. She had wanted to leave and deserved to fulfill that desire.

I turned on TV for some noise and realized I was on it. The reporter dubbed me as the Hello World Hacker. When they claimed officials didn't know if the recent attacks were the work of one person, or a group, I couldn't help but smile a little. The attention did nothing for my pride, but I could take solace in that fact that I drew attention off of Sonia. Only attacking UltSyn's interests meant everyone wanted to talk to them. I hoped they thought she was still with me, or even better, had forgotten all about her with this new problem.

Despite continued attempts to stay focused, I found myself distracted by Sonia. Worried even, but more so, I knew if I didn't keep track, she'd fall off the map, completely lost in the clutter of the world. Just because she wasn't here didn't mean I couldn't be sure that UltSyn wasn't on her tail. I programmed Hallie to keep watch, but slowly more and more of my time was spent watching the feeds looking out for trouble. Responsibility nagged at me, telling me to get back to my own search, but reason could wait long enough for me to claim a moment for myself.

It was like the population of the world had doubled. Now there were two people I felt responsible for and needed safe.

While searching down both paths, I found a young girl in Wales that seemed to fit the description of my sister. I hadn't gotten a clear video of the girl's face yet, but with a little math, I figured out she was at least the exact same height. It might not seem like a lot, but it did fit with the other pieces of the puzzle I had. In the data stolen from Paris was a listing of placements. Hundreds of employees were led by that Operational Director; their titles made them seem like nothing more than glorified assistants or interns. In truth, they were like the cogs that kept the whole corporation running. All the names I looked up so far had higher degrees. These weren't filler positions; they were likely just as handpicked as HIDs. Cross referencing the lists showed one matched against the testing facility I first hit. Like Sonia had said, good but not HID level.

I was close, I could feel it.

"Sir," Hallie said, interrupting the music that was playing in the background.

I looked over the multiple screens for a proximity alarm or some other message. Nothing was found, meaning this was different somehow. "What is it?"

"An UltSyn team is being deployed to Denmark. I picked it up when they scheduled a flight plan."

"Same city as Sonia?" Maybe they were going for routine business.

"Yes."

"Damn it." I looked over the screens that showed Wales and clips of CCTV in the area where my sister might be. My focus had been so singular that I even now hesitated when given a choice.

"Switch the feeds," I ordered as surveillance of the UK was replaced with available footage from Denmark cameras. Their system was limited by licensing laws, paperwork, and public safeguards al resulting in fewer windows for me to spy in. One perk, however, was that citizens made a crowd mapping app that listed nearly 3,000 cameras. That made it far easier to know where to get in, and when I needed to jump to see where Sonia was and what was around her.

On one of the cameras I spotted a marquee with a screen that scrolled through different commercials. A tourism advertisement caught my attention with its suggestion to "Come Back for the Holidays."

Sonia was a few blocks down by my best guess, currently in a void between two cameras. But, if her pattern stayed true, she'd pass this sign. The marquee was connected online so they could upload new ads when needed. Instead of hacking in, I pulled a good old-fashioned DDoS attack to lag the system enough that it would freeze on screen when it read: "Come Back."

I didn't think she was going to see it at first, but her mind picked out the oddity, and paused at the sign. "Come on, Sonia. Figure out what I'm doing," I whispered. She watched it for a moment before walking past. I wasn't trying to exactly stop her; I just wanted to warn her that others were coming.

"Why can't you ever make things easy for me?" I grumbled, and jumped ahead to the next closest camera looking for other clues I could leave. I found a theater that was putting on a play of "Great Expectations." The words "Sold Out" filled the second line. It took me a little longer to hack into that sign, but its distance away gave me the time I needed.

I waited with my fingers on the keys until she was in close enough to see the digital marquee before blinking off various letters so the new message collectively spelled: Get Out, a sign so clear that Sonia had to know it was me. The only other explanation would be the advertisements around her were possessed. Occam's razor suggested otherwise.

It was clear that Sonia got the message this time. She looked up at the sign, as did several others, but instead of continuing to gawk at the sign like the pedestrians; she turned away, looking for the person responsible. While I was all the way back in London, she did spot the camera. She looked directly into it before flipping it off.

Didn't need to know sign language for that one.

Sonia looked around again as if planning. Having decided on a path, she headed to a more public area away from the shops. Normally, it would have been a real shit idea, except this county didn't allow cameras in such areas. I wasn't sure if she actually knew that, or if she was just trying to lose me in the crowd.

"Find her," I demanded, and Hallie blinked an acknowledgement. "And if you can't, get me to Denmark."

Sonia was a bit more careful after that. I spotted her briefly twice throughout the day, but she was doing better to avoid being seen, even if just to spite me. But, it was still enough that I knew where Sonia was. I didn't understand why she didn't go to ground. If I could find her, UltSyn would be able to as well.

I was pacing in front of the desk as I thought of ways to protect her from so far away if I tried to run a distraction that wouldn't pull the team off Sonia. "How long until that flight lands?"

"Scheduled to land in four hours and twelve minutes."

"How long would it take to drive there?"

"Roughly twelve hours."

I breathed in like the numbers pained me. There were a host of reasons I wanted to drive there. Less paperwork, able to carry a gun, and not being trapped in a metal bird for hours were among a few. I debated all the factors, calculated a move in my head, and pictured how that would ripple across before I imagined the counter plays from their side. With hands basically tied, and there weren't any good moves to be had.

My phone started to ring, and I stared at it over on the desk. Who was calling me? No one *calls* me. I walked over to it, gawking down at the caller ID which had the audacity to read: UltSyn.

"That's new." It might be a secure call, but since I didn't place it I had no confirmation of that fact. I answered without a word. If the corporate devil wanted to talk to me, I'd listen. There were a few seconds of silence before they decided to speak first.

"We know you've had one of our assets and we are close to you," a deep voice tried to provoke. I simply wondered who exactly was given the job to call me. I wasn't interested in old news.

"How did you get this number?" I said in an attempt to take control of the conversation. My guess was that asshole Jesse finally gave it to them. Wonder how much he got paid this time.

"Now, now, Mr. Gray. You didn't honestly believe you could elude us forever."

Lie number one: that wasn't my real last name. They might be close, but it was clear they hadn't pegged my real identity yet. The alias was still working in my favor, and likely keeping my sister safe.

"What do you want?" I asked, my voice not moving off an unwavering tone.

"It's more about what you want. Why don't you come in? We can work out an agreement, give you whatever you are looking for," the man offered, but I wasn't going to buy it this time.

"Why would you give me anything?"

"To be frank you see, you are costing us a lot of money. We'd like to come to an agreement. Turn white-hat for us and we'll work something out."

I laughed. "I don't want a job."

"We already reclaimed our HID," the voice continued, and my heart stopped beating.

I leaned over to the mouse, giving a shake to pull up the video feeds. It estimated Sonia's current location, despite the gap between cameras that spotted her not that long ago.

That was lie number two. I bit down so I didn't breathe roughly out as the worry radiated off of me.

"Point?" I asked, sounding like that wasn't what I wanted either. I couldn't let him know I cared; they'd just use one of us to get to the other.

"Thought you'd want to know," the man replied, a little thrown off. I think he expected more of a reaction. Lucky for me, I excelled at not giving a shit in dire times.

"Since we can't bargain, are you going to call the cops, or is your job that dull that you had to pester someone?" They hadn't called to make a deal. UltSyn just wanted me out of their hair while they acquired Sonia again. It was their goal to either pacify me or get me to run.

"I think you know enough about our company to know that's not how we'd deal with you," the voice vaguely threatened. The mob used to bust kneecaps; I don't think I wanted to imagine the sort of torture a company that could play with memories could cook up.

"Now that does sort of worry me, but…" I said, letting the last word linger for a moment. "If you aren't going to start being honest, I don't think this relationship is going to work." I didn't care what they'd reply. Once the threats started, I hung up before that third lie showed up.

I looked down as my phone blinked a "Called Ended" message. Despite the GPS in my phone being turned off and having a couple burner phones as buffer, if those were compromised, one could triangulate my location from the cell towers. "Hallie, scrub the phone. Delete everything except that auto-dialer."

I ran out of the hideout past the car, and hit the parking garage on foot. Out here I felt like an exposed nerve with the hounds of hell on my heels. I walked to the street, and spotted a woman getting out of taxi. I ran toward it so no one else flagged it down first.

"Take me to the bakery two streets over, please," I said, settling into the backseat of the taxi. The driver nodded and drove. I utterly silenced my phone, and activated the auto-dialer before discreetly stuffing it down in the seats. If UltSyn wanted to track the phone, they could follow it all across London.

I tipped the driver well for a ride that was only a little over a mile. It was raining out, and I thought of it as both a blessing and a curse. I pulled up my hood, glad for at least the excuse to look huddled up and eager to get inside.

By time I made it back, I was shivering and soaked. I checked to see if anyone was on my tail. At very least, they had to check the surrounding towers which would buy some time. No way to tell how much though.

I ran upstairs and changed into dry clothes faster than I ever had before, then moved into my tech closet and dug around a box parts until I found a pair of glasses, blinking a few times as their systems loaded up. Embedded in the glass was a heads-up display that augmented anything around me with any relevant information it thought was useful. I headed back into my room grabbing a backpack, and stuffing in a jacket, tablet, and chargers. Then I ran downstairs, making sure I had various tools I needed before standing in the living room, giving everything a once over. The hours of safety before now only felt like minutes.

"Lock down everything. If anyone returns besides me, fry it all," I said, almost bitterly. This was my home in a way, and I wasn't thrilled leave it as a rook for someone to try to capture.

"Please declare any access points," Hallie asked indifferently.

"Glasses and tablet only."

"Any other requests before procedure is activated?"

"Book me a plane ticket."

A flight straight there was risky, but since UltSyn tipped their hand, I didn't have the time to bluff a trail. They had been able to get me to run, but not away.

<chapter twenty>
<! -- Scott -->

Have I mentioned I hate flying? Because I really do. The whole process rubs me the wrong way. Every person has to check in at the gate, and if UltSyn didn't have a personal vendetta, there likely would have been cops ready to greet me on the other side. Not surprisingly, pistols weren't allowed on the plane, nor in Denmark, forcing me to travel unarmed since it wasn't worth the risk to smuggle one in.

I pulled my backpack off the scanner's belt, realizing I didn't have much of a plan. No weapons, no car, and limited access to my systems. All I had was a belief that I could warn Sonia, either in person, or by running interference between her and UltSyn's team.

My seat was next to the window, pinned in by a man who looked twice my age in the aisle. It was easy to tune him out in favor of tech. At the head of the plane I could hear a flight attendant talking, and soon after, the plane took off. But despite all of this, the man next to me seemed intent on getting my attention. He stared, then cleared his throat loudly a few times when I didn't look up. If I had to put up with four hours of this…

"What?" I snapped, since he refused to give up.

"You're not allowed to have that on," he said, pointing toward the tablet.

"Ugh. You really don't believe that, do you?"

The man tugged on his scarf like my words were repugnant. "Everyone knows you aren't allowed to have electronics while flying. It could mess with the plane."

"Could it?" I tried not to be memorable to strangers, but putting up with misinformation was too much to ask of me. I held the tablet up with one hand and carried on. "You think a device like this could crash the whole plane? They don't give off nearly enough radio or electromagnetic interference to do shit. Modern planes are completely shielded against the amount they do give off. I could go on, but I think you get the point."

"Well, I wouldn't test fate," the man replied as he puffed out his chest.

"It not a matter of fate. It's science. Maybe next time you hear something, you'll look it up to see if it's true first. You're only afraid of it because you don't understand it."

"People these days have no manners," the man grumbled before leaning back in his chair.

Why a fact was considered rude manners must be generational bullshit. My new "friend" and I split up as soon as the plane landed. He headed toward baggage claim, and I headed for the street. Now all that was left was getting to Sonia first.

I actually hadn't thought of where to go after this. I walked over to a listing of all the flights that were boarding, delayed, or coming in. My glasses added another list of al the privately chartered planes that also had checked in with air control. The secondary list was a bit translucent, but I could see the section scroll until it highlighted the private plane that UltSyn had hired.

Despite the time saved, they still had a three-hour lead on me. "What do I have going for me?" I asked myself, probably sounding like a tourist who was having a hard time with things. No car, no phone, and limited tracking abilities. But I did have one thing. Unlike anyone else, I knew Sonia.

I knew why she picked this country. She was lost and wanted to be found. No better way of doing that then showing up on the grid. To best do that, she'd go somewhere public. Somewhere that constantly is getting a new supply of people.

"Only check the public transport areas. Buses, subways, and anything this country has that is similar," I said to Hallie, holding my hand up to my ear like there was a Bluetooth headset there. Hallie didn't have a lot of horsepower to give me right now, but if I narrowed my scope, it would be easier.

I left the airport, ruling it out right away. If you wanted someone who lived here, odds are they wouldn't be at the airport too often. Since I didn't have a set destination, I just walked. A taxi would have been nice, but I didn't have an exact location to give; choosing one at random only to likely change it later would come off as strange.

A small park is where I ended up. My tablet had beeped several times finding close matches, but they weren't confirmed hits. I sat on a picnic bench, searching any system I could get into to help the search. Another alert popped up, this time finding her. A security camera picked her up at the subway system. The bottom corner displayed a time stamp of thirty-three minutes ago. "God, I hate lag."

I got up and hunted down a taxi, this time with a location in mind as the driver pointed the car in the direction of Copenhagen Metro station. The subway's lanes made for a fairly clean map. Despite studying the station on the drive over, I hadn't been prepared for how big this place felt. There was mile after mile for me to check, split over multiple levels. My glasses were able to scan the crowd of faces faster than I could, which was helpful since I also had to look out for UltSyn people.

Glancing around, I wondered if I should wait Sonia out, or keep moving. I slipped over to the elevators behind me, where several passengers and a worker joined. As I waited for it to go down a level, I spotted a key card hanging off the worker's belt. My fingers twitched at my side before I fell forward like someone else bumped me, and unclipped the card from the rest of the keys.

"Sorry, mate," I mumbled. I slid the stolen goods up my sleeve, and pulled back resituating myself.

He turned back frowning briefly, and understandably so after being touched, then nodded and faced forward again.

The elevator chimed and the doors pulled open as I looked beyond the text displayed on my glasses, and to the group standing past the elevator doors. People funneled past me, but I didn't move as I stared straight at Sonia. The corner of my mouth twitched the briefest smile.

Sonia seemed surprised that I was here in Denmark, only a week after she had left on her own. Neither of us moved, irritating those who had to move past the both of us. I wasn't sure what to say after watching over her these past days as she moved city to city looking for answers. I hadn't come to stop her, or bring her back to me. I just wanted to make sure she was safe, to be here to make sure she didn't get hurt. Needed to make sure UltSyn didn't make off with her. I cared enough to want her out of danger, even if she didn't want me there.

The door chimed again as it started to close, and just like that, Sonia turned on her heel, wiping the shock away to an annoyed expression and backed off. I jumped at the closing doors, squeezing between them to get out of the elevator, and followed as fast as I could behind her. She was trying to lose me, but I managed to keep up.

"Sonia, wait. Just hear me out," I said, and fell into a quick step at her side.

She simply glared harder at the distance in front of her. "You're only making things easier for UltSyn being out here. You're not safe."

After several more strides of her focus being solely dedicated to putting distance between us, I ran ahead enough to step in front of her, blocking the way for a moment. "They've found you, and I can't watch that happen, Sonia. Just come back, be safe. At least until they're gone."

She met my eyes for just a moment before turning to look for a new route.

This time I reached out to her. "Just give me another chance," I said, as I caught her hand to prevent her from leaving.

A crinkle caught my attention as I looked down to notice the small bit of clear cellophane that covered a fresh tattoo on her wrist. It was small, but I could tell it was a bird in flight. "They didn't give you an inch for yourself, but you took one anyway," I said, finding myself smiling now at her choice. I don't know when she got this, but I knew one thing: this is what freedom looked like. It was messy and complicated, and sometimes left a permanent mark. "Let me help you."

She spun back around, and I felt like maybe she'd try to backhand me, but what happened next took the air out of my lungs harder than any slap ever could. I don't think I would have processed it if I hadn't watched her lips move perfectly to the broken sound of the voice that erupted from her. "Stop!" she yelled at me, commanded me. Just like that, I obeyed, frozen as I stared at her. She lifted her hand to touch her throat in surprise.

Sonia wasn't in much haste this time. She didn't have to be, and I watched her take an escalator to the floor above us. I tried to collect myself, but was having a hard time understanding what had just happened.

She could speak? My head cycled the thought over and over like it was stuck in a loop. Al this time, all these months of silence, the only words she shared had come from her hands spelling it out for me. But this time, nothing was explained, and I was left behind trying to understand.

In an attempt not to be completely floored, I glanced around at the people, some who looked on suspiciously. Others seemed concerned with Sonia, who didn't even look over her shoulder at me as she moved up the escalator. Do I just walk away and listen to her? My feet felt heavy as both leaving and going after her each felt like the wrong choice. I took a few steps backwards and out of the crowd as I tried to remember to breathe.

There was a commotion apart from me as someone yelled from the escalators. Who, I didn't know. I just knew it wasn't Sonia, even if I had only just now heard her voice for the first-time seconds ago. Just as I felt like I may not move from this spot in the station for days, someone grabbed at my hand and crashed into me.

Sonia was back. Fear painted her eyes darker as she glanced over her shoulder before trying to pull me quickly along with her. I glanced back as well, seeing the men in outfits far too familiar descending the escalators Sonia had just

156

been on. Just like that, I stumbled back into a world full of sound.

She didn't say anything as she tugged eagerly, but even without the words, I followed her. We moved over to the train tracks, and even though she brought us this way, it was clear she was lost as to what to do now.

I lead with a tug on her hand. "This way." I could stow away my surprise for another time. The real world called. I remembered seeing a maintenance door, and I headed back to it, swiping the card I had stolen earlier over the lock. We ducked inside, and I peered out through a tiny window in the door, watching the UltSyn jerks rush our way. Sonia had let go of my hand, and was standing a few steps behind me with antsy bounces on her heels. "Wait for it," I said, stealing looks from the men to the lock's controls. The men nearly slammed into the door, tugging at the door handle as I finished jamming it not to open again.

I watched as one of men shouted, but I couldn't hear him. I think he was signaling to one of the others in the back to fix the lock, making me grin at my handy work. Sonia laced her fingers with mine, leaning away to get me moving again. We quickly wove down these back hallways, passing on the first few exits before arbitrarily deciding the next was safe.

We took a second to get our bearings, but didn't need a fraction more than that, since my heads-up display showed one of the trains was leaving in forty-two seconds. We ran for it, sliding in right before the doors closed. As the automated train started to move, I closed my eyes, thankful for a closed transport this once.

I turned to find Sonia; she had backed herself into an open seat near the front, her chest heaving from all of the running. I nearly fell into the seat next to her, and just barely took off my backpack before sitting down.

These rides weren't long, and I looked over at a sign to see which line we had jumped on. A little ETA of just under thirty minutes was listed for its farthest point. Despite helping her escape like I had wanted; I still didn't know if she wanted to leave. But it was clear there wasn't a lot of time and either way, there was one thing I owed her before she decided.

"I lied when we were in Germany, about finding something." I pulled out the tablet from the backpack, unable to look over to Sonia as I just stared down at it. "Didn't have it in me to say anything, but you deserve to have the answers you wanted. Even if you won't like them." Once selecting and queuing up the file, I held the tablet out to her.

She took it from me, I dug around to offer headphones as well. When I finally looked up to Sonia, I saw that she was looking at me with a wary expression.

"I'll give you a moment."

<chapter twenty-one>
<! -- Sonia -->

I watched Scott move away from me, staring at him for a few seconds as he settled alone at the very back. He caught my gaze and he took a moment to give me a silent nod. There were a lot of things I felt toward him before, and since leaving. Anger was amongst them, but right now I felt very confused about what he was doing.

And what I was doing? What would I do after getting off this train? Would we separate, or should I return with him? I frowned and turned my attention to the tablet. I put headphones in before beginning, curling my fingers around the cord nervously after I pressed play. What had he found that he wanted to hide?

A man placed his things on a desk, and flashed his ID at the camera, really just taking his time before sitting down. "Please state your age for the record."

"Eighteen," a girl replied as the camera switched to her. Or rather, *me.* I could recognize myself in the video feed, even with wavy hair past my shoulders. Maybe even fresh out of high school. I leaned forward in my seat, feeling like I could connect to the girl sitting there and understand more than what the video was showing me.

"Name?"

"Lydia Kolding," I said in the video, not making eye contact with the man. As I analyzed my body language, I could tell there was a certain sadness in my eyes. A clear disinterest in everything, as I paid more attention to the jacket cover than the interview. I was dressed appropriately for an interview, despite my makeup showing wear.

"You had denied our previous job offer. Why did you change your mind?"

The girl blinked a few times, adjusting in her seat. "I had declined the offer because of your requirements, specifically the one about letting go of my former life."

It sounded like I was applying to be a spy, but even though I didn't say it, I knew what that meant now. Forgetting my past, memories, and loved ones. "That rule doesn't bother me anymore."

The man leaned forward. "May I ask why the change of heart?"

"My family passed away last week in a car accident," the girl said, her voice dry of emotion, but I knew myself enough to see past the mask she wore. "If I agree, I won't have to live with that fact."

"Well, then, welcome to UltSyn, Ms. Kolding," he said to her. To me.

I closed my eyes and felt the tears that were already running down. I pulled at my sleeves, and began to wipe them away as best I could. I found myself clutching at the tablet harder as I listened to the video clip repeat as if this time, it would play a different tale. I attempted to stifle any sobs that escaped when the story retold the same way again.

So much to process, connecting myself to that girl, and feeling the loss of people I already had lost. I could hear myself in the voice of the girl who used to be me. I could hear her heart break, the sadness as she found a way to try to remove that very thing. It seemed incomprehensible that this was once me. How I had given up on life so easily, on individuality, simply not to deal with the loss of loved ones?

I barely stopped crying enough to see clearly back to where Scott was. I didn't know what to say to him, or what I wanted to do. I just didn't want to be alone anymore. I've been alone for an entire week already. Now I needed someone, more than ever.

I shuffled my way through the car before getting to Scott. He looked up at me with sad eyes, saying nothing himself. I managed to hand the tablet back before crumbling into the seat next to him.

Why didn't...you tell me? I signed, my breathing breaking the sentence into parts as my lungs only let me get a few words out between heaving. In truth, I was having trouble keeping myself from erupting into a crying fit. I was willing to settle for silent tears.

Scott didn't look away when giving me an answer. "I didn't know how. I didn't want to see you... give up. Thinking I lost my sister broke me in ways," he said softly. "A person needs hope."

I forced a slight smile as I looked down at the floor. "Running away from this pain again does seem tempting." My voice sounded as broken as I felt.

"Yeah." Scott reached over for my hand, holding it tightly as my eyes drew back up to him. "I know it does."

I stifled another sob, and leaned my head into him. With each whine or wheeze or shake I couldn't control, I found myself closer to him, until I was pulled onto his lap completely, curled against him as I cried into his shoulder.

Louder and more shaken than ever before, Scott held me tightly, almost squeezing with each fit my lungs pulled.

"Please don't leave," he whispered into my hair. The intent behind his words was blurred between wanting me safe and just wanting me around. Either worked. I nodded into his shoulder, not moving away to give any more of an answer. I wasn't leaving this time.

We hailed a taxi to get out of the station after getting off at a random stop. It was late now, and they seemed to be getting harder to find. I was worried the driver would be annoyed with our request, but when we asked to be driven a city over he looked like Christmas came early. I guess that meant he didn't have to worry about finding a countless number of fares tonight.

The taxi drove up to a hotel that barely had enough rooms to warrant two stories. I could have used the excuse of it being a single small bed, but being tucked against Scott was for my personal comfort. I just wanted to hold onto someone that I knew cared about me.

The TV droned on, but it didn't seem like either of us paid attention. I didn't even know what show we were watching when it flipped to a commercial, and Scott hadn't commented on it in an hour or so. Actually, he hadn't commented on anything in for a while.

I must have spaced out for a while because when I started to pay attention again, the channel was definitely different.

"So, what do I call you?" Scott asked after I stirred.

My birth name came back to mind, and I shook my head a little at the idea. "Sonia."

The corner of his mouth tugged up, and I think that was the answer he wanted to hear. "You should get some sleep. I'll stay up and make sure we stay safe."

He looked tired, but I knew there wasn't any point in arguing with him, so I just nodded and laid my head back down so he couldn't slip away.

<chapter twenty-two>
<! -- Scott -->

I was quite happy when Sonia decided to come back to England with me. I knew it was a low bar since the other options were UltSyn or homelessness, but I was going to mark it down in my book as a win all the same.

A part of me doubted we'd make it back there. We got yet another taxi to drive us back to the parking lot above the hideout. We got out, and I watched the car drive away before I started moving again. "You're going to have to hang up here for a moment. Everything's locked down and if Hallie's brain gets fried, I'll never get her sorted out again."

Sonia was carefully watching another vehicle look for a parking spot; when they traveled up a level, she gave me a nod.

Getting in the back way felt a lot like breaking into your own house. There was an access shaft hidden away from foot traffic. It scanned my ring before opening.

I dropped down and took no more than a step before scanners activated. Lights rolled over me checking identity and signaling to be still.

If confirmed, it would unlock a door in my real garage. I had thought about rigging the system for Sonia *and* myself, but you didn't want to tie a self-destruct sequence to a variable that could be overly harsh at times.

Since everything was working, it didn't seem like anyone had tried to access my systems. When I was given a green al clear, I smiled a little. "Hi, honey, I'm home," I mused before climbing back up to retrieve Sonia.

She moved cautiously until she stood almost exactly between the desk, the kitchen, and the living room. Maybe she expected things to look different after returning, when in reality, they didn't.

"Everything okay?" I asked. Sonia nodded, taking a step toward the couch to run her fingers over a folded-up blanket she often used. "Yeah?"

"Yeah," she said. The voice was soft. It didn't crack from lack of use, but it also didn't have the same volume as most. Sonia hardly talked even now, but every time she did, I found myself smiling a little. She was so many things they tried to take, and there was just something about the way she held herself, not despite that, but because of it.

"I still don't know how you do that."

"Do what?" she said, face scrunching in a frown.

"Talk."

"Oh," Sonia breathed. She looked down at her hands, likely so used to talking with them over the years. "I don't know if it was pity or mercy. After I was wiped of my memories, a case worker who read my file said they didn't want me to lose everything, which I wasn't ever sure what they meant by that until now. I thought maybe they just meant if I performed properly, it was my reward. Anyway, they had switched some papers around to make it look like I had the surgery. It was our secret for a time. I think they quit soon after."

What could one even say to that? I was wordless for a moment before something finally came to me. "Sometimes one act of kindness can change everything."

* * *

The search for my sister resumed. First in Wales, then I moved on to thoroughly search Cardiff. A solid trail picked up again in Cambridge. The city was only slightly over sixty miles from here, and it took all I had not to storm the place now. I refused to fuck things up on the one-yard line.

I caught Sonia's reflection in one of monitors. I spun around in my chair to see her coming down from the stairs, her hair wet from the shower. "Hey," I grinned.

"Hi," Sonia replied, looking a little amused.

"Want to see what I found?" I said, unable to keep excitement out of my voice.

"Yes," Sonia said in an even tone as she walked over next to me. I pulled up a clip of the girl I had showed her that first day. It clearly showed my sister getting into a fancy black four-door SUV with an UltSyn executive. "Wow, you found her."

"Don't sound surprised."

"I'm not," she chuckled before going on. "Just, she doesn't look like a captive at all. You wouldn't think she was missing."

"Yeah, I was thinking about that. Maybe she doesn't know I'm looking," I said weakly, staring at the screen again. How did you save someone who didn't know they needed to be? My excitement died down as reality set in. Tori wasn't dressed like the two HIDs I saw, but she was definitely tied up with UltSyn. Sonia hadn't instantly wanted her past, would my sister?

Sonia put her hand on my shoulder, and I tensed forgetting she was next to me. "You'll figure it out. If she isn't an HID, there's less architecture so I'm sure there is a way for her to remember." I was still unsure of the logistics of it, but at least Sonia's words helped me again see the hope in this.

The two of us kept tabs on my sister's movements for a week. If there was a pattern, we could find a way to exploit it. Victoria was never alone, but at times, she was only accompanied by one other person. Most of their time was divided up between a professor at the university, and an UltSyn building that focused on software and bioscience in Silicon Fen.

Both were made up of a collection of buildings, and my sister seemed to be serving as a liaison between all of them. I focused on the Silicon Fen area since it had more privately-owned buildings of tech companies. Startups were born and often died here, but instead of letting that stifle the area, they used those ashes to build something new. Innovation at its finest.

I knew walking into the UltSyn building would never work this time; Sonia and I were too visible on their radar already. But, I bet I could get into one of the other businesses. So, like any adult must do from time to time, I got us an interview at one of the companies that my sister often stopped by. I added us in the company's schedule, making the appointments back-to-back with an hour in between to give us plenty of wiggle room. As clever as I thought my plan was, I think the best part was Sonia's half tempered annoyance at the suggestion of her getting a job.

The next day, Sonia and I were sitting in the lobby of a 'rival' tech company. There were cameras around, but since the firm was in direct competition with UltSyn I knew they wouldn't be privy to any of the feeds. I would even be willing to bet that if I properly introduced myself as the one tanking UltSyn's stocks, the CEO would shake my hand. As two people who were posing like they wanted the same job, Sonia and I didn't act too chummy. If we needed to say something to the other, we could tap it out in Morse against the armrest.

I was looking down at the camera feed outside on my replacement phone. My interviewer was fifteen minutes late, but I couldn't care less as I spotted Victoria and her escort approach. It seemed like both our schedules would clear up soon.

My heart was racing as Victoria and her partner stepped inside. I was sure her partner worked in operations with her, presumably intelligent to have the job he had, but I couldn't remember a thing about him as I looked past him to my sister.

As he talked to the person at the desk, Victoria idly turned to look our way. When her eyes widened in recognition, I stopped breathing. "Are you coming?" asked her partner. Surprise only seemed to hold Victoria's attention on me for a few seconds more.

I'll be right there, Victoria turned and signed to him. The man looked puzzled, but in the end, followed after the receptionist.

"It's you." I was already on my feet, even though I don't remember standing.

I knew you'd find me, she signed, before colliding into me to give me a hug.

I wrapped my arms around my sister, almost afraid the slightest touch would crush her. But when she didn't disappear like a cruel dream, I held on tighter. "I'm sorry it took me so long," I choked out. "God, let me get a look at you."

If I didn't know better, I would have sworn she was taller. My eyes drifted to her name tag, and I tilted it up to read it better. The picture was clearly her, even the name of Victoria Gris was correct. I had expected to see an alias, not our real last name.

"We need to get going," Sonia urged. I dropped the ID as she spoke, my eye line rising to see where the others had gone. He wasn't a typical guard, but I'm sure he wouldn't be happy with me whisking his partner away.

"You're coming with us, right?" I checked with Victoria. My ratio of taking UltSyn's assets was a hard 50/50 success rate, and I figured I should ask this time.

Victoria's eyes flared wider, as if she was worried I hadn't planned to for a second, then she reached out to take my hand.

"Let's go." I headed for the door and jammed the cameras this time. It was a little tricky to do with only one hand, but I refused to let go of my sister. The three of us ran over to the car in the nearby parking lot. Sonia was in the lead, and Victoria was only a half-step behind me.

When her hand slipped out of mine, I instantly stopped. "Tori, come on. We need to get out of here," I said, as she seemed to be stuck on the other side on an invisible fence.

She took a step back away from me, her disposition changing completely. *What sort of nickname is Tori? Vicky would make more sense. Don't you think anything else is a stretch?*

"No?" I said and signed at the same time, completely confused on why this was important now. I might be the only one who called her by that nickname, but this was the first time she yelled at me for it.

God, you are stupid, Victoria said.

Still, utterly lost, I turned to Sonia to check if I remembered the signs correctly. My stomach erupted with pain. I stepped back with a gasp and fought the urge to throw up. I knew I shouldn't have pulled out the knife, but had trouble believing it was real until I felt the handle under my fingers, until I saw my blood glisten against the blade. The knife effortlessly fell out of my hand as I looked up to my sister.

"Why?" Had I failed her so completely that she now hated me? My head felt too light and I stumbled back further, bumping into my car, which was the only thing keeping me upright.

Did you really think you could cause all that chaos and get away with it? We figured out what you wanted, and used it against you. UltSyn warns you to leave well enough alone, unless you want a bullet in this pretty little head of mine.

Each word Victoria signed was killing what was left of me. My mind was just clear enough to realize that if Victoria was with UltSyn then Sonia wasn't safe here either. I turned to her as I started to slide down the car. "Sonia, go, run," I demanded, my voice cracking from the pain in my gut. There was an added wince as I ended up on the asphalt.

Instead of leaving, Sonia twitched toward me, but when Victoria moved toward me as well, Sonia pulled the gun I gave her. They both froze, the knife now at my sister's feet as Sonia aimed.

"Don't hurt her." Their standoff turned its attention to me, likely curious who I was trying to protect with that comment. "Please," I clarified to Sonia.

Her face tightened before she holstered the gun. She dropped down to my level, putting her hands over the wound since I was barely putting any pressure on it.

"Stop it," I fussed and batted her hands away. "Just go." My attempts to shoo Sonia away proved ineffective since my eyes barely left my sister. They wanted to close, but I willed myself to pay attention.

Victoria looked amused and had a bitterness about to her that I'd never seen before. *Don't worry,* she said, *I wasn't sent for her. I was sent specifically for you. Enjoy what little is left of your life, brother.* She might have gone on, but at the last word I closed my eyes, unable to take anymore. I couldn't tell you what hurt more... my stomach or my heart. All I knew was that my world just scattered.

<chapter twenty-three>
<! -- Sonia -->

I think Scott was ready to bleed out right here, but not if I had anything to say about it. I called his name until he weakly looked up at me. "It's all right. You'll be fine, we just need to patch you up."

"There is no point," Scott said, sounding beyond defeated, already accepting this fate. "Please just leave me." When he blinked, tears ran down his cheeks, but I was the only one to notice.

I put my hand on Scott's cheek, in an attempt to keep his attention, and he shivered under my touch. "I *need* you to stay. Okay? Just give me some time."

"I'm sorry, Sonia. I'm so, so sorry."

"You've seen worse than this. Don't give up yet. Can you do that for me?" My tone was a bit firmer this time. He sniffled, and shook, before a nod came.

I looked over my shoulder to where Victoria had run off. I knew there would be at least a few minutes before she returned to her handlers. If it could somehow bring her back, if I could somehow take her with us, it would do Scott a world of good.

When I turned back, his head was down, and his hand had fallen away.

"Scott!" I yelled. The sheer volume gave me a start. He twitched and picked his head up just barely enough to look at me. Christ, this boy was going to give me a heart attack. "Just… don't close your eyes."

If I could only run off to get his sister, but I knew getting him out of here was more pressing. He didn't protest as I wrapped his arm around my shoulder. The groan he made when I stood us up seemed involuntary. It made me feel bad for moving him, but I didn't have a choice.

After awkwardly managing to open the passenger door, Scott collapsed into the seat. I ran around to the driver's seat, looking around to where a med kit was hiding.

Without any preservation of the neatly ordered supplies, I dumped everything out. The main concern was Scott losing too much blood, especially with him holding the injury more out of pain than conscious effort of preservation. He was slouched enough that I was able to wrap gauze tightly around his torso. If he had any objections, it was lost to his quick, shallow breathing.

None of this was good in the slightest, but both stab wounds and shock were survivable. If I could get us back, they'd be more supplies there. I searched around the steering wheel for how to start the car. Right, the ring.

I reached over to Scott, and he almost curiously watched me take it off his too cold finger. I held the ring up to the ignition and car blinked to life with a series of colorful lights.

"Unauthorized user. Access denied," Hallie replied, seeming heartless for even a computer.

I wanted to slam my hands against the dashboard, but stopped myself, certain that it wouldn't gain me any favors. "Can't you override it?" I asked, but the error message continued to stare back at me. About ready to teach myself how to hotwire the thing when help came.

"Just," Scott winced. "Let her do what she wants."

"Thank you," I whispered. At least he wasn't so determined on giving up that he wasn't even going to let me try. He tried to mirror my expression as I looked over, but the ghost of a smile didn't reach the rest of his face.

"Authorized user. Access granted," Hallie said changing her tone now.

"Confirm biometrics." A picture of a fingerprint appeared on the screen and five circles lit up on the dashboard.

"Yes, yes, just fucking go already!" I placed my hand up on the dash. Of course, Scott's tech would have some sort of fancy scanner. If he was feeling better, he'd likely complain how most fingerprint scanners were faulty and therefore stupid in some way.

I moved my hand back to the wheel and the engine started. I pulled the car out and glanced to check on Scott again. He was staring off and looking passively amused.

"What?"

"I was thinking," he started and licked his lips. "How strange it would be if the last thing I heard was you cursing at the computer."

I was in no mood for gallows humor right now. "Stay awake," I ordered and starting speeding. I got us back to London as fast as I safely thought I could.

The miles still felt like they took too long, and I think Scott passed out during the ride over, because he looked confused when I lifted him out of the passenger seat. That's if I wasn't reading more into it. Every reaction was so slight, I was worried I was just filling the emotions in.

We made it two steps upstairs before he felt like deadweight, and I strained to keep us upright. "Come on, don't be a baby," I said, trying to get some sort of response out of him.

Scott groaned as his feet found their footing. "I hate you so much right now."

Not quite what I was going for, but I'd take it, since it meant we were moving, and I wouldn't have to figure out how truly bad things were on the floor.

I managed to get him on the bed before dashing into the bathroom for more supplies. I found a bottle of liquid stitch, and flipped it over to be greeted by the UltSyn Bio logo. Their advancements had got us into this. Maybe they could help get us out. I cut the gauze around his waist off to check the bleeding, and make a proper judgement call. It wasn't a completely clean cut, but not a jagged mess either. "Here, bite onto this," I said, and brought over a washcloth.

"You're wasting your time," he said to the ceiling.

"You made it this far."

As I began cleaning the wound, Scott gasped from the pain, before he remembered my advice and bit down. The muscles in his jaw were so tight it looked like they would snap like a rubber band; only a bit of fabric saved his teeth. After I had cleaned, stitched, and bandaged the wound, there wasn't an ounce of tension left, just a cold sweat.

"If you are done torturing me, can I sleep now?"

His tone make me realize I was wrong. There was an anger rising above an otherwise earnest request.

"Shortly," I signed, and pulled off plastic gloves. He didn't listen that time and was out before I did anything else.

I tried to clean up, but got frustrated, and wanted air. Unfortunately, being alone downstairs was as close as I was going to get. I wish I could say that Scott was being simply being dramatic; I've seen him work through things with wounds that would put other men down. However, this loss of innocence cracked his foundation, and without legs to stand on the mind crumbles.

"I'm going to need help," I mumbled.

"How may I be of service?" Hallie replied, giving me a fright. I looked over to Scott's wall of monitors as a ribbon flowed gently between the screens. I hadn't expected her to hear me, or volunteer to help.

In reality, I don't think she had. Scott's comment in the car had been far more reaching than I had imagined. "I guess we are partners now." The system just blinked in acknowledgment. "Does Hallie stand for anything?" I asked, affording my curiosity a second.

"Heuristically Algorithmic Logical Interface," she replied, and I did a quick mental check which letters were used before giving a little nod at the name.

"All right, let's get to work."

<chapter twenty-four>
<! -- Sonia -->

While sightings of Victoria lessened, UltSyn didn't seem to care if they hid her entirely. After all, the company's wheels had to keep turning. Or maybe they figured keeping her visible prevented Scott from further action.

It felt taboo to sit at his desk and made me want to get him back in this seat even faster. Scott had finally figured exactly where to look. It was strange to think how little of the world we saw at one time.

If I could only find a way to bring her in. Scott was a master of turning a system against itself, he even mentioned concern about setting off an EMP around our architecture. This led me to a theory of my own. I could use a similar tactic on the chips UltSyn implanted by finding a way to disable them without damaging the surrounding tissue.

But how? I tapped my fingers against the desk as I tried to think. I paused, staring down at my hand. That's it. I could use sound.

"Could I make a device that emitted a sound that could temporarily disable anyone with a shared implant?"

After a few seconds of processing I got the 'Yes' answer I was hoping for.

"Do I have such a part?" This would be my only chance; any failure and UltSyn would just cut their losses and scrap Victoria before they let us try to harm their profits again.

I wanted to tell Scott about my idea to give him hope, but I knew he wouldn't want me to do it. He'd rather have me leave it alone, instead of risking mine or Victoria's life. He had thrown in the towel, but I was only just getting started. If I told him, he might force a promise to not even try.

"Unknown," Hallie finally reported. "Not enough information about HID infrastructure is known. An experiment would have to be performed."

"An experiment?" I did not like the sound of that. "What sort?"

"The scanners reserved for disabling tracking chips could be altered to confirm your theory."

That system had a bite to it; that was for sure. I looked over my shoulder to the stairs that led up to Scott's room and wishing he was here before I started tweaking things. With a sigh, I turned back to the computer. "Set it up."

Thankfully for me, Hallie was programmed well enough to make most of the changes herself, so I didn't have to spend all day teaching myself how. However, doing it myself would have made me less nervous about stepping in front of the scanners.

The system would first look for any metal or signal type that could be exploited, followed by a test of my "sound" theory.

I hit the start sequence on the tablet before putting it on the counter and positioned myself in the exact spot I was made to stand before. Tensing as the scans started, instinctively nervous that the system would mess up and zap something I needed. The scans took longer this time, and I let out a shaky breath as they finished.

"Viable alloys found in the temporal lobe. Would you like me to begin work on a suitable frequency?" Hallie asked.

"How long will it take?"

"Six hours and forty minutes."

Is that Microsoft time or real time?"

"Query not understood."

"Never mind." I frowned and picked up the tablet again. "Just let me know when it's done." I headed back in from the garage as a yawn escaped me. It was easy to see how Scott could lose days down here.

I went upstairs to check on Scott, finding him still asleep even though it was half a day later. Normally, he had headphones in so he was still paying attention to everything around him on some level, but they were abandoned on the nightstand, a sign he was choosing to disconnect from the world completely.

Scott was roughly on the middle of the bed on his side, and I decided to take up the bit of room that was left. I eased myself slowly closer, until there was only a few inches left between us.

"I'm going to find her, Scott," I whispered, and studied his face to see if there was any hint that he was hearing me. None was to be found, but I didn't care. "I'm going to bring her back."

I wiggled a bit until I was in the right position to place my hand on one of his, and closed my eyes as I decided to kill some time with him.

I woke, feeling his hand twitch under mine, and opened my eyes to see Scott waking up. He sleepily pulled his hand away, and I don't think he had even registered the extra weight on it. As his eyes focused, his brow tightened briefly as he looked over to me. I hoped it didn't come off as weird that I was watching as he woke up, but it probably did.

"Good morning," I whispered.

"Is it?"

I frowned, and he closed his eyes again, looking intent on going back to sleep.

"Here," I said and sat up to reach over to the nightstand to grab the painkillers that had been pushed toward the back. I pressed the bottle into his palm.

Scott rolled the container up to his fingertips to read the label. Looking unsatisfied, he palmed it, and tucked both arms against his chest. It was like he was trying to punish himself by not taking them.

"You said I could do whatever I wanted," I started, not sure where this sentence was going. I just wanted to get him talking, and if I was lucky, maybe even joking. "So, I decided I wanted to share the bed."

"Okay." Scott groaned as he rolled over to his back. I wasn't sure if he moved to give me more room, or to turn away from me. I heard the tablet beep with a message, knowing it had to be that Hallie finished up. Instead of leaving right away, I stuck around until Scott fell back asleep, which only turned out to be another ten minutes or so.

The garage felt cold compared to the bedroom, so I made a slight detour, and stole Scott's jacket off the back of his chair before going out again. "How safe is this, Hallie?" I stood cautiously by the door.

"This is an untested experiment with a high probability of success, but the risks include hearing loss, vomiting, headaches, and other possible sensory phenomenon."

"Sometimes it's better not the read the fine print," I mumbled.

"Would you like me to wake Scott to serve as your spotter?"

"No!" I said without even thinking. "I mean, it's fine. Let's just get this test started." I walked over to the testing area listening nervously as the system explained that two possible frequencies had been written, each lasting ten seconds before alternating to the next, with a two second break in between.

"Would you like to proceed?"

I nodded. For the first few seconds, I thought the test was a bust, but when the signal hit me, it was undeniable that something was happening. Fear clenched my chest up tight as my vision went black.

It came back almost right away, but in its place, I saw Scott sitting in the car the night he asked me to kiss him. Every detail had been recorded, most notably the breathless expression on his face. It had been a look that made me blush, a feeling that stayed on my mind for days after. The memories jumped further back to when Scott had been baiting me that first night. I think some of his attitude transferred to me that day since I had been taunting him in return. I couldn't hear him now, but memory of the words stuck. "A computer part with attitude. Real cute. Adorable even." Next, I saw a few seconds of the SUV convoy right before it crashed.

My vision cut back in after what must have been the ten second mark. I was unable to even get my breath back during the break that was far too short. The ringing that followed threatened to bring me to my knees. It was the loudest sound

I'd ever heard, and I swore Hallie's test was going to alert the whole city. I pulled my hands up to my ears to help block out the sound, but it did no good.

I tried to think why, but couldn't hear myself over the sound. I took a step forward to try to turn the damn thing off before instinctively covering my ears again. It still did nothing to ease the pain, but this time I realized why. No sound was actually being projected; the noise was coming from inside my head.

The tone stopped exactly when it was programmed to, but that had certainly been the longest twenty-two seconds of my life. Brimming with anxiety, my hands were shaking, and I tucked them protectively against me.

"Did either signal produce your desired results?" Hallie asked, clearly oblivious to my trauma.

"Yeah," I gulped before my voice found its footing. "Second one." Personally, I never wanted to experience either of them again. What good would my weapon do if it took me out with it? I leaned against the wall for support, trying to calm down enough that I could think again.

There had to be a way to shield myself from it. I took a break before researching everything on the matter that I could think of. One method suggested a different metal to block out the signal, but a whole tin foil hat approach wasn't as eloquent as I was looking for.

I managed to think of a different approach. I didn't much like the sound of it either, and I knew Scott would hate the idea of it even more. I laid next to him in bed again, debating for hours if I should wake him up and say.

"Scott," I said softly. He had been sleeping lighter, since no one man needed as much as he was getting. I think I heard a mumble of a something, but nothing substantial. "There is something I want to tell you… in case my plan fails horribly." I took a long moment before I could finish. "I love you."

I didn't expect an answer, but I waited, chewing on my lip, for one anyway. They pursed together, as I reminded myself that the point wasn't to hear it back, but to simply say it.

Without waiting any longer, I got up and headed downstairs. I walked into the garage, and stopped to stare at the area that had become my personal circle of hell. If I wanted progress I had to do this, despite my fear.

I set Hallie up to interface with the connectors UltSyn had installed, but the whole idea of letting another computer into my head gave me the creeps. I was worried that she might trigger some sort of left-over security. Hallie wasn't going to read or write over any of the data simply to turn the clip off, so I hoped it would work out fine. I hooked up the cord at the back of my neck, and the weight of it made me nauseous.

"I need you to concentrate a powerful signal to disable it. You are… connected to localize efforts the best you can. Don't need you to be banging around up there. Are you certain you can alter the frequency that destroyed my tracking chip to a safer threshold that will only disable this chip?"

"Yes. However, it is unknown if it will affect the temporal lobe, or any other parts supported by the chip. Dangers range from memory complications, changes in behavior and personality, loss of language comprehension, and problems with visual and auditory processing."

"How sure are we it will affect things?"

"Fifty percent risk."

This was a serious risk. I walked over to the tablet with a sigh. "Just remind me what I'm supposed to do if I forget. Set up the frequency."

Hallie only took a few minutes this time before reporting the new frequency was ready. Like ripping off a bandage, I pressed the command to begin. I knew there was no use in hoping that disarming my chip would be kinder than the signal that zapped my arm before, but I stood there silently, trying to prepare myself. Now that I had found my voice I wanted to use it to scream, but I didn't want to give any machine that satisfaction. UltSyn never got a peep, and these systems wouldn't get one either.

I lost what happened between me standing and where I was now, currently curled against the ground. Could barely describe what I was feeling, because any pain I had known before was different. It didn't feel like a headache, more like I was losing a piece of my mind. I pressed my forehead against the cold floor, willing the feeling away as best as I could. It felt like both a second and a century had passed before I was able to even try to stand.

"Successful deactivation of implanted chip," Hallie said.

I managed to open my eyes and remove the cord, despite the intense ice pick migraine that now persisted. As far as I could tell, my memory was still intact. I moved over to the tablet to tap away the warnings Hallie brought up.

"Think the chi—i—ip disarmed success."

I stared at the tablet, a little confused at what I just heard myself say out loud. The sentence I had formed in my head sounded nothing like what came out of my mouth.

"Temporal for scan damage." I wanted to scan for damage, but each word was out of order, or completely dropped from my sentences. This wasn't going to make any sense. I guess not everything went as smoothly as I had hoped.

It wasn't difficult to understand what my brain was doing. My temporal lobe was taking my words, and spitting them out as a mess of a sentence. Damaged language processing now meant my verbal communication skills were more or less ruined. I could still do this; I went without them before.

Hallie hadn't responded to anything yet. I cussed silently. The tablet was still around, and I figured I could at least communicate via text to begin developing a portable device to emit the previously tested signal. I wasn't sure how soon I'd head out to try to find Victoria, but right now, my head ached for one of those pain pills Scott had in his room. I prayed my problem with language comprehension would wear off with sleep.

The idea of a bed sounded really nice, but the closer opportunity to just sink into the coach won out. I had also been worried that if I went upstairs, Scott would suddenly be chatty, and I didn't want to get into it. Realistically, the couch also just took far less work to get to.

I woke up to the rustle of someone in the kitchen. I quickly sat up, looking over the back of the couch to see Scott downstairs for the first time. He was staring into the refrigerator looking unimpressed, then just grabbed a water bottle. With a sigh, he moved over to grab a bag of chips from the counter, but ate only a few before giving up on the whole eating thing.

His eyes finally lifted to see me sitting here. I didn't say anything, because I was afraid it would come out as a word jumble. Scott looked away from me as if noticing everything down here was on and running. The monitors had a progress bar that read 82% complete on the middle screen. Scott turned back to me as I tried to look as inconspicuous as I could.

"What's going on?" he asked flatly.

I shrugged at first, but knew that wasn't going to be enough. So, I brought one of my hands up to sign, *Nothing.* I could see something shift behind Scott's expression, like he wanted to challenge me, or take a few steps over to see for himself.

"Whatever," he grumbled, and headed back upstairs.

Today seemed to be my day for close calls. I don't think I had slept for more than four hours, but I got up anyway and sat over at the desk.

Awake, but bored, I started looking through the desk drawers, finding old papers, a few stray parts, and countless external storage. My little invasion of privacy wasn't proving to be that much fun, but curiosity urged me to finish my search. On top of bunch of papers was a book, but not just any book…it was *my* book. A copy of the da Vinci codex I had mentioned wanting in Belgium. When did he get this? I thought about going to ask since he was up, but found myself smiling, more interested in flipping through the pages as I waited.

Hallie was able to use the 3D printer to make much of the device, but I had to still search around the house to find parts that couldn't be fabricated. Most were in the computer room upstairs, but I did save some time by spotting one of the pieces in the desk drawer earlier. I don't think I've ever done anything like this before, but armed with a tutorial, I could pretty much do anything.

Nervously, I flipped the device on to test it. Instead of a sound loud enough to make my ears bleed, I was met with just a low hum from the device. At least messing with my head wasn't completely fruitless, and now I had something that could temporarily disable UltSyn's prized tech.

I had to drive to Cambridge by myself. Every mile I expected to get a text asking where I was, given I had made it that much harder for Scott since I traded my tablet for his phone. The last thing I wanted was to fight with it over permissions issues while out here. By the time I made it to the university, a message still hadn't come.

Fine by me. If everything went according to plan, I'd be back within two hours anyway. Victoria and her partner were scheduled to meet with an admissions officer today to help ensure that UltSyn got their choice of freshman in the school.

I sat outside on a bench waiting, scrolling through his contact list that only had two names. I wasn't sure the first entry of "NIC" was a person. Wasn't that an acronym used for network interface cards? For a man so connected to the world, he didn't talk to many people.

Surveillance picked Victoria up before I did. The phone happily displayed

"Assets Located," and followed their movements on campus. If I stayed right where I was, they'd walk in my direction, but I wanted to be able to get the drop on them. I worked my way around a building, cutting them off as they entered the parking lot.

I triggered the device, and they crouched down like the glass in the buildings had blown out and would start raining down on them.

In the parking lot, there is a blue car. I want you to run to it and get in. Only then will I turn this of, I signed to Victoria. She recognized me, and clearly wasn't happy to see me. I looked over to her partner to deliver a message to the both of them. *If you run off or try any other attempts to escape, I'll shoot him.* The two managed to look over at each other, and I wondered if they were friends.

Go, now, I ordered as Victoria begrudgingly headed into the parking lot. With some distance, she tentatively moved her hands away from her ears. Students were starting to gather as it looked like I was standing in judgment of a man who was having an aneurysm in front of me. A part of me felt bad that I was leaving him behind, making this twice someone had tried to save his partner and not him. I didn't even know his name. *I'm sorry,* I signed, before running to catch up with Victoria.

She hadn't followed directions as well as I had when been forcibly liberated, and was currently standing next to the car instead of sitting inside.

Victoria deeply cringed as I neared again, and she hastily got in the passenger's seat. I turned the device off and got in myself. Her legs were up onto the seat, hands shakily wrapped around them. Ten seconds for me had been terrible, poor girl now shared the nightmare I both suffered and created.

We hadn't talked since the first threats I had made, but about halfway back to London, she turned to me like there was something she wanted to say. I looked over, and had to steal a brief look back to the road before she signed anything.

Where are we going? Victoria asked.

I pressed my lips together not exactly sure how to answer that. I didn't know if she was still rigged to activate violently toward Scott. I thought about it for a second, and decided what to say. *Home.*

UltSyn?

No. I frowned, remembering those days. *Your home before that.*

Victoria turned back to look at the road looking like she was still having trouble figuring out where we were going.

I brought her into the house much like Scott had brought me that first day, gesturing for her to step over so her tracking chip it would also get fried. She mouthed a clear "ow" before angrily rubbing her arm and glaring at me.

"Sucks; that part I know." I paused for a second. That hadn't been exactly what I meant to say, but since it worked, I went with it. Victoria was stubborn, and I had to urge her several more times to keep moving and to get in the holding room. I locked the door behind her, watching from outside as she looked around her new surroundings.

Scott had been right; there was a day where he needed the room again. My plan had only gone as far as bringing his sister back. I was hoping he could do something more now that we had her. I ran upstairs to go get Scott, nearly colliding with him on the stairs.

"Where do you keep going in such a hurry?" he asked, raising an eyebrow as I backed off a step.

I have something for you, I signed, taking a few more steps down the stairs again to get him to follow me.

"Did you go somewhere? Hallie keeps beeping about the door," he yawned as he felt around in his pockets for something. "Did you take my phone?"

I breathed out an 'oh', reached into my pocket, and handed it back to him.

"That answers one of my questions," Scott said, and scrolled through his phone, trying to see what I did with it.

I got something I need to show you. When he didn't budge, I pulled him in the direction I wanted, and he didn't resist further.

Once Scott was close enough to see his sister inside, he took his hand away from me. Instead of being relieved, he looked like he had stumbled across a ghost.

Scott looked over to me wide-eyed, and I wondered if he was asking if I could see her as well. I smiled reassuringly.

"You did this?"

I didn't understand. I nodded as his blunt accusation made the smile fall from my face.

"You shouldn't have done this." His chest heaved before he took a half step back.

I looked over to his sister as she sat slouched in the chair, arms crossed. When I turned back to him to sign my answer, I saw that he wasn't looking enough at me.

"Scott." His eyes darted over to me, fevered, afraid. "Knew wanted you this," I said, all jumbled up again. His face tightened, confused about what I said, and I don't blame him. That wasn't quite right. I took a breath, and went back to using my hands. *I knew you wanted this, so I found a way to get her away from their control.*

Scott gave me a funny look before taking my hands in his. "What did you do?"

I tried to move to answer him, but he held my hands in place, looking me in the eyes as he waited for me to speak.

"Rigged," I started having a little trouble getting the words out correctly. Being flustered made things harder, and Scott's whole body was coiled so tight it was making me nervous. "A device to… disrupt chips, in our heads. Speech off, but it's okay. Your sister, safe."

I could see Scott's chest sink as he took a breath. He let go of me like my hands burned him. "You shouldn't have done that," he said looping back to one of his first statements. "This isn't what I wanted."

"But—" I stopped right away as it didn't seem like Scott was listening anymore. He hands rested on top his head as if there wasn't enough air in the room, breathing in such fast, short breaths that I don't think his lungs were getting much. He'd even taken a few more steps away.

I wasn't completely ignorant to what must be going on in his head right now. It's exactly why I hadn't told him what I was doing at the time. However, I hadn't expected a panic attack. "I'm getting better," I said, and to my credit, got the words right when I really needed.

"Don't do these things," Scott said. Now I could hear the slight aggression I had expected all along. "I like to work alone, because I'm not putting anyone besides myself at risk. And then you—" He looked around, seeming at a loss for words. "You did something dangerously stupid! And for me."

I wanted to, I signed, not wanting to fumble.

"Why would you do that?"

I thought that the reason would have been evident. I could think of an obvious answer, but I think saying it again would only add to the hysteria. *There comes a time when everyone needs help,* I said, *You taught me that being independent doesn't mean you can't lean on someone when you have to. Look at her, then tell me that you don't want this.*

Scott held my gaze for a long moment before looking over to Victoria again, even venturing a little closer than before. Feet were now up on the table as she was cleaning the dirt out of her nails. She showed so much more personality that I was certain he'd see more than just UltSyn's tool. He saw me when I didn't even know I had anything to show.

"I don't see my sister," Scott said softly. I furled my brow, not following as he turned back to me. "There isn't even a trace left." He looked away for a moment before heading back toward the stairs, pausing before he rounded the corner. "Just let her go."

Balling my hands into small fists, I watched him as he started going back up the stairs. I quickly squeezed past to stand in front of him, and placed my hands out so he couldn't pass. "Scott. I will find a fix. Give time, you will see."

Scott didn't say anything. A twitch rippled through his expression, before he glanced away. My heart was breaking as that hopelessness left a chill in the air.

I had felt bad this entire time, and nothing was convincing him to try again, even his sister being here. It seemed he needed just as much convincing as she did at this point. Be firm, I told myself before signing. *Don't sleep. I'm not working when you refuse to.*

"Fuck off," he said and pushed past me to go upstairs. I wasn't trying to give him a hard time, but I couldn't let him sulk around now that we had more work to do. I don't know what to look for in his sister, so he had to help.

I walked back down to Victoria as she remained as casual as casual could be. If I had a family to find, would they have turned me away because I had changed? Would they have not wanted me back because something in my head was keeping me from being Lydia?

Scott loved his sister. He would come around, even if he had to wait for her to warm up like I had. This could work, just as soon as he stopped blaming himself.

I headed back, wasting no time as I pushed Victoria's legs off the table. That got her attention. She started to get up from the chair as if she was going to throw a fit. I put my hands on her shoulders, and pushed her roughly back down into the chair.

She didn't like that either, but did nothing more than try to brush off my hands. *Not going to baby someone who is violent. So, forget it,* I said, and sat down myself.

What do you even want?

I'm trying to help you remember who you were before UltSyn.

She scoffed. *Sure.*

You have your brother here to help, and I can help you forget UltSyn. I was an HID, so I understand your loyalty to them.

You're not mute, and you don't seem very loyal. Don't act like you understand anything.

I was, which is all that matters.

Victoria crossed her arms in front of her chest, almost like someone slamming a door in your face. I sighed. *What did they tell you about Scott, before they instructed you to hurt him if he ever came for you?*

She shrugged, making a sour face like she didn't care to know about him. I didn't know if UltSyn filled her with lies, or just tore the siblings apart some other way.

You know he's your actual brother, right?   Victoria shrugged again so I went on. *You can't seriously be okay with UltSyn manipulating you for the rest of your life.*

How do I know you're not lying?

I leaned a little more into the table, taking a second to think. *Because I know what it's like to have my memory wiped of anything and everything I think might matter, or of the things you don't want to have matter. You think they'll give you freedom, or happiness, just a little later on, if you earn it. It never happens though. They tricked you like they tricked me once. You just need to find yourself again.*

She didn't respond this time, and just looked away. I knew it wasn't going to be easy, but I was hoping I didn't have to force feed her back into remembering her past, crack out old diaries, and baby pictures like I was introducing her to herself.

"Leaving for now. Let know if you need things," I said, leaving before she mentioned my mistake. I went upstairs and found Scott sitting on the bed using his tablet. He was just staring down at it. When I moved close enough to see, he was watching a feed from downstairs. He locked the screen and the image faded to black.

I moved to the edge of the bed, and looked over at him carefully. "Is there things to show her? To jog memory?"

Scott twitched again, and still didn't look at me. "Will you ever be able to talk like before?"

I glanced down at my hands. They been my communication for so many years, and now Scott was acting like I'd have to end up only using them again. I didn't know why sometimes words were right and sometimes they were beyond me. I shrugged slightly. "Not a big deal," I managed, and found it encouraging.

"It is to me."

I shot him a look, thinking he was being unusually rude. Now he had a problem with my lack of speech?

"I never should have let you do this. I should have been paying attention. You could have seriously hurt yourself because of me." As his words finished, they were barely loud enough for me to hear.

I put my hand on top of his, since everything else just felt like it would be too much. "You can't control everything," I softly reminded.

<chapter twenty-five>
<! -- Sonia -->

I watched Scott as he sorted through old things that might help me jog Victoria's memory. We agreed things that were once hers or group pictures would work best. Scott had a random collection scattered through various drawers. A stray trading card and a beaded bracelet were mixed with mostly photos.

Scott's hand hovered over the pile that had gained a folded-up note since the last time I looked. "These will do the trick," he said without enthusiasm. "If this works."

I picked up the things and gave him a quick peck on the forehead. "It will."

With the stuff in hand, I walked downstairs to Victoria's room. "Want anything before start? More tea?" I offered, and placed the items down on the table.

A better view? That sarcastic attitude apparently was new, and part of the reason why Scott wasn't in the room with me right now. As stoic as he tried to be, Victoria easily could get a reaction out of him. Never anything more than a visible discomfort, but she played into this weakness whenever she could. It didn't seem to benefit either of them, so I rarely pushed for him to join us.

I sat down at my side of the table and crossed my arms. Victoria eyed the pile for a second before turning her bored attention back to me. "Seriously, look at them," I said, and leaned closer to spread the items out. One photo had an unusually happy Scott and an excited looking Victoria tucked close to each other so she could take the photo herself. She was at least five years younger in it with bright eyes, but the photo was clearly of them.

Victoria leaned forward to get a better look. I swore I saw a glimmer of something in her eyes before she sat back. *Photoshop is a very old program.*

You'd think we'd manipulate such candid photos? You're smart enough to tell if these are fake, I signed, and picked up another photo. Sure, some of these could be edited to make a convincing lie, but it was a bit of a stretch to edit Scott into a selfie. I reached for the folded note, turning its odd shape over in my hands. It seemed rude to open someone else's letters, but I wanted to show her the absolute best, so I unfolded it. I skimmed it before handing it to Victoria.

"You had a crush," I said, and waited a long moment for her to eventually take it. The words switched between Victoria's and Scott's handwriting. There had been a mention of a girl and the seventh grade. Since neither of them had given me any sort of backstory, I imagined one myself. I pictured a barely teenage girl writing a note to her newly twenty-something year old brother at the kitchen table. Folding it up and discreetly passing it over to Scott, since Victoria wasn't quite ready to tell her parents about her new crush.

From what I understood from Scott's more scribbly handwriting, he handled her anxiety well, citing it was nothing to beat herself up for in the first place. He even got playful at the end by asking if she needed a ride to sample cake choices for their future wedding. The note ended with an unconvincing 'haha' in Victoria's handwriting. I figured Scott had just tucked the note away, forgetting about it over the years until it fell out of a book, only to be secured somewhere else safe for a few more years.

I watched Victoria's eyes scan over the whole note. Instead of aggression, her posture hinted at melancholy. She could have dismissed the notes as fake too, but what would be the point? We weren't asking for her to do anything besides remember.

Any UltSyn secrets she managed to gather we didn't even touch, didn't care what her net worth might be.

Victoria looked up at me, her jaw set tight before she shoved the items off the table. I ignored the outburst, giving it little more attention than simply watching it happen. While I would give anything for things from my past, I could empathize enough to understand how sharp the edges of those broken pieces could be. How scary it could be to feel them again.

I'll leave you to it, I said, and headed out of the room. Victoria could be as bitter as she wanted. I knew it was only a front to protect herself. Once she knew it was safe, the real Victoria would come out.

I closed the door behind me, and stopped short not expecting Scott to be right outside watching through the glass. Everything from the set of his brow, to the hand hoovering over his mouth radiated a tenseness. He gave me a hint of an acknowledgment before moving away.

Scott went over to his desk, messing around with something I couldn't see from this angle. The rattle of the bottle gave it away. He reached over to a day-old water bottle, and took a painkiller. When Scott turned around, he must have noticed my frown. "Don't give me that look," he continued as if I had said something. "Everything is really hard right now and… I'm having trouble tuning it out like before."

As long as you're safe, I said, and took a few steps closer. *Then I don't care what you do.*

Scott just blinked at me for a moment before I wrapped my arms around him, trying my best not to put pressure on the wound. I felt a slight tremble roll through him, but couldn't tell what was responsible.

Scott leaned away first, breathing in hard like he was trying to steel himself against the world. Planting both hands behind him on the desk to support himself. "I'm going to go lie back down, okay?" he said, eyes narrowing a little with the question.

"Okay."

I found Scott a few hours later where he said he would be. I was almost surprised he didn't wake up when I sat down on the edge of the bed. I looked down at him for a moment before I decided to kiss him. It was a soft gesture, but it was enough to stir him.

He let out a contented sigh. "Lately, you're so close," he breathed against my lips. I smiled and leaned in again. This time, he parted his lips to cradle my kiss. It was a soft, fragile moment, and I desperately wanted it to last.

My thumb caressed his arm, and Scott moved back in the same breath. "What are you doing?"

The words left me confused, since again, I thought it was obvious. I sat back and thought about it until I had a better answer to give. *Making sure you feel cared for.*

"You really…" Scott searched my face for something, but I wasn't able to figure out what before he finished. "Don't need to do anything for me."

I pushed my hair back, and got up from the bed without another word.

"Wait," Scott uttered, catching my hand before I was able to take a step. "I'd rather you just hang out with me for a bit."

I could do that. I sat back down, and he wiggled over to give me more room on the bed, stifling a wince from his injury. Pain meds made him drowsy, but as we watched some stupid show, it was clear he was making a conscious effort to stay awake to be with me.

When I started to drift off myself, I knew it was time to get up or the whole day would be lost to sleepiness. So, I did, even bringing Scott along with me with the promise of food and I enlisted his help to make something more than our standard.

Dinner was a quiet affair, for us at least, and I was gathering what was left to make Victoria a plate. "Let me do it," Scott said, breaking the silence with his offer. I smiled and handed the plate over.

His eyes lingered on the food for a moment before looking up to the room his sister was in. I think he was trying to find his courage. He headed in and I followed, taking up the spot he had earlier to watch.

Oh, it's you. Victoria crossed her arms again. It was hard to believe the tough act now that everything had been neatly returned to the table. Scott simply put the plate down. *You know, I don't care if we are related,* Victoria taunted.

He was turned enough that I saw his jaw tighten, but he didn't engage her any further. Instead he took a step toward the empty cup of tea. I figured Scott was just going to bring out the dirty dish, but his fingers swirled around the rim. "When you were six, you'd always make me have tea parties with you." His eyes didn't lift from the cup. "I always said no, but then you'd give me this puppy dog look, and I caved. Every single time."

Victoria's eyes were wide with an emotion I couldn't read. Recognition, I hoped. Scott swallowed unevenly and didn't look up before leaving without the cup.

He didn't get far however, sliding down to sit on the floor once he had closed the door. I wondered if he had forgotten about those times too.

I stepped closer, stopping when our toes nearly touched. "You okay?" I asked softly. When he nodded, I offered my hand to help him up, but he shook the offer away.

"Uh..." Scott looked up at me, and seemed livelier than I had witnessed in a while. "I sort of want to just stay here for a while."

"Okay." I smiled and settled down to sit next to him for a bit. I leaned my head on his shoulder and laced my fingers in between his to help hold onto that flicker of hope. My eyelids grew heavy after a while, and if I became any more tired, I'd end up sleeping on the floor with only Scott's lap as a pillow.

"I should go to bed," I mumbled, not wanting to drag him away from his sister, since this had been the first time he actively wanted to be near her. So instead of offering my hand, I just asked if he needed anything.

"I'm okay," he said softly. "Thank you, though."

<chapter twenty-six>
<! -- Scott -->

I didn't know how long I was going to sit outside her room. Maybe all night.

Just wanted to be nearby in case she needed anything. It didn't matter if that reasoning made sense or not. I bummed around on my phone for a few hours. To be honest, I really didn't know what to do on the thing, since everything I had worked for was behind the door I was leaning against.

It was a strange feeling to be rudderless. I can't say I had ever planned beyond this point, and to be frank, I never would have even gotten here if it wasn't for Sonia.

There was a knock on the door behind me, and I shifted to turn toward the sound. I stared at it thinking maybe I was just hearing things, but three more quick knocks came, followed by a pause then two more.

"Hi," I breathed out as I recognized the Morse code. My chest felt too tight and I had to remind myself to inhale. I turned fully toward the door and repeated the pattern back.

There was a long pause as I waited for anything in return. Just before the flicker of hope dimmed, a much longer pattern of my name was tapped out. I quickly shuffled to my feet, moving to the window to see Victoria as she was crouched down by the door in the low light.

I tapped "here" back, worried I'd fuck up any longer of a reply.

Her head turned up to the window and she hesitatingly stood up. The distance was too much to bear as Victoria signed, *I'm sorry.*

It wasn't until after I unlocked the door that I worried about my own safety. A bitter memory made my stomach knot up as I stood in the doorway and whispered her name.

She nodded as her hands trembled. *I didn't think you'd be on the other side.*

"I'm sorry if I scared you."

Victoria shook her head and glanced down.

I took a step closer, and she quickly took one back. I stopped just as fast.

"I'm sorry," I repeated. "Do you...remember anything?"

Bits of a tea party. I don't remember the photos. Or the note. But I know it's true, Victoria started signing in fragments. *I think I remember when you found me. Did I really—* She didn't finish that sentence as her whole body seemed to quake.

Ironically, I had to take a stab at what she was referring to. "Yeah," I managed, and tears ran down her cheeks. I took another step closer to comfort her before I forced myself to stop short. "It's okay, Tori. Don't cry," I tried to reassure her, when all I wanted to do was hug her. "I'm okay now. I promise."

Victoria backed up further, despite me making no advance, until she was hunkered down in a corner of the room. I couldn't stand it anymore. I slowly moved closer and crouched down to her level. I opened my mouth to say something, but I didn't have any words.

It didn't seem to matter though, since all I could do was let out a puff of air as she collided into me for a hug. I tried not to crowd her, but it was hard not to hold her with everything in me. After a moment, Victoria sat back, staring off somewhere as tears continued to fall.

"It's okay. You don't need to figure it all out in a day," I said, as I smoothed her hair down and wiped her face. "I've just missed you. Nothing else matters now that you are safe."

I—, she started, but stopped as she looked up at me with a sad and twisted expression before sniffling.

I let out a short bitter laugh. I think she was going to say she missed me too until she realized that would have been a lie on some levels. Tori looked so tired now, so worn down without that hard as nails act. "Don't worry about anything. We'll take care of whatever you need," I promised. She nodded a little and wiped her nose with the back of her hand.

I smiled slightly, thinking she looked like a child again. Like that time her knees got scuffed when she fell off her bike. The situation had been scarier than it physically hurt.

"Are you tired?" Given the time and her panic, I figured she was bound to be. Tori nodded a little again. "Where do you want to sleep, sweetie?"

Her eyes ventured toward the door before she pointed over to the bed in here, which wasn't more than a thin mat. When I asked if she needed any extra blankets or anything, there was another nod as Victoria stood up with the help of wall.

I hoped that she wasn't just agreeing to everything, but pushed the thought aside, figuring cooperation was at least better than fighting. "Be right back," I said and headed out to grab a blanket off the couch.

When I returned, she was curled up. "When Sonia sleeps downstairs, she always steals this blanket, so I know it's a good one."

I got a small smile out of my sister at the remark. *Where is she sleeping?* she signed, before taking the blanket.

"Oh, uh…" I stammered. I hadn't thought about it until now. "In my bed, I suppose."

Tori looked confused, but didn't press further. "Do you want me to stay down here with you?" This time, she shook her head and I smiled. So, she wasn't just agreeing with me.

I wondered how much she believed. What she thought about UltSyn. About me. How much of it was right, how much was tinted over with emotion, or removed from it. "I'm here if you need."

Okay, she signed, before adjusting the blanket.

* * *

Each day my sister got better, although I can't say she was back to herself completely. At times, she was cold and distant. Sometimes, as much as I would try to play around with her, she would just stare at me like she didn't understand. I don't think staying in an unfamiliar place was helping, but it was still the safest place for the lot of us right now. Sonia was getting better too; her words were becoming less displaced as she spoke.

Most of all, I was starting to get used to the fact that the three of us hadn't made it this far without getting dinged up along the way.

And that was okay, too.

* * *

Today was one of those rare, good days. I had grown comfortable enough to let Tori roam around without having to worry about her for every second of it. It was a lazy morning, where Sonia and I had woken up early for no particular reason beyond we just had. It made neither of us in a hurry to get out of bed.

"You know what I haven't heard?"

She hummed an answer.

"I haven't heard you laugh yet."

"Be funnier," she said grinning.

My jaw dropped at her remark. "That was so mean," I laughed. "You know what? I'm going to get you for that." She raised a brow, but didn't seem worried about the threat.

I moved around so I was practically on her lap. My fingers searched her sides until I found a really ticklish spot and seized on it. She squirmed and tried to hold her tongue until she couldn't help but laugh. It was a soft, almost soundless laugh, but I didn't give up until I heard the true giggle I had wanted to hear.

I leaned back with a growing smile to give her room to catch her breath. "I love you," I said, effortlessly, as if it wasn't the first time I had said it. Wait. *What?* I looked away, taking a second, and realized those words had actually come out of my mouth. I don't think I've loved more than a single thing in years. It was a bitter, downright painful realization.

"I love you," I repeated, more deliberately this time. Sonia smiled and amusement seemed to sparkle around her eyes. "What? What's funny?"

"Nothing," she said and propped herself up on her elbows. "It's just I said it out loud before."

"You did?" I racked my brain for that memory.

She nodded. "It's o—"

The certainly of my kiss got a surprised and pleased little sound out of her. I pressed my forehead against hers. "Say it again," I whispered, or maybe prayed. My bottom lip caught on my teeth, as I both wanted to kiss her again, and wait.

She took a breath before taking a peck. It left me wanting more, but the hushed words that followed didn't. "I love you, too."

<chapter twenty-seven>
<! -- Scott -->

The news came on after Victoria's soaps. Since she had been binge-watching them, I had found myself sort of glad as the platinum blonde reporter and her co-anchor, a man old enough to be her father, came on. "After recent attacks from the hacktivist group dubbed Hello World, UltSyn's stocks are once again on the rise.

Despite allegations of human rights violations—" the women reported, but my mind stopped tracking.

"Hacktivist group?" I asked myself really, even though Victoria and Sonia were close enough to hear from the couch. I wasn't an activist. Nor was I a group. I did, however, know what violations she was about to mention. I had given the information to Terry a while ago. Recruitment plus coercion plus exploitation is a textbook definition. I suppose this news story was just as much his doing as mine, if not more so. Hell, even Sonia recently moved against UltSyn's interests. Maybe we were a group.

When did that happen?

"The chairman revealed at a press conference yesterday afternoon," the reporter continued, stealing my attention back, "a revolutionary new way to store data. Imagine if you could store those wedding photos on a device you are certain never to lose—your own DNA. That's exactly what the UltSyn Bio division promises to be able to do in the coming quarter. To prove this theory, sonnets from Shakespeare were stored on DNA then read off at the conference. They say the technology isn't quite ready for consumers yet, but will be soon."

"Just what everyone needs," the older reporter joked. "Our mothers having our baby photos always on hand." Their shared laugh made me cringe.

"They already have that tech," Sonia said, as her eyes stayed glued on the screen. "They've had it for years. It was the early stages of the HID program until they decided the reader would be as hackable as anything else. Its usage turned purely commercial after that."

The reporters' laughter ended as the man turned in his seat to face a new camera. As if not even a 90-degree turn could wash his hands of their banter.

"Officers are still unsure what took place early this week when a body was found by houseboats in Cambridge. Some reports seem to suggest an accident, but suicide has not been ruled out. Foul play is not suspected."

"If you have any information on who this man is, please call the police," the female reporter finished, as a picture of a man was displayed next to her. He looked familiar, but it wasn't until I saw Victoria gasp did I place him. He was barely an adult in the photo they used, but with the reference point, I could tell he was clearly my sister's coworker.

I looked away. It had never been my intent to save him, but now I felt guilty that I hadn't. Both Sonia and I had been there, but we didn't do anything for him.

Fuck, I didn't even learn his name before his employers found him defective and tossed him. A fact that UltSyn was distinctly not telling the media. I wondered if he had a family who would only now find out what happened. If they even saw this broadcast before the headline got buried under other news.

Sonia called my name and I looked up to her. Their positions had changed. She was on the edge of her seat, looking unsure of where she should be, but it became clear she had said my name for my sister's benefit. Victoria was now leaning against the back of the couch, waiting for me to look her way.

His name was Chris. I'm not sure if that was his real name, but I know they must have done that to him, Victoria signed. *We have to do something.*

"We?"

Victoria looked over her shoulder to the TV which carelessly moved on, then touched one shoulder then the other to sign "We" again.

I knew it was the right thing to do. The somber and almost angry expression on Sonia's face suggested she agreed. As I looked between the two of them, I couldn't help but want to leave it alone.

I joined UltSyn because I thought it was a way to help. I lost myself, instantly. I would have fought differently if I had been given the whole picture, Victoria said. *The truth can outlast us.*

I was afraid to lose them, but fear shouldn't be the way of the world. "We are going to need some help," I said. I didn't know how well she knew Chris, but I knew one thing. Only vowing "never again" would never be enough to stop things from happening. We could fight, for as long as we could, in all the ways we could.

"With Victoria's help, I should be able to adjust the frequency to incapacitate without it hurting so much," Sonia said, to my horror. "Harming people we are trying to help isn't the best approach."

Shit is loud. Victoria added, and now I was bordering on queasy.

"What are you planning to do?" I asked as I watched my sister trail after Sonia.

"Go make your calls." She placed a hand on top of Tori's head. "I promise not to figuratively tase her brain." My sister turned around to sign *A*gain before she was out of sight.

"Not cool, guys!" I took the available distraction and called Terry.

"Hello?"

"Hey, do you have time to talk?" I sat on my desk and glanced toward the garage. "I'm thinking that maybe we should start combining more than just whatever I find under overturned stones. I know you've worked with The Unseen; maybe together we could get more done."

"You have my attention," he said, sounding unsure. "Is this about finding that uh, friend of yours?"

"No, that's finished. Look, I know I always said no to getting more involved, but I'm done being selfish about things."

"You weren't selfish," Terry corrected. There was a pause and I was straddled with the weight of him defending me, to myself. "I'm always in the mood for help that is actually willing to get shit done."

"Maybe I can bring some uh, new friends over, too?"

"That sounds great." I swear I could hear him grinning over the phone. "I'll give you the address of the Hive."

I wrapped up the call before walking to the garage since I was itching to see what was going on. Sonia had wires in her hands, and Victoria was sitting on an upside-down bucket. I didn't know if they were starting something or finishing up. "Did you fix your signal problems?"

"Not yet," Sonia said as she glanced toward my hands. "Making progress."

Confused, I looked down and noticed I was nervously spinning my ring around my finger. I don't think she was judging me here, but shoved my hands into my hoodie anyway. "Oh, cool. If you are done, we can head over to Terry's."

* * *

Nic was waiting outside for us, puffing on a cigarette. He nodded in greeting and started walking in the hope we'd follow. "I thought you didn't like having friends. Who's your new crew?"

We stepped inside before I answered. "This is my sister, Victoria, and this is Sonia." I gestured over to both of them. Nic raised an eyebrow with a silent question, and I knew what he was getting at. "Tori was the one I was looking for. Sonia and I kind of just found each other. She's been helping me for a while now."

Sonia smirked. *Technically true.*

Nic raised a brow, not understanding, and I opted to just ignore Sonia's teasing. "Hey, Ter. They're here," Nic called over. Once close enough, he leaned over Terry's shoulder. "Also, it *was* his sister. Pay up."

Terry grumbled and reached into his pocket taking out fifty pounds from his wallet. Nic's cigarette bobbed as he laughed, and he quickly stashed the money. I can't believe I was a bet.

Terry got up from his seat in a rather lazy way after his loss. Nic pointed to which girl was my sister, if our age difference hadn't already given it away. He nodded with mild interest, before his eyes lingered on Sonia in a way that made me uneasy.

"I'll introduce you to the other guys."

This place reminded me of my old high school. Rooms along the sides were ignored as we walked like they weren't our class. Nic hung back enough to put out his cigarette. The hallway opened up into a bigger area, which if this was a school, I'd imagine would lead to a theater.

Gathered around like a group of theater kids I suppose, was a handful of people. Not counting Terry and Nic, there were three more. Two stood around talking to each other, while another guy was leaning against the wall. I didn't recognize any of them as Nic broke off to stand by the duo. They welcomed him back, but didn't say anything else as Nic took out his phone.

Terry told me their names, but I didn't catch them over my nerves. Victoria had huddled awfully close to me, practically glued to my side, and was being a total distraction to what was being said. Maybe Sonia had caught it.

"This is Scott," Terry continued. "You know him as the Hello World Hacker." That sparked their interest. It burned through the group's inattentiveness like a dry piece of tinder. First a bet, and now a legend.

"And these are his—" Terry's lips puckered as he tried to pick the right word. "—friends. They're here to help us take down UltSyn." The collective focus shifted from me to the girls, as they sized them up in what I hoped was a completely analytical way.

"If you'll excuse me," Terry continued, his accent beginning to wear on me in a way it never had before. "I'll go get our little group's leader." He headed for a set of doors to the left and I wondered if him being the only one talking added to my nerves.

There wasn't much time for silence to settle as the person who had been leaning against the wall dragged a foot up against it. "Nice work you did fucking with UltSyn. Had us entertained at least."

I opened my mouth to reply, but my attention was turned as one of the men broke off to walk closer. "We thought you lost the HID for good after what Jesse did," he added in a less complimentary tone. The words were clipped and held a challenge between the extra crispness. "Now why this HID," he continued and pointed to Sonia, "rescued that USB worker is beyond me."

"Maybe neither of them are HIDs," I countered roughly. Squishing UltSyn Bio into USB was a bit much for my taste.

"Maybe they both are," the man dared. "I wonder if emotion has corrupted any of the data UltSyn gave."

"Maybe they don't have any."

"We saw a video of that recent little rescue. Being sorry is showing sympathy. You can't program that, Scott." He said my name sharper than any of the other words, like he had talked about me before, but never had a proper name until now.

"I meant data, asshole." At the cuss, Nic looked up over his phone at us.

When I saw movement again, I drew my gun as the aforementioned asshole moved even closer. "You sure seem to know a lot. Would be a shame for a bullet to make all of that useless."

He took a step back and put his hands up. I heard the door open again, and he looked over as my eyes stayed put. "Are you sure about this guy, Terabyte?"

"Scott's ferociously protective," Terry replied. "Just be glad he's finally decided to protect the world. You must've been a creep, Ash." When Terry looked toward me, there was a hint of pride that seemed out of place. I tried to figure out where he had gone and why, but the only clue was a sleek piece of tech tucked snugly in his palm.

"Terabyte?" I repeated like it was a joke. "What— *you're* the Unseen leader?"

Terry's eyes lowered just slightly to the gun, silently telling me to put it away.

Nic had moved closer, quiet enough that I hadn't caught him. My gut told me it was to stop Ash more than me. Reluctantly, I put the weapon away.

"To answer you, not quite," Terry said. "The Unseen is designated not to have an official leader. Can't cut off the head of an organization that doesn't have one. But for this case, yes, I guess you could consider me their leader."

"Why didn't you tell me?" I asked, realizing the question wasn't that important in the grand scheme of things.

"We both had our secrets and kept them for similar reasons." Terry took my silence as a cue to continue, looking at Sonia and Victoria for a moment. "How much do your new friends know about the insides of UltSyn?"

"Not much if you keep acting like we're not right here," Sonia said.

"How does she even do that? Talk, that is," Ash said, now from the sidelines.

"None of your fucking business," Sonia said, turning to shoot him a glare. I grinned. That's my girl.

"Guys," Terry said, putting his free hand up like a patient teacher. "I'm sorry, it seems we all need to brush up on our manners." He glanced at the others, before turning back. "What do you know about UltSyn?"

Victoria started signing, and Sonia translated. "About the networks and who calls the shots—" Tori shook her head and signed a word again to correct her. "*What* calls the shots."

Maybe we should've been debriefed before coming here. But only Sonia and I seemed surprised somehow.

"We have a similar theory, thanks to Casio," Terry said. "Come on, let me show you my tech." I didn't know what he meant until I spotted a wristwatch on the guy who hadn't spoken yet. The watch was a darker shade of black against his skin, and clearly Casio in brand. That nickname made sense.

Terry led us through the set of doors he had ventured alone before. As we walked, I whispered over to Sonia to pick up the name of the person I had missed.

Script. That's who spoke before. Which left me with one question.

"Hey, Nic," I called. He had been walking ahead of me, and when I said his name, he turned my direction and waited. "What outcome would have made Terabyte win the money?"

He grinned. I'm not sure if it was from the code name usage or the question.

Maybe both. "He guessed partner. Girlfriend, boyfriend, whomever. I had a feeling my money was safe with sibling."

"Did Jesse bet?" Sonia asked. I wasn't sure if she was really interested, or if she was trying to make sure she was seen and heard.

Nic's smile faded as he looked over to Sonia, something that concerned me at first. "Jesse was a dick," he said. "I'm sorry about what happened. We didn't know. We didn't even play around with him like that."

Sonia seemed content with this answer, even though she didn't voice it either way this time. Tori however was looking up at me confused, lacking the tale. "Don't worry about it," I tried to reassure her. There was a lot we didn't tell people. A lot we hadn't shared since her return. Maybe we were afraid to.

We stopped as Terry opened a door that made my security systems look lacking. The piece he had gone to grab fit into a section of the wall, its honeycomb shape turning like a gear. Tori leaned in on her tippy toes as she tried to peer around to get a glimpse. I grinned despite myself, remembering a similar pose when she tried to take a peek in the closet where our parents hid Christmas gifts.

Once we took a step inside the Hive, the gesture seemed even more fitting. It was like a tech wonderland in there. Hanging from the ceiling like a chandelier was a ring of eight monitors attached by a thick base, each with a different news station on. When my eyes lowered, I spotted two rows of workstations. Instead of being split up like blocky cubicles, they were one solid piece with inset monitors and an illuminated keyboards tilted forward toward the user. Their screens were dwarfed in comparison to the large displays above. More impressive was that I could see through the displays as they idly waited for commands.

"Wow," I breathed, turning my attention to the others. Terry stood with his arms crossed high on his chest, al too pleased with my marveling. "I thought the point was not to give the Unseen an official HQ. This is… amazing."

"And it's all mine," Terry grinned as he pushed forward to one of the consoles.

"Terabyte is our favorite," Script said to Sonia and my sister before looking over to me. "On slow days, we throw LAN parties."

I smiled and headed to see what Terry was working on. I expected people to follow, but Victoria didn't. Her steps were slow and almost thoughtful as she made sure to keep a wide berth away from the other unknown tech or hackers.

"Everyone thinks a CEO leads the company. For obvious reasons, right?

"Well, Casio found evidence that suggests otherwise," Terry explained as he found the file. He flicked it over to what looked like a framed plate of glass before it lit up to show various tax files, memos, and video surveillance.

Victoria silently stopped pacing, landing in my eye line as we both looked toward the screen.

"I checked," Casio said, his voice coming from my left. "No one at the company is doing the job. We are always told to follow the money since that's where the corruption is. No one is getting paid to do the job."

"We just haven't figured out who, or what, is running the show," Terry added. Tori turned toward me and signed a C shape over her forearm.

"It's a computer." My sister smiled weakly as I felt everyone's eyes turn to me. Only Sonia wasn't and went to talk to my sister.

"A computer runs UltSyn?" Ash asked.

"I think she's suggesting a system was put in place, and everyone is just operating under it."

"I heard when the founder passed on," Sonia said, "he made sure his vision would be carried on, but to imagine it so literally. Even if it's all pre-programmed the system could be designed to carry out his wishes far after death."

I heard someone mumble a curse, but I didn't know who the voice belonged to. There was a distinct coldness that settled in with the news despite the warm and buzzing tech everywhere. A person could be exposed and removed from a company, but a system could be upheld, protected, and sometimes literally restored with far greater ease.

"Binaries can be smashed," Script said, "And systems can be subverted."

"They are right," Terry said with a nod to Script.

"If we can access the program," Nic grinned as he undid the buttons at his sleeves. "It can be hijacked like anything else."

<chapter twenty-eight>
<! -- Scott -->

If you ignored the industrial espionage at every turn, it was just like any other sleepover. I encouraged Sonia and Victoria to head back for a real night's sleep, but they decided to stay with me. We worked solidly for nights on end.

They helped out when they could, but the most amusing part was how fast they picked up games that the others had been playing for months. Nic and I never played, both refusing to take a real break. Sometimes people came and went in order to find a real bed. The only occasional distraction I had was Sonia snaking her arms around me from the back of my chair. She'd ask how things were, and I'd fil her in. This normally ended with her telling me not to work too hard and kissing me by my ear.

The lot of us made a pretty good team, but it wasn't a flawless effort. I didn't catch how it started, but Sonia's rough tone tipped me off that something had happened. I leaned back in my chair, looking over at Terry and Ash. My sister was frowning, and Sonia had fire in her eyes.

"You think neurodiversity leads to violence?" Sonia glared at him.

"I didn't say that," Ash said.

"You sure as hell did."

I thought the two might start a staring contest to decide who'd be forced to sleep outside. Also, I was fairly sure they were talking about me and I did not want to get into it. Depression doesn't make me dangerous. It makes me not want to exist. Not caring if others exist is what makes someone violent.

When Terry stepped in to keep the peace, I was off the hook. "We need to be accountable if our goal is to show the world the truth. That's the plan."

Ash looked scolded, Sonia didn't seem convinced, but at least Tori seemed to perk up a little.

"Hell yeah, it is!" Nic yelled loudly next to me. He hadn't said much this whole time, so the outburst surprised me. His tone had the confidence that I know Terry had wanted to show, but didn't want to seem like he wasn't taking Sonia seriously in the process.

Nic turned away from his screen, and smiled over at me. I smiled back and mouthed thank you. He waved his hand as if it was nothing and we got back to work.

* * *

It's funny how so much effort can be stored on something so small. I turned a flash drive over in my hands thinking about how all our time had been put into the virus that sat on this tiny thing. It was the physical proof that something important doesn't have to be big.

"What should we dub it?" Script asked.

Some ridiculously bad names were thrown about. Names that could show up in a *Transformers* movie. "Apocrypha?" Ash suggested, looking pleased with his suggestion. Casio and Script nodded in agreement, but I made a face at it.

"From the Greek, apokryphos. Meaning 'to obscure or to hide away,'" Nic read off. Terry looked puzzled, as if he wasn't sure if that meant Nic liked the idea or didn't like the idea.

"We could call it the Hello World virus," Casio said.

Tori signed a quick yes.

"No, that's a horrible name. I don't get why you guys even want to name it," I laughed. "It isn't a puppy."

"Why shouldn't we name it? The media will if we don't," Terry said.

"I think it fits," Nic said. I looked over at him like I had been betrayed. We usually agreed. As if trying to explain his treason he went on, "I like the poetic meaning behind it."

A Hello World program was Programming 101 for any language. The fact that the first and simplest program one writes suggests a ghost in the machine actually did fit.

"I'd vote for it," Sonia replied, as my usual allies went down to zero. When we did tally, only Ash and I voiced nay. Being outvoted was the true danger of working in a group.

"Now that we have our doomsday device, what's our next step?" Script asked, getting us back on topic of bringing down giant corporations.

"We can't access the mainframe from here, and using Victoria as a Trojan horse would be both dangerous and likely ineffective. We've seen what UltSyn does with people. Our best bet is to upload it directly ourselves," Terry said.

Terry, or rather Terabyte, made a good leader. Always planned for the next move without being too tightly wrapped up in his cause. My thought ended abruptly as I noticed everyone's focus had shifted to me. Right, I was the expert in the ways of storming these buildings. "Well buckle up ladies, gentlemen, and my new non-binary friends." I smirked. "This isn't going to be easy."

* * *

Everyone was invited back to my place to get a few things. Halie nearly threw a fit at the unusual number of people. Sonia started working with Victoria again to make sure the sonic device could safely be used for longer durations.

I was just glad that my sister couldn't join us. Staying busy was the only thing that stopped me from checking up on them every three seconds. Ash said he was going to train those who didn't know how to use a gun to be at least decent, which worked for me since I was tired of touching them. Since the garage was taken, I guess Firearms 101 had to meet in the living room today.

Knowing Terry had been silently dying to see more of Hallie, since he couldn't keep that kid in a candy store look off his face, I decided to oblige, and we headed upstairs. My phone beeped a grumpy note, and I looked to see it was low on power.

"I'll be right back," I said, and continued on to my room to plug it in.

I had just hooked it up when I heard someone come in. I turned to see Terry looking down at the floor with amusement. "I like your modifications."

"Yeah, well, where one's sleeps is their home, or whatever," I said, as went into the closet.

"That's not the quote at all," Terry chuckled. "This must be really weird for you." I didn't care what the saying was, so I simply raised a brow, now with a jacket in tow.

"All people around. The lone wolf has found his pack."

"Ugh, that's worse. Please keep the coffee mug sayings away from me."

Terry looked like he had something more to say, but when Sonia leaned into the room, he opted to let her speak instead. She gave him a pleasant smile. "We're ready."

I wasn't ready for this. But, my personal issues last time resulted in me not being there for Sonia, and I refused to let it happen to my sister. I instantly headed down to the garage and found Victoria nervously fidgeting.

"Ready?" Sonia asked at the controls.

Tori nodded, while a loud no rang through my thoughts. Sonia flipped the switch. My sister's eyes clamped shut. Her face held a twisted expression before she gave a thumbs-up. *Less loud, but still workable.*

I could tell when Sonia had turned the signal off since my sister's face instantly calmed. Without much care, I hugged her to my chest. "We're done with the DIY neurosurgery, right?"

Yes. Tori playfully pushed my hug away. *I think I can tin hat from here out.*

"About that—"

"Hold on," Terry said from the doorway. He had been splitting his attention between us and the rest on the team on the first floor like a lookout. The people inside seemed to be winning his interest at the moment. "I need to gather the guys before they start hitting on your operating system."

"What? Why?" I asked no one in particular.

"If Hallie was a hologram she'd totally be hot," Sonia said.

For sure. Victoria grinned.

"That makes zero logical sense." I shook my head and let it go.

"No drooling on the tech," Sonia teased as she walked back inside.

Nic had been back a ways, failing in his attempt to look disinterested, while Script and Casio pulled back from the desk like they were caught red-handed.

I tilted my head and moved closer to see what they were looking at. By their search results, it seemed they were hunting exclusively photos and videos. "What were you two doing?"

They looked over at each other, but didn't say a word. Ash walked out of the kitchen with a glass of water. "They were looking for your porn stash."

"I—what?" I stammered, looking over to Sonia who snickered. "Is this what you guys do? Take on the world and look at dirty photos?"

"Sometimes," Ash replied after a sip. "You should see Nic's collection. Super weird." Nic's eyes went wide and he shot Ash a look that could kill, which only made Ash smirk.

While the advantages of a specific queer sexuality was debatable, I, a non-porn watching asexual, had a secret advantage here. They may have thrown me off, but I was determined not to lose my footing further. "Hundred dollars says you'll never find a trace."

Casio appropriately seemed interested by the number, likely mentally converting it into pounds, while Ash looked intrigued by the challenge alone.

"I'm not taking that bet," Script warned just when I was sure easy money was going to come my way.

"All right, *ye aw*," Terry interjected. "Let's head out before Scott starts to rethink his choice in friends." The lot of them headed for the garage but Terry stopped in front of me. "I know it's a weird bunch, but we won't let you down when it comes to showing UltSyn what's what." He turned to Sonia and Victoria. "Any of you."

Thank you, Victoria signed and headed upstairs now that everyone was leaving. Sonia watched everyone leave. "Were they ever going to find any porn on your computer?"

"Nah." I grinned as if it was ridiculous to think they could hack into something I wanted hidden, despite it not being that at all. "My security is aces."

Sonia tilted her head slightly. She was brilliant enough that I was sure she'd put it together. I just loved making her think. "You're joking," she said through confusion. "Explain please."

"I, uh... I'm asexual." There are plenty of people who didn't understand that, or assumed they did to a bigoted extreme. Many times, it wasn't worth correcting, especially in the days where fighting to exist came first. When her expression started to grow concerned, my nerves threatened to revolt. The fact that gender meant nothing to me romantically would have to be saved for another day.

"I'm sorry," she said, and I felt sick as she put her hand on my arm. "I feel like I might have pressured you in Paris. If you don't want to do something, please don't feel like you ever have to."

I looked up from my arm and blinked at her. While I knew what I wanted to say, my tongue was tied by the instant acceptance. "I wanted to be with you in Paris. In that moment, I didn't care in what way. This life is full of pain and I wanted to feel and give something that didn't add to that."

"Still," Sonia smiled. "I'll make sure I'm considerate of this fact next time."

I hadn't cared about being liked, or understood, or even accepted in a long time. But the fact that she did on all fronts brought a peace of mind I hadn't realized I lost. "Thank you."

If the weather was any indication on how well a day goes, things were looking good. London was gorgeous today. Crisp and clean air seemed to follow everyone as they converged at my place again, this time bringing more than tech with them.

Victoria was lingering around Sonia and Casio as they went around to everyone making sure they had everything they needed.

When Sonia stepped away for a moment, I gave her a little nod to come over.

I turned my back to everyone else and signed. *I need you to help me. We can't take Victoria with us.* I glanced over my shoulder to my sister. *I just can't imagine—*

Sonia interrupted by touching my shoulder. *I know. I mean, I had the feeling you would want that.* She took a step back out, looking over at Victoria before the rest of the group. "Someone should stay behind and help out from here. Any volunteers? -- No? Then I'll go ahead and pick." She feigned a pause. "Victoria, you'll stay."

My sister came over almost immediately, saying how it wasn't fair, how she wanted to come, and how she could help a lot more if she came along. Sonia's stern expression was unyielding as she let Tori finish. "I'm sorry, but you aren't as trained on being the other side of this war. You're the freshest face on their roster list of missing assets; you can better help the team from here."

I never was the best at telling my sister no, which left me at a disadvantage when it came to arguing with her. Victoria turned to me like I'd argue with Sonia on her behalf. "I don't disagree," I said, pretending like the whole idea wasn't mine in the first place.

Victoria's expression begged for me to understand. Sonia came to my rescue before I was able to cave. "Let's get you acquainted with the computers. It's a pretty cool system," she said, and I was off the hook as Victoria reluctantly agreed.

* * *

Hours later, we piled into our cars and drove to the European headquarters for UltSyn, waiting it out until sundown. Casio and Script were in the car with me and Sonia, watching the area with weariness.

I fiddled with my earpiece that connected our group together. "Can you hear me?" I asked to the other car where Terry, Nic, and Ash waited.

"If this connection was any clearer, I'd be able to hear what you had for breakfast," Terry said. I smiled, while Sonia rolled her eyes at the remark. I watched the building as my sister's reply rolled across my glasses saying she also could hear me loud and clear. Victoria could use Hallie's systems to speak aloud, but we weren't too fond of the computerized version.

My phone beeped an alarm that marked an hour past when most of the workers left. While we were armed, I didn't want to hurt anyone. We just were looking to corrupt their main computer. I turned in my seat to look at everyone in the car, and each gave a silent nod to signal they were ready. Sonia was last, but fil ed me the most with confidence.

My eyes lingered on her as I spoke to the other group. "We're ready."

"Thank god. I've been dying back here, let's fucking do it," Ash said. A silence fell for a moment. I couldn't see Nic shoot Ash a look, but I could hear annoyance in his voice when he formally replied that they were ready.

We all got out; my group headed to the east side of the building while the others went to the west entrance. We huddled around the door as Casio started unlocking it. I'd admit that it was nice to watch someone else do the hacking for once.

A piece of me might have even preferred that I wasn't alone this time.

Sonia's face was tight as she adjusted her grip on her gun. She was close, ready to head inside right after me. I touched her arm to get her attention as Casio finished up. *This is it. We'll finish this now, and everyone will be free of UltSyn,* I signed.

Sonia's expression wavered for a moment as if searching my face to tell if I meant it.

A half smile flickered on her face, before Casio signaled that he had the door ready. "All set here," I said to Terry, who was leading the other team.

"Ready," Terry said, letting a beat pass. "Go."

Casio opened the door, and I lead the way into the back storage entrance.

Sonia and I checked each other's corners as we made our way through the hall before getting to a warehouse-like room. It wasn't really wide, but was impressively tall, probably enough to make up the first two stories of the building.

We stopped for a moment, waiting for Script and Casio to regroup after checking that the door had locked and no one was coming in behind us. Sonia looked over to a map on the wall that showed the emergency exits for the bottom floor, likely comparing it to the maps we reviewed before coming. We hoped the offices would lead to where the main server room was. No map would obviously say "Plant Virus Here" but they should have clues. Even a blank spot could help deduce where we needed to go.

"Make sure the police stay distracted for me won't you, Sis?" I took a quick look around the room again. This place would be littered with security, and the last thing we needed was for police reinforcement to show up. "Trip every alarm in the city if you have to."

The words "On it" displayed before scrolling away.

"Seems like we are going to have to go up," Script said.

"Funny," Terry replied even though he was at the other side of the building.

"I thought hell was always down."

I shook my head, despite my amusement. "What did you guys find?" I asked, as my team headed toward an elevator.

"These offices are empty so far. We pocketed our weapons in case we run into any late workers. Maybe we can pass for Geek Squad if anyone asks." I think I heard a snicker from Terry's team as I just acknowledged that I heard and carried on.

First things first, we needed to plug in the sonic device. That should get people with UltSyn tech in their heads out of the way, and therefore safe. We bundled into the elevator, awkwardly waiting for it to go up to a new floor. "You know,"

Script started to say, and I half turned to look at him. "If Terry ran this place, this elevator would be impossible to use."

"Aww, thank you."

"You know this is the stealth part of the mission, right?" Ash whispered.

Couldn't say I disagreed actually. The radio chatter went down after that. Our team focused on planting the first device while Terry's team worked on securing even more evidence. We had the hard data, but the news loves a spectacle.

We made it into a security booth, and found two men sitting in front of the monitors. One had his head tucked down sleeping, and the other was scrolling through his phone. Neither of them heard Script and I move into the room, making it that much easier for us to knock them out. I went for the computer that controlled the cameras and the intercom system as Sonia and Casio moved the guards into a closet in case they woke up.

Sonia came up next to me, watching as I booted up the sonic device that would ring through the rooms here. I wasn't sure if Sonia just wanted to watch her contribution go into action, or if she was just worried something in her head would activate the frequency again. I didn't ask, since we both knew that she was good enough not to make that sort of mistake.

I started the frequency, and glanced at Sonia nevertheless before turning back to the computer as it queued up the second executable. There was heavy bass that streamed through the speakers as the Glitch Mob's remix of "Seven Nation Army" started playing. I wanted everyone to know we were here. I wanted to give them the chance to either flee or come at us.

For a couple seconds, I savored the music, took a calming breath. When I opened my eyes, Sonia was looking at me with an incredulous expression. I had told everyone of my plan, but I don't think she realized I was serious until now.

"Was the song necessary?"

"Sonia, it's a classic."

"Classical denotes cultural importance, not age."

Script gave us both a funny look and pulled out their phone. "Used to refer to a period from 1750 to 1820."

"Yay, they are both wrong," Casio said, now holding the door open for everyone. "Let's go."

"Hallie, do you have those hotspots populated yet?" Hopefully, the system had crunched the new data and decided where our target would be. Instead of a vocal reply, my glasses fil ed with a transparent map showing the most likely locations for the mainframe. There ended up being five in total.

I swiped the information away as Terry suggested we should split up to cover more ground. I wasn't completely sold on the idea because of personal reasons, but I knew it was the right tactical choice. "I've been in these buildings enough to wade around on my own. One of you go meet up with Terry's team, and other needs to have Sonia's back."

Casio stopped mouthing the lyrics as he looked to see who'd get which assignment. She turned quickly to me, a clear objection forming on her lips. I wasn't sure if she protested leaving my side, or the idea in general. I shook my head to anything she was about to say. I've done this enough to have confidence in myself, and I doubted I'd be able to focus if Sonia was the one not paired up.

Sonia didn't argue before she turned to Script. "Guess you are with me," she grumbled. If their feelings were hurt, they didn't show it as they followed her.

232

"Who does that leave me with?" Casio asked, over the earpiece.

"With me," Ash said. I checked the little map looking how far apart the hotspots were. Wouldn't take more than a few minutes to reach unless they ran into a snag. I headed toward my target which was up several floors and over a ways. The song repeated twice, but the hidden signal underneath wouldn't go away. I came across two possible HIDs hunkered in the corner behind a guard who looked completely lost, possibly racking his brain for what a training manual said to do. When I stopped in the room, he jumped back.

My hand went to my gun before he could take the baton off his belt. Instead of drawing it, the guard just raised his hands. "Hunker down with them or leave," I said, with a careful eye on the lot of them.

The man looked over to the two, and I wondered if he wanted to help them, but in the end, he carefully skirted past. Poor choice.

I had to hack a security door that was in front of my destination. The inside was warmer from the small server farm. While these machines were likely connected to the one I wanted to take offline, it wasn't worth poisoning a puddle when I needed to reach the ocean. If I placed the virus at too low of a terminal the anti-virus would kill it before it did enough damage.

Terry cussed, and for a moment I didn't know why. "Nic and I could use some help if anyone could spare it."

"We are closest," Sonia said. "There are only noncombatants in this area. I know the layout well enough that I can spare Script."

I mouthed a curse of my own. Instead of volunteering, Script's com stayed silent. Maybe they were waiting for my approval, or maybe Sonia had been glaring because her tone was a lot harsher when she spoke again. "Do I look like I'm a damsel? Go help the boys."

"The sooner would be better," Nic added.

"I'm headed your way," Script said.

Ash and Casio were roughly a floor above me. I was left torn between joining Sonia and going to help the others, too. Sonia was technically a little closer, but they were in opposite directions. Or maybe I should stay with the servers searching for breadcrumbs that might save us time in the long run. Ugh. I would get nothing done if I suddenly doubted every choice. "I'm coming to you, Sonia."

She exhaled sharply, but said nothing. The escort wasn't so much for her, as it was my own peace of mind, so she'd have to deal with it.

Mapped out on my glasses, I saw a shortcut to Sonia. It would require me to go through a large office, but there was no sign of anyone being currently in it. So, I ran in that direction.

When I walked into the room, I instantly knew I fucked up. Three men were lying in wait. They weren't so much hunting for us as they were a nest of snakes I'd simply run across. I pulled out my gun again, but was beat by a Taser that hit me with enough current that I dropped it.

Before I was able to pick myself up, two of the men grabbed my arms and swung me up to my feet. If it was anyone else, I might be grateful for the help, but right now I just wanted their hands off me.

They shoved me against a desk, scattering a cup full of pencils and papers.

The third guy had moved over to pick up my gun. If they were as serious as they were letting on, I might be dead already. The two who pinned me to the desk moved away, and the fucker with my weapon situated himself in my blind spot. The threat of being shot in the back kept me down.

"Well, look who it is," one of the two that I could see said. "It's that hacker. Your sodding face has been posted in our break room for a month." He grabbed my chin like he was trying to closely compare it to the picture he saw before.

"Wow, so original," I said, as his crooked nose and dark eyes filled my view.

He ripped his hand away with enough force that it turned my head. I used the opportunity to try to see how close the guy was behind me. If I could kick him, or something I might be able to wrangle my gun back. Unfortunately, I only caught a glimpse of his uniform before slowly turning my head back.

"What should we do with him?" the other man I could see asked. While I was glad they didn't shoot me yet, I didn't understand why they hadn't. Was there a reward for me alive, or were they just that sadistic?

"One of the reports suggested he controls his tech with the ring on his finger," said the first. The man nodded toward my hand. My eyes followed, not sure what he was getting at. "If he thinks he is a legend now, wait until the hacktivist community has a nine-fingered man."

Oh, that's what he was getting at.

Shit.

"Look guys, I'm sure we can talk this out," I said, and dared to take a clean look over my shoulder. The guard was standing just far enough back that I wouldn't be able to interfere with his shot.

"Got a knife?" asked the man, whose nose I'd like to break on the desk he had shoved me against.

"That really isn't necessary." I hoped I could either talk my way out of this, or buy enough time before help came. The guard behind me passed forward a folding hunting knife that wasn't big enough to properly do the job unless they planned to saw through my bone. "I mean, do you realize what year it is? This is a bit barbaric for people who work for a medical company."

When the gun's muzzle was pressed into my back, I figured they didn't want to talk. One of the men held down my wrist as the other worked on uncurling and sprawling my fingers out flat. I gritted my teeth. A wince escaped from behind them as the knife sliced into my ring finger. Fear held me still as they were being precise with their plan, trying to literally cut it off instead of just blindly cleaving. Maybe losing more than one finger would ruin their joke.

I closed my eyes as a message from my sister scrolled by, and risked a second to mute my mic with my left hand. The small gesture felt like the only bit of control I had. If my com hadn't raised concern, the spiking heart rate would surely do the trick. I've done a lot of borderline suicidal things before, but this was something I didn't want to see through.

Despite not being able to read the messages, I could still hear who made them. Stray sounds from Terry and Nic, an elevator ding from Ash, yet Sonia's mic wasn't picking up anything as if she was holding her breath. Al of which was somehow okay. I didn't actually want any of their help in fear that these goons would turn their attention to them. I'd rather be the only plaything tonight.

My right hand would have been shaking if it didn't feel like it was vise gripped to the table. "We can work this out," I breathed out in a single breath. My blood stained the papers beneath it, yet they didn't stop. My body wanted to struggle under the force of everyone holding me down, but I forced myself to endure so no one became trigger happy. All I could do was wait for the next cut that would surely hit bone.

The weight on my shoulder was suddenly gone. A gunshot made my knees buckle as I believed I was the one at the end of the barrel. I turned to find Ash standing with a gun over my assailant. The other men were almost as stunned as I was, but with another shot, Ash took down the one with the knife before he started scuffling with the last one.

I crumbled the rest of the way on the desk. My lungs tried to keep pace with my heart, sporadic enough to make me lightheaded. I just wished both of them would slow so I didn't feel like a man who never had a gulp of air before.

Shakily, I pushed myself off the desk. Ash was the only one standing now.

"Thank you," I panted.

Ash whistled. "That was fucking sick."

I was going to vomit if he found shooting people enjoyable. How anyone found pleasure in the violent details was beyond me.

"He's okay."

"Scott?" Sonia's voice cracked over the line.

I unmuted my microphone. "I'm fine. I promise," I assured her, and maybe myself. The idea of her frozen with worry was painful in a whole different way.

Pain bit down as I pulled my ring off, and moved it to the other hand so it at wouldn't rub against the cut.

"Take this," Ash said, and held out bandana.

"Thank you," I said, looking up to his blood-speckled face. "Again."

There was a modesty about him as he kept watch of the door. I cleared my throat. "Report?" I tied the bandana around my hand the best I could, wincing as I pulled it tighter with my teeth.

Ash handed my gun back as I stepped over the asshole who threatened to use it.

"Nic got hit pretty bad," Terry added, "He'll make it, but I'm going to take him back to our cars to make sure he stays that way. Are you all right, mate?"

"Yeah, I'm good."

Sonia sighed in relief; maybe I was more convincing that time. "Come here, I think I found it."

"Work, work, work," I teased, but it came out more of a wheeze. "I'll be right there."

<chapter thirty>
<! -- Sonia -->

The area I had been sent to was eerily bare and sterile looking. The few consoles that were around me were set perfectly on sharp right angles to each other.

I imagine that the wiring underneath would have looked even stranger placed in such an unnatural perfection.

Scott came into the room fast, and stopped even faster in front of me. He almost didn't look convinced I was truly here until his good hand reached out and touched my cheek. I could feel the tension in his fingers as if they wanted to pull me closer.

My smile faded as I looked down at his other hand that had been crudely wrapped, but didn't mention it. What needed to be done first, he'd say. Always, even before checking on ourselves.

"What did you find?"

I nodded toward the door at the other end of the room, but my eyes quickly returned. "This has got to be it."

Scott glanced over, shrugged a single shoulder, then led the way. The door lock was such a minor inconvenience, and Scott had it open within a minute.

Inside was a mass of cords reaching across the floor and up the sides. They covered the available surfaces like vines in an old, abandoned garden. I looked at Scott, who had wandered further into the room.

"Hope this works and doesn't end up as a virus in just about every UltSyn employee's brain," I said, carefully watching from the door. Maybe it was abundance of electricity, but this room made my hair stand on end.

"It won't affect you, or anyone, I promise. The virus is written to only infect this console and anything directly connected to it," Scott said, as he began to type away at the main console. "I think." He turned enough to flash a grin over at me before connecting a USB.

I narrowed my eyes at his jest, but he had already turned back. His devil-may-care attitude didn't fool me. Scott only acted like this when he was certain he knew all of the factors.

I stepped over a mass of wires that were near my foot, but misjudged it. My shoe got hung up in the tangle as it held my whole foot hostage. If I didn't know better, I'd say it had reached out to wrap around my ankle.

With a grumble, I pulled a little harder. I even placed my hand against the nearby wall for support as I reached down to get myself out.

I jolted my hand back as I swore the mass moved again. Maybe snagging my foot hadn't been an accident. Hesitantly, I reached back down to free myself. A cord began to curl around my fingers like a small snake, and I shivered as it moved up my arm. "Uh, Scott. This is creepy."

"What is?" He looked over and got his answer. Another thin wire moved up my forearm, winding its way until it came up to one of my scars. It was a blur as I tried to bat it. Scott was running over as it broke the skin. I gasped, if only to try to keep myself from screaming. The feeling only multiplied as I swore it dug into my muscles, and into my bones.

"I've seen these before." Scott was next to me now, holding my hand almost clinically as he tried to remove the wire. "They're used in automation."

"Ow, stop!" It hurt too much to pull out, and seemed to latch under my skin like a leach wanting blood. I didn't care where they came from right now. I thought about suggesting he cut it out, but I didn't want a bit left behind. "Just, just get my foot free." I felt another cord making its way around my leg as it made a light hissing sound. Without question, Scott kneeled down, and ripped away at the cords.

Another came for my other hand so quickly that I wasn't able to react. It wormed its way into my skin, and this time, I screamed at the feeling. They felt like needles that once lined up with my scars dug teeth in.

"I didn't know they made robotic arms this tiny and flexible."

"I don't care!" The pain and sheer fear was too much as tears welled up.

"It's going to be okay, hold on, you're almost free," Scott said, with unwavering conviction. His confidence almost made me believe it. I heard Script in my ear asking us what was going on, as everyone was either fighting back security, or keeping watch over the exits.

Neither Scott nor I responded. Both of us were too busy trying to get me out of this mess as a cord now reached around to my shoulders. "Let go!" I said, but they were not my words exactly.

Scott didn't stop. "Calm down, we've almost got it," he said, even though I could now hear the lie to keep me from giving up whatever hope I didn't know I had been losing.

Before I said or tried anything else again, a wire wrapped around Scott's throat. He had been paying so much attention to me that it caught him by surprise.

Scott gasped, but the sound didn't seem to have any air behind it.

I just watched, unable to show worry. While he was still looking my way, his eyes didn't seem focused on anything as he was forced to think only of himself now.

Light narrowed around my vision, until it disappeared completely. I thought I might faint, but the wires had more than enough help keeping me still. There must have been one for each old scar UltSyn had marked on me.

I struggled to even keep my eyes open against a current as strong as a riptide.

The last ones moving along my spine caused a shiver, and when the last one at the base of my neck sunk in; I became its rag doll.

There was a moment before I could clearly see anything around me again.

Time was hard to track; it was a measurement too fluid and convertible. I tried to focus on simply watching for a moment instead of thinking, and I saw Scott back at the main console.

"Scott Gris. The infamous Hello World Hacker," my voice said, but the words were not mine. "Not a pleasure."

Scott whirled around; his face painted with horror. I think from my monotone he could tell it was not me speaking. Or at least not completely me. "Who are you?" This something inside my head had no thoughts of its own. I couldn't listen, couldn't ask for a name. It just sent a weighted charge and my nerves fired to its design. The presence smothered me, made me feel as void as UltSyn had trained it to be, what I tried to be before Scott. Maybe even worse since I could only stare as everything around me went on.

"Who is semantics," I said, "You are a threat to this program."

"Stop it!" A calculation told me that he was breathing heavy, eyes dilated, and nearly unblinking. An emotional response.

I thought the AI would have something to say, but it didn't care. It felt like it was probing around my mind for something, but I didn't know what information it would want that it didn't already have. Scott advanced.

"Don't."

Scott didn't seem to be listening to it anymore. A pain prickled through me, shaking my whole form. This time a whimper came out of my mouth that felt like neither mine nor the machine's. A reflex.

He froze. I could distantly feel an acknowledgment that his emotions were a better catalyst than if he would have been programmed to stop. "What do you want?"

"Knowledge of this system has been compromised. A backup must be created. Wind her up and send her off, as you said before." I wish I could say I felt something...fear, horror, or even heartbreak over the pain on Scott's face. But I felt too shallow for any of it, just barely holding onto my own sentience.

"I need help," Scott said.

"Please, just leave." My voice sounded natural this time. The system was now mirroring patterns, reading every emotion, thought, and memory like I was its manual on how to survive his resistance.

Scott looked back, a silver lining of hope in his eyes that I was still inside, begging, fighting to be saved. I might be a puppet, but I could learn, I could rally. I pushed for control again, and gained an inch. My fingers twitched enough to catch Scott's attention.

Lie I tapped in Morse. Repeating the pattern in case he missed it, or didn't trust himself.

Agony washed over Scott's face again, but he raised his chin back up and got back to work. He took a deep breath as he tried to concentrate on the console in front of him. His shoulders were tight, and his hands hesitated over the keys. Script came into view, and I hadn't even realized he had come into the room. "The fuck is going on?"

"Just, shut up, I need to think," Scott said.

"You asked for help!" They stepped closer to me and I let out a loud whimper as a shock rolled through my body again.

"Don't," Scott warned, my—the machine's advocate now. "Don't go near her. Just step away, Script. She's hooked in and is being controlled."

"He's controlling me," I said. "Like he's always been in order to get his revenge. Please, stop him."

Scott's mouth opened, but no words came as he looked a hair width away from breaking. "That's low. Even for pre-programmed bullshit."

Script looked from Scott, to me, to Scott again like they were being shown horror on alternating cards. "You're telling me the ghost in the machine is processing her?"

"Attributed to Gilbert Ryle," I said. "Most commonly used to support the concept of sentience beyond the body, when in reality it was coined to mock the separation of the two."

"God," Scott seemed to pray as his hands formed a steeple over his nose. "I can't hear that *thing* control Sonia and concentrate."

"I did not plan to give a CAPTCHA test in person today," Script said and headed toward Scott. "Move."

There was a moment of silence as they worked, and the system controlling me must have been too busy calculating situations. Script mumbled something. Scott nodded, and the invading program kicked into protective mode. "If you do this, she dies. If you don't, she can live. Can you kill an innocent human? One you know wants to live?"

Script hesitated. They looked over to Scott as if questioning the most classic of moral dilemmas.

"Not like this," Scott said to Script. He glanced my way, before his hand hovered over what I assumed decided my fate. "She wouldn't want to live like this."

The shifting mixture of emotions was too human to read, but the lasting one had the telltale signs of sorrow. "I'm sorry, Sonia," he whispered before hitting the key.

There was nothing more than a slow ache at first, but like an actual illness, it crept up on me with a growing fever. I screamed, but I could only distantly hear my voice through the delirium.

I wasn't sure how I was holding onto consciousness as everything was slipping away around me. The room was a hue of red. Enough senses came back that I understood an alarm was going off. My eyes almost looked past Scott as I searched for something to hold onto.

Then I realized Scott was here, ripping the connections off of me as easily as dying vines now. My focus settled on him in a haze that could only be death. I tasted blood in my mouth, and I could see some on him. There was a strong smell of something burnt, but I didn't know if it was me, or the tech around me.

"We have to go," Script said. I didn't have it in me to look over. All my will power was used to concentrate on Scott.

"I don't care." He didn't look away. Carefully, he laid me down, so I wasn't bunched up against his chest. There was frantic search for an injury that could be patched up. I wanted to move closer, but I found none of my muscles responded.

"Victoria can't hold off the cops for much longer. Bring her, we don't have the time for anything else," Script said.

This time Scott looked absolutely certain. "I'm not leaving. Get the others out," he said, before turning back to me. I hadn't realized I closed my eyes until he said my name and tried to soothe me. There was another voice. He cringed at the sound and ripped the earpiece away before doing the same with the glasses.

"I need you. Just…" He picked up one of my hands and squeezed. "Don't close your eyes."

I remembered this repetition and forced a weak smile. "I couldn't have known what it was… even like to fear death without you." My breaths were short as Scott looked confused, almost more hurt from my choice of words. So, I tried my best to go on. "You gave me a life to fight for. I'm happy— I got to spend this new one with you."

"No, no, no," Scott breathed out involuntarily before talking louder. "I'm not letting you go. Let me fix this."

He sounded so sure of himself. It was a nice thought to hold onto as he pulled me against his chest again. My senses dulled until most just floated away. I leaned into his chest, not

246

ready to let go of him either yet, but even that will was drifting away too.

The last moments I could understand were concentrated on the sound of his heart against my ear. If I could bring a memory with me wherever I was going, I'd want it to be this strong sound and the reminder it gave me that as long as his heartbeat went on, mine would continue to echo through it.

<chapter thirty-one>
<! -- Scott -->

This place looked exactly the same, like a copy created from my memories. Well, almost the same. There was a broken gate missing that my mother always complained about. Getting back here was a string of long plane rides, and the road here had been even longer. The world continued. It had moved on to tell stories besides our adventures, but I wasn't.

It had been so long since I'd been here. While I dreamed daily of my sister's homecoming, I don't think I ever took a moment to think of my own.

You all right? Tori signed.

I exhaled, slow and controlled before managing a nod. "Come on, let's go."

I pulled on a smile and offered my hand. She gave me a funny little expression. We weren't kids anymore. We were adults. Ones that were given broken toys when we had been promised the real world.

"Sorry," I added. She wasn't a little girl anymore, far too grown up now after everything. It was just so easy to picture someone how they used to be. Even more so after they had been gone for a while.

Victoria's expression turned into a light smile as she took my hand, and we walked up to the door. Standing on the porch is when her own resolve cracked. Her attention moved to a flowerpot that once had blooms, but now only had a cracked base.

I rang the doorbell, such a simple device compared to the world I had been buried in. Time dragged as we waited, even though it couldn't have been more than a minute. My mother opened the door, her brown hair pinned messily in a clip. She looked older than I remembered, the wrinkles around her eyes had deepened, but the surprise was clear. "Scott?" She looked past me.

"Victoria?" Her voice grew more excited, despite a strong waiver of disbelief in it. My sister didn't even manage a nod before Mom threw her arms around her. "My little girl, you're back."

Tears fell without care as she pulled back just enough not to yell in Tori's ear as she yelled for my father.

Movement in the house caught my eye as my Dad rushed to the door worried something was wrong. He gave me a questioning look before realizing who my mother was hugging. My dad isn't an overly affectionate man, but within a second, his arms were draped around the both of them, stifling his own sobs.

The group hug took up enough room that I was forced to take a step back. My heart felt like it was up in my throat as I tried to find the words I had only a moment ago, "I… told you I'd find her." The words sounded shallow for how happy I knew I was. Somewhere I couldn't reach right now. "I know it took me a while." I wanted to take a step back. Logically, I knew I belonged, but unlike my sister, it had been my choice to stay away. I hadn't said a word to them since going to London, now I just showed up again with my sister in tow.

"Oh, Scott," my mother said softly. Her tone made me twitch, and I looked away to my father. He asked Victoria for what must be the third time if she was all right.

My mom hugged me, and it took me a second to return the gesture. "We've missed you so much. The both of you." She turned back to my sister, but made sure to leave a hand up on my arm. After wiping away her tears, she told us to come inside.

There was more crying once inside. My father asked more about what happened, but neither Tori nor I seemed to want to explain. Our withdrawal seemed to alarm my mother, and she declared that it didn't matter now that we were home.

When pushed for more by my father, Victoria just replied that I saved her. Mom treated Tori like she did me when I used to stop by during college. First, she asked if I was eating, then proceeded to make a home cooked meal despite the answer. She tried to get me to sit down at the table as well, frowning deeply when I refused.

It was enough for me to just watch them. I didn't think I could explain it to them, but their existence was enough. I didn't need to be a part of it, maybe I didn't think I deserved to be on some level. Either way, I hung around in the living room with an ignored TV that had been left on. Our mom was waiting for the oven to heat up as Tori sat in the kitchen talking with her. It was sweet to see Mom try to sign again, apologizing profusely any time she forgot one of the words. Tori smiled, and kept saying that it was okay. And while not meant for me, I believed for a moment that everything would be okay.

The sound of the TV captured my attention. "After the recent launch of a worldwide investigation, estimates suggest the recent attacks on UltSyn not only left the company in ruins, but cost billions. The FBI reports that, on average, viruses cost businesses over $113 billion a year. Estimates believe this attack alone could make up a forty percent of that."

Guess we finally got UltSyn where it hurt. We screwed their bottom line up enough I doubted they could ever repair themselves, at least not by that name. Not after investigations were finding years of human trafficking violations. No one would trust them. And I couldn't help but smile.

"That was you, wasn't it?" my father asked, likely seeing that my attention had been stolen away. I looked away, toward Victoria who was now helping my mother make something. When I turned back, my father's eyes were still squarely on me, waiting.

"Yes," I breathed. I wasn't sure what he would think. I got shit in high school when I modded my phone. He not only thought I'd break it, but that it was ethically wrong to do it in the first place. I couldn't tell what he was thinking now, couldn't imagine what he'd think about me breaking far more than TOS.

He once believed I was obsessed with the quest to find my sister, said I was upsetting my mother, that she would end up suffering the loss of both of her children if I continued.

Now the prodigal son had returned.

He looked over his shoulder to the television as a pundit compared my work to the civilian version of Stuxnet. With a scoff, he turned back to me. "I'm proud of you," he said, and held his hand out low as if to shake. When I took it, he pulled me into a hug.

"It takes a lot to keep believing when everyone else has given up," he said. I didn't quite follow why he was saying this. "You brought our family back together, and if the reports are true, you did the same for many more people."

"I…" What could I even say? "I just needed to bring Tori home."

"You did a good job." He smiled over at my mother and sister. "Come on; let's go lend them an extra hand." My father took a few steps to the kitchen, but I didn't follow.

"Dad…" He turned back, frowning as he noticed I hadn't moved. "You must know I can't stay."

His eyes fell to the floor and nodded a little. "Stay for dinner."

"Deal."

I wanted to spend forever in this family that could once again be whole, but I didn't want to bring hell to their door. One person's whistle-blower was another man's traitor.

<epilogue>

UltSyn knew I was here.

Or rather, what was left of it did. The only reason they hadn't come banging on my doorstep with guns drawn was because the men they did have left were being closely watched by the government. I knew some of them wanted me dead; others were just too busy throwing their money at the problem to distance themselves from it all. It would work for some, but the world was watching. They were awake now.

I knew I shouldn't stay in London in the safe house turned home while I had been searching for my sister. The United States and the UK had extradition laws, meaning America was no longer free for me either. I should already be in some foreign country. The others already were.

I couldn't leave yet though, I needed to be here.

She needed to be here, and I feared it was our only hope after she lost everything, or almost everything, to the program that infected her brain.

I looked over to the holding room where it all started. Where it al might end. There was still work to be done, and I headed to it.

"Do you know who I am?" I asked the woman inside. She didn't say, or sign, a single word. Recognition of who she was burned through me, down to the soles of my shoes. If anyone wanted revenge, this would have been the way.

I shook off the question, and tried to go with something else. "I need you to tell me if you know about this girl," I said. I tried to use words I had before, although I didn't remember them exactly after all this time. I slid a picture across the table of a blonde girl with slightly shorter hair.

She could memorize anything within a few seconds; she definitely didn't need help understanding why someone would go through the trouble to acquire her. But seeing a photo of herself seemed to throw her off. *I don't follow,* she signed.

"I know you can speak," I said throwing the script out.

She leaned back in the chair, more startled than if I would have thrown something at her. *You have the wrong person.*

I pinched the bridge of my nose. "Why can't I have a perfect morning, just one of these days?"

Right, okay, I had to play this like last time. That remarkable brain of hers should eventually pick up the familiar pattern. It worked before with my sister. UltSyn tech wasn't written to handle deja vu without considering it missing data. "You can roam around the first floor as long as you don't touch the tech or wander upstairs."

I'd rather stay in here.

"Too bad," I said rather coldly, gesturing to the door. Sonia got up before she was dragged into the other rooms, inching down the room like a careful little mouse.

I needed her to get better, because I didn't know how long my head, or my heart, could take this. I stayed up nights on end wondering if Sonia would recognize this place before someone arrested me. Or worse.

Almost a week had gone by, and I was starting to feel like a poor copy of myself as I tried to keep the pretense of work up. I was glad when one of Hallie's parts crapped out. It gave me something new to do before monotony was my official cause of death. Finally, something tangible I could fix.

I had been up there for an hour, and wasn't paying attention to anything besides the problem at hand. When I finished, some food seemed to be in order, but I stopped only a step outside the door. The lights on my bedroom floor were on, and unless they were glitching, I couldn't tell you why.

They lit the way, and I ended up standing at the foot of my closet. Sonia was staring at what had become her half. The black dress she had worn in Paris was delicately between her fingers. I was speechless as to what I should do. This wasn't what had happened last time. I didn't know if I should comment about her 'not being allowed' up here, or try to encourage her to remember. My greatest sin was hope, and I found myself powerless to it.

I held my breath, and did nothing until she made the first move. "I love a good challenge." Her voice was soft enough that I prayed this wasn't a dream. "That's what you said the first day we met."

"That's right," I said, not sure how far to push my luck. "Do you... remember me?"

Sonia moved away from the clothes, and I feared the spell that brought her back was broken. Instead of pushing past, she stopped in front of me. Her hand reached up to my cheek, then trailed over my lips like she had been blind before. The gesture was almost enough to convince me I was dreaming, but the tightness in my heart was all too painful. "Scott."

I let out a small laugh as I took a step closer, wanting to touch her. Just to hold her for a second. I rested my forehead against hers, my arms tucked around her back as I wanted this second to lag on. I might have kissed her if I could have stopped smiling for a moment.

"It's just I said it out loud before," Sonia smiled at her own joke.

I chuckled at the memory of that day. I don't know if I ever felt this happy, especially at someone teasing me. "I love you, too."

* * *

That's the thing about the mind. It's resilient. Memories can be lost; they can be overwritten by time or design. Yet, there is one thing that can never be fully eroded.

No amount of biological difference or tinkering can write code over the soul. Time may advance us until we are completely merged with the technology around us. But, whatever wrapping life might try to cover us with there will always be something of that person beating underneath.

Acknowledgements

To aces on tumblr, I found myself as I wrote this story. Since then, I've learned so much about the greater queer community and what it means to fight for something with your whole heart and soul.

To Rachel Sharp, my former pub sister, who literally makes every sentence I write better without fail. Thank you on so many fronts both personally and professionally.

To friends, who likely listened without context to things like jokingly tracking how many crimes are in this book, or who knew that the fruits of this labor of love wouldn't help feed anything except my own morale for years.

To my co-author, who let me name this book after a programming reference. Before we even wrote a word, I knew I was in love with this story and what it could be. The fun we had with it has been a gift that keep on giving.

- Rose Sinclair

***

My mother, grandmother, and grandfather for encouraging me and feeding my interests in the arts throughout the years. I don't know what I'd be without your help and influence.

Tricia for being a lifelong friend that I could lean on during bad times and celebrate with during the good times. I would write you into a character someday, but you're too amazing so I'm not willing to share.

To my family in Greece, who I miss very much and taught me valuable lessons about life you could never learn in America. My understanding of the world is because of you all.

My co-author, who pushes me to be a better writer and person. The joy I've had knowing and working with you is worth every hiccup along the way.

And most of all, Steven, my husband who builds me up when I'm crashing and holds me higher when I'm soaring. Existing without you would be crap, thank you for being you.

- Alexandra Tauber

About The Authors

Rose Sinclair is the profane community leader that started Fuck Yeah Asexual in 2013. The biggest noise maker they spearheaded was the #GiveItBack protest in 2015 that made GLADD step up for asexual, aromantic, and agender people, paving the way for future acceptance of those communities and on-screen representation. They are an active member of their communities, popularizing terms such as allosexual to serving as a decentralized support system with a "Dear Abby" style approach. They are the author of HELLO WORLD, leader of community projects such as WHAT YOU SEE, with more to come.

Loving cat mom and wife, Alexandra Tauber grew up with a strong love for science fiction, comic books, and games. A growing love for storytelling helped formed her aspirations to write novels, driving her at an early age to practice writing in online roleplay forums. Alex plans to work on and develop diverse, compelling narrative driven video games as another exploration for her love of storytelling. Most days, Alex spends her free time cuddling her cat, cooking a bomb ass meal, or playing a whole lot of video games.

***

Thank you so much for reading Scott and Sonia's story. Their adventures continue in VARIBLE CURRENT coming out in paperback and ebook in Fall 2021. Keep reading for an exclusive preview of HELLO WORLD's sequel.

VARIABLE CURRENT

<chapter one>
<! -- Sonia -->

"You meet three types of people in an airport: Travelers, lovers, and lawyers," Scott said. I'd have liked to say we were the lovers in this quip, but after fleeing multiple countries to reach Japan we were definitely the travelers. The lovers were a foreign couple celebrating their honeymoon and making the Japanese people returning home silently uncomfortable. That left the lawyers. Unless any of the other passengers were going to stand up and identify themselves, I was not sure who else he was referring to.

"Remember when you said I was controlling?" Scott added. All of his attention narrowed in on me, when it had been splintered among the array of nervous tics he had picked up on the way here like it was his carry on. "I might have done a thing."

I looked at the queue of people leading to customs, but my eyes fell directly over two Japanese police officers that stood with a woman in a suit. Panic set in fast. When I turned to Scott, he gave me a slight smile. "It's all okay. Just be yourself, and remember whatever happens it's completely your choice."

Baggage claim was in front of us, and I wanted to be there. I've done that before, I knew how it went. Scott kissed me on the cheek before the officers ushered us in separate directions. I kept looking over my shoulders, expecting them to arrest him, before my escort stopped in a small interview room.

Through the glass door I could just see Scott. He was now seated and very still, as if a step removed and frozen as he watched everything.

I hadn't paid much attention to the assumed lawyer but after a glance I knew I'd be able to recall the pattern of her freckles. Her English was very practiced, suggesting she has done international work before and introduced herself as Otsuki.

"What is going on?" I asked.

"You are going to be interviewed about what Mr. Gris had requested."

I met her eyes. "What did he request?"

She blinked, the tiniest hint of being thrown off, and I noticed a small scar like I've seen on others from implants. I knew an answer was about to come, at least that was until an older-looking officer walked into the room. It took everything for me to reign in my emotions, a skill I had once been far too good at. When I looked for Scott again, he was missing.

"Kon'nichiwa, Otsuki-sama," he greeted her before addressing me. "Do you speak Japanese?"

If he knew about HIDs, he knew that answer. I nodded slightly, but he switched to English all the same. "Probably best to interview you in English either way. It is your native tongue, is it not?"

"As far as I know." He smiled, but I wondered if he truly understood or was trying to be personable. "What's going on?"

"We are expediting your naturalization," Otsuki-san said.

***

Continue Scott and Sonia's story in Variable Current coming Fall 2021 and be sure to check out Bone Diggers also from this author duo.

If you've enjoyed Hello World please consider leaving a review on Amazon, or your website of choice.
Thank you!